THE DOCK GIRL'S SHAME

ANNEMARIE BREAR

Boldwood

First published in Great Britain in 2024 by Boldwood Books Ltd.

Copyright © AnneMarie Brear, 2024

Cover Design by Colin Thomas

Cover Photography: Alamy and Colin Thomas

The moral right of AnneMarie Brear to be identified as the author of this work has been asserted in accordance with the Copyright, Designs and Patents Act 1988.

Every effort has been made to obtain the necessary permissions with reference to copyright material, both illustrative and quoted. We apologise for any omissions in this respect and will be pleased to make the appropriate acknowledgements in any future edition.

A CIP catalogue record for this book is available from the British Library.

Paperback ISBN 978-1-83751-240-9

Large Print ISBN 978-1-83751-236-2

Hardback ISBN 978-1-83751-235-5

Ebook ISBN 978-1-83751-233-1

Kindle ISBN 978-1-83751-234-8

Audio CD ISBN 978-1-83751-241-6

MP3 CD ISBN 978-1-83751-238-6

Digital audio download ISBN 978-1-83751-232-4

Boldwood Books Ltd
23 Bowerdean Street
London SW6 3TN
www.boldwoodbooks.com

1

WAKEFIELD, WEST YORKSHIRE, ENGLAND

March 1871

Closing the ledger, Loretta Jane Chambers, Lorrie to her friends, sat back and sighed. No matter how many times she added up the figures, the bottom line was always minus. Her father's business, Chambers Boat Builder and Repairs, was in deep trouble.

She stared out of the window at the bustling boatyard edging the River Calder where it swept in an arc near the weir. To her right was Wakefield Bridge with the Chantry Chapel, St Mary's, perched beside it. On the left, on either side of the river stood the docks and wharves, malthouses, all types of mills from cotton to corn and sawmills, plus the odd brewery, such as Henderson's Brewery, owned by Christian Henderson, the husband of her best friend, Meg.

The river itself held an array of vessels, the cargo barges and canal narrowboats, the repairs of which had kept her father in business for twenty-five years, a venture he'd taken over when she was only a baby. However, the busy waterways of the River Calder and the Calder and Hebble Navigation canal, which cut through behind the mills beyond the boatyard, were dying. The railways had come and stolen the cargo from the canals and, each month that passed, Lorrie saw the fall in boats being brought in for repair, and even less call for new boats to be built.

Her father, Ernest, kept denying the changes, saying work would pick up and ebbs and flows of business were to be expected. But Lorrie needed her father to see that the railways were affecting their income, and that the way they ran the boatyard needed to alter, or they could lose it altogether. They had an investor, Oswald Lynch, a man Lorrie disliked, but who had done a deal with her father to buy into the business. The investment money bought them some time; however, Lorrie felt it had simply delayed the business going broke completely.

A tap on the office door preceded Jimmy, a young labourer who worked for her father. 'Sorry to disturb you, Miss Chambers, but your father wishes to know if the rope order has been sent off as we're running low.'

Lorrie forced a smile and pretended to look through the paper-work on her desk. 'Tell Father I'll double-check and come out to him.'

'Rightio, miss.' Jimmy closed the door and Lorrie stopped moving the papers about.

The rope order hadn't been sent off because the last invoice hadn't been paid. She opened a drawer, which held a wad of bills not attended to. The stack grew each day.

How long could they hold off the inevitable?

The door opened again and her father, Ernest Chambers, stepped in, rubbing his hands from the cold. Spring warmth had yet to make an appearance, even if the daffodils were blooming.

'Dearest, the rope order?' Father asked politely, as he did with everything.

'You know we haven't paid the last bill,' she reminded him. 'They won't take another order until we do.'

'Then pay them.'

She stared at him in amazement. Did he not remember the conversation only three nights ago when she told him the money was all gone? 'We have nothing to pay them with, Father, not until the Johnson invoice has been received. Did Mr Johnson mention when he was paying us for the work on his boat?'

Father, looking older than his sixty years, took off his hat and rubbed his sparse grey hair. 'Walter said he'd pay this week. Are we that short of money that we must wait for his payment to do anything else?'

'Yes.' Lorrie stood and poked the coals in the little fire at the back of the office. 'We spoke about this only a few nights ago.'

'I don't understand it. Are you sure you're not mistaken? There has to be some money left?'

She bristled. 'Father, I have been doing the account books since I was sixteen. It is rare for me to make a mistake. I might be terrible at cooking and other things, but I know figures.'

'And what of Oswald's investment?' he asked of their partner.

'It's nearly all gone. We have enough to pay the next month's wages.' Lorrie kept her back to her father and added more coal on the fire. She didn't want him to see the revulsion she felt for Oswald. For the last six months since Oswald Lynch had invested in the boatyard, Lorrie had had to constantly hide her feelings towards the dreadful man. Her father had shaken his hand on a deal to invest in the business, but although the money had been welcome, Oswald's overzealous and obnoxious nature had become a problem, at least to Lorrie.

'How can that be?' Father sat heavily on the wooden chair by the desk, his face pale, his shoulders drooped. 'I promised Oswald a return on his money within a year.'

'I told you at the time you were setting yourself up for failure. Our trade has dropped in recent years.'

'You don't have to tell me that, dearest.'

'Then why did you make a deal with Mr Lynch?' She'd asked herself that question a hundred times in the last few months, but never openly questioned her father, believing that there had been a suitable reason to go into further debt.

'Lynch had new ideas, modern ideas that could save us. Buying new equipment, taking on more men to do the jobs faster, it all sounded good on paper.'

'All of that would have worked if we had the work to show for it, only we don't. Oswald's ability to find us more clients has failed so far.' Lorrie went to him and placed her hand on his shoulder. 'We have to cut back on labour.'

'We need the men to finish the projects to bring the money in.' He lifted his hands in the air, as if in surrender.

'I understand that but we need to lessen the number of wages we pay,' Lorrie said with a little frustration. 'We must find ways to cut our costs, Father.' She felt she was repeating herself at least daily and yet her father never seemed to take it in.

'Of course.' He stood and replaced his hat and walked out of the office.

Lorrie wondered if this time their talk might have had the desired effect and her father would start to economise, but she doubted it.

Leaving the office, she went outside and stood for a moment, watching the scene. Father had employed more men with Oswald's investment money than they'd ever had, and the yard resembled a thriving business, but she knew the truth. Seeing the workers happily whistling as they went about their tasks or hearing the hammers hit wooden pegs into planks or smelling the burning tar should have given her happiness, yet it kept her awake at night.

The cold breeze had her pulling her shawl closer about her arms. The low grey sky threatened rain and she hurried up the outside staircase to the living quarters above.

Inside, she raked the main fire in the sitting room and added more coals, before doing the same to the cooking range fire in the kitchen. The living quarters boasted two bedrooms and one large room which was the kitchen and sitting room combined.

A mutton stew simmered on the range hob, and she tasted it with a spoon. It needed a touch more salt.

Setting two places on the round table which sat in the middle of the room, Lorrie smoothed the red damask tablecloth, knowing it had belonged to her mother and was something her father held dear, as he did with anything that had belonged to her dark-haired and dark-eyed mother, Arianna.

She remembered very little of her mother, who died when Lorrie was young. Father told her she came from an Italian family, and he'd met her in London when he was an apprentice for a ship builder on the Thames. When he finished his apprenticeship and returned to Wakefield, he'd brought with him his young bride, much to her family's despair. Arianna died within six years of Lorrie's birth. Lorrie had been named after her Italian great-grandmother, Loretta. A woman Lorrie had never met, nor had she ever seen any of her mother's family.

When her mother died, Ernest Chambers said he'd look after his own daughter, and he did. He employed a weekly cleaner and a cook who came to the flat three times a week until Lorrie was old enough at twelve to take over the running of their home, and a few years later, having a head for numbers, she started work in the office.

Besides working in the office, Lorrie had attended a small

privately run girls' school. Miss Rodgers in Westgate taught Lorrie to speak well and educated her enough to become a suitable wife for an upper-working-class man, such as a clerk or a scholar or a solicitor if she was very fortunate.

Years later, Lorrie still wondered when that man would enter her life. She longed to be married, to fall in love and have a family of her own. For a while she thought that might be within reach. She'd gone on a few walks with a kind man, Tobias Parker, but Tobias's interest waned when he saw that the boatyard was in fact a noose around Ernest's neck and not a successful business he could take advantage of by marrying Lorrie.

She should have been heartbroken when he stopped calling, but she wasn't. She wanted a heart-stopping love, the kind of adoration her friend Meg had with Christian, and would settle for nothing less.

The door opened to voices and Lorrie spun to see her father usher in Oswald Lynch.

'Lorrie, dear, set another place at the table, Oswald is joining us for our meal.'

'This is an unexpected visit, Mr Lynch?' Lorrie wasn't expecting him until the end of the month.

'I could no longer deny myself the pleasure of your company, dear Miss Chambers.' Oswald, red-faced from climbing the stairs, bowed towards her as much as his rotund stomach would allow. Shorter than her father, who was only five foot nine, Oswald had a proud manner, as though he was the son of a king instead of the firstborn of a backstreet grocer. Words she'd heard the men in the yard say about Mr Lynch were not flattering because he spoke down to them in the belief he was better than them.

'Sit, sit,' Father encouraged him to the sofa. 'Will we eat soon, daughter?'

'A few minutes. The stew is ready, I shall cut the bread.' She busied herself at the small square kitchen table, slicing the loaf, aware of Oswald's eyes watching her every move.

'The yard shows a hive of industry, Ernest,' Oswald stated. 'A fine sight to see indeed.'

Father nodded enthusiastically. 'We have repairs aplenty.'

'But do we have orders for new builds? We should be building vessels, that is where the money is, not these piddling little fixes.'

Lorrie brought the bread to the table. 'It is those little fixes that keep the yard afloat,' she defended.

Oswald's face brightened. 'I do so enjoy it when you interrupt our business talk, Miss Chambers, with your... *knowledge*. I do forget that even though you are just a woman, you do have, remarkably, a brain in your head.'

Lorrie bristled at the insult.

'My daughter is very much the centre of the business, Oswald, as you know I am the one who oversees the yard, but Lorrie runs the office.'

'Yes, so I have learned.' He turned to looked at her fully, his eyes narrowing like a hawk about to catch a mouse. 'Then you will be able to tell me when I shall get my first instalment of the profits?'

Lorrie hated him for putting her on the spot, but before she could answer him with the unpalatable truth, Oswald laughed and slapped his thigh.

'Isn't she most delightful, Ernest? What a daughter you have. Beauty and mind. Some men would find that daunting, but not me. No, I admire such creatures.'

She turned back to the kitchen side of the room and took bowls from a cupboard. Seething that he had demeaned her yet again, she took a deep breath to calm herself.

The meal passed in general conversation about national events, such as the upcoming wedding of Princess Louise, Queen Victoria's daughter, to John Campbell, Marquess of Lorne, the unrest in Paris and the news of the member states of North Germany joining with the southern German states to become a nation called the German Empire.

When they had finished the meal and her father and Oswald returned to the sofa to drink tea, Lorrie stayed in the kitchen to wash the dishes and tidy up. The conversation on the sofa was too low for her to hear, and that worried her. She didn't trust Oswald. He'd pestered her father into investing in the business. That he owned a half share in the boatyard sat like a rock in her chest, suffocating her. Why he'd wanted to buy into a failing business, she didn't know, but there had to be a reason and she wanted to find out what it was.

Oswald took his leave shortly after. 'Thank you, Miss Chambers, for a lovely meal and your delightful company.'

'You're welcome, Mr Lynch.' She forced a smile as he bent over her hand like a gallant knight.

'Until we meet again, which I hope is soon.' He went out with a chuckle.

Lorrie glanced at her father as he put on his hat, ready to go back down to the yard. 'Father, what were you both talking about just now?'

'Only business, my dear. Oswald has some cargo he wishes to send down the river and asked my opinion of hiring a boat or buying his own. I told him I have a couple of my own boats in the yard that, once repaired, he can use.'

'The ones you use for scrap parts?'

'Yes. If it keeps him sweet, I can repair one for him to use as he pleases.' At the door, he paused. 'Oswald has a keen interest in you, dearest. I would hazard a guess he is thinking of marriage.'

'Not with me,' she blurted out in shock.

'Of course with you. Why wouldn't he? You are beautiful and clever. You'd make any man a fine wife.'

'Except him.'

'Don't be too hasty, Lorrie dear. He may be the answer to our prayers.'

'I say no prayers which include Oswald Lynch, Father.'

He let out a long sigh. 'Then perhaps you should.' He softly closed the door behind him.

Lorrie stared into nothingness. Marriage to Oswald Lynch? She'd rather die.

2

After shaking Mr Rendale's hand, the vicar of the church she attended on the other side of the river, Lorrie hurried up to catch her friend, Fliss Atkins, while Father spoke to old friends.

'Lorrie.' Fliss embraced her. 'I'm sorry I couldn't come for afternoon tea yesterday, my aunt is in bed with a dreadful cold, and I had to wait on her.'

'You look tired,' Lorrie commented, noticing the darkness under Fliss's blue eyes. Even her freckles seemed faded today. 'Are you unwell?'

'No, I'm fine. I'm just exhausted from looking after Aunt and then working my shifts behind the bar.' She spoke of her uncle's public house, the Bay Horse, where Fliss lived and worked.

'Have you seen Meg at all?' Lorrie asked. 'Last I heard she was going to Huddersfield to visit Mabel and the baby, who was sick.' She had kept her voice low, for Meg's sixteen-year-old sister Mabel had found herself pregnant and unmarried. Meg and her brother, Freddie, had sent her away to have the baby.

'You haven't heard?' Fliss whispered.

'No? What?'

'Freddie came into the bar last night to tell me that he and Meg had just returned from Huddersfield. Mabel's baby girl died a few hours before they arrived.'

'Oh no!' Lorrie's heart broke for them. 'Poor Mabel.'

'The funeral was yesterday, and they brought Mabel home with them afterwards. None of them have come to church this morning.' Fliss looked around as if to make sure she wasn't mistaken. 'Freddie said he had failed as a brother, but how can he blame himself? It wasn't his fault his sister got into trouble or that her baby died.'

'Perhaps it is fate?' Lorrie murmured sadly. 'Mabel can get on with the rest of her life now without the torture of giving up her baby and knowing it was living out there somewhere without her.'

Fliss nodded. 'Mabel's young. She can start again. Though Freddie will keep a close eye on her now. No more messing about with lads for a few years.'

'Indeed. Though how he'll be able to do that when he is a landlord of a pub and men are in and out day and night, I don't know.' Lorrie nodded to her father, who had finished his conversations. 'I'd best go.'

'Me too. My aunt will be wanting me.' Fliss grasped Lorrie's hand. 'Meg will be needing us.'

'Yes. I'll send her a note to come for tea one day this week. What day suits you?'

'Thursday? My aunt should be well enough by then.' Fliss stiffened as her cousin Gerald came up to her, scowling.

'Hurry up. Father and I are waiting for you.' He didn't acknowledge Lorrie.

'Sorry.' Fliss's gaze dropped to the ground. 'Bye, Lorrie.'

'Until Thursday then.' Lorrie smiled at Fliss before giving

Gerald a glare, hating how he always ordered Fliss about like a servant.

Walking home with her father, Lorrie tucked her arm through his. She enjoyed Sunday afternoons, the only time they were alone together. The yard commanded all of her father's time and when he'd finished for the day, he was usually exhausted and fell asleep before the fire. She spent most evenings in silence, reading or sewing while her father gently snored in his chair.

However, Sunday afternoons she could cajole him into a walk or, if the weather was bad, a game of cards. 'Shall we be extravagant and go to the theatre one night this week?'

He chuckled. 'You're the one saying we should watch our spending and now you want a trip to the theatre.'

A flare of guilt sparked but she quickly squashed it. 'It's rare that we treat ourselves, Father. Can we, just this once, do something that is nice for the two of us?' In truth, she felt that if the boatyard went under they would never go to the theatre again.

'Dearest, if that is what you want to do then we will.' He patted her hand where it rested on his arm.

Excitement made her grin. 'I'll go into town tomorrow and buy the tickets.'

Entering the boatyard's iron gates, they paused on seeing a man leaning against the wall near the staircase.

'Are you expecting someone?' she asked her father.

'No. Not on a Sunday.' Father quickened his step. 'Good day, sir. How may I help you?'

Lorrie's footsteps slowed as she neared the man. He was tall, lithe, and when he took his hat off, the sun shone off black hair, as dark as a raven's wing, like her own.

'Good day, Mr Chambers.' The man held out his hand and Father shook it. Then the man gazed at Lorrie for a long moment. 'Miss Chambers.' He bowed.

For some strange reason, Lorrie's heartbeat doubled in time. The man was handsome, with classic Latin looks, dark hair, dark eyes and tanned skin as though he spent all his time outdoors, but his suit was well made and of good quality, so he wasn't a labourer looking for work.

'And you are?' Lorrie blurted out. Something about him raised the hairs on the back of her neck.

'Matteo Falcone.'

'Italian,' Father said, stiffening beside her.

'Yes.' The stranger bowed his head to her father. 'You married a member of my nonna's... my great-grandmother's family.' His accent was slight, but detectable, as if he'd spent many years away from his home country.

'My wife is dead,' Father told him. 'I wrote to Arianna's family many years ago.'

Shocked that not only was an Italian standing before her but that he was related in some distant way to her own mother left Lorrie reeling. She had never seen anyone from her mother's side of the family.

'And the family have wondered how her daughter has fared since then.' The man's dark gaze strayed to Lorrie.

'Shall we go inside?' Lorrie led the way upstairs and unlocked the door. She took off her coat, gloves and unpinned her hat, all the while aware of the handsome stranger who stood just inside the doorway. 'Please, come and sit by the fire.' She hurried over and raked up the coals, adding bits of wood to get the blaze going.

'Why are you here?' Father took over the concerns of the fire while Lorrie went into the kitchen and did the same to the range fire.

While she tended to the tea things, she kept glancing over to the man, listening to every word.

'My great-grandmother was an important friend and distant

cousin to your late wife's grandmother, Loretta. My great-grand-mother has sent me on this errand to visit you while I was in England on business.'

'Why now?' Lorrie took a step from the table, eager to hear any mention of the family she knew nothing about.

'Your great-grandmother...' He bowed his head for a moment and then stared at her. 'Loretta died recently. She was of a good age, lived a good life. She always talked about you and wondered how you were.'

Sorry that her great-grandmother had died, but not sad, for the woman had barely registered in Lorrie's life, she folded her hands and tried to make sense of his visit. 'My great-grandmother never wrote to me.'

'Her English was very poor.'

'None of my mother's side of the family wrote or visited me.' That fact hurt, no matter how old she became. She knew she had relatives in London, yet had never seen them.

'I am sorry for that.'

Her hands trembled a little as she placed the tea things on the table. 'So why have *you* come and not a member of my mother's family?'

'My great-grandmother sent me. She promised your great-grandmother she would do so because of their lifelong friendship. I am honouring that promise.'

'To see if I am alive?' Lorrie shrugged. 'Why do they care now?'

Father straightened as much as his slightly stooped back would allow. 'Well, you've seen my daughter, and she is well. You have fulfilled your promise and can leave.'

'Father,' Lorrie admonished. She'd never heard him, a quiet and kind man, speak so rudely.

Father held his hands up. 'I'm sorry, Lorrie, but I want nothing to do with that family. I didn't back then, and I definitely don't now.'

'I was told there is...' Mr Falcone seemed to search for the right word in English. 'Bad blood between you and your wife's family.'

'Bad blood?' Lorrie stared, wide-eyed, at her father. She knew nothing of that.

Mr Falcone gave her a small smile of sympathy. 'It is not my story to tell.'

Besides being intrigued by this family history, Lorrie wondered where he had learned to speak such good English.

'No, it damn well isn't.' Father turned away to gaze at the fire. 'I want you to leave. Please.'

'Very well.' Mr Falcone bowed his head, then looked at Lorrie. 'I have something for you. From Loretta. Perhaps I can call tomorrow and give it to you? I did not bring it with me in case you weren't living in this place.'

'She needs nothing from you, or them,' Father said, not looking at him.

'That is Miss Chambers's choice, yes?' Mr Falcone's dark eyes were tender as he gave a nod and walked out.

In the silence of the large room, Lorrie sucked in a breath. What had just happened? Her mother had died when she was a child. Pneumonia, Father had told her. Arianna hadn't ever adapted to the bleak and damp northern weather. Arianna was a lover of the sun and warmth. Yorkshire didn't provide enough of that for her to enjoy, Father said, and Arianna missed her family in London. Her spirit eroded over the years, and she grew unhappy; that last bit of information came from Jed, the old man who worked in the yard and who had seen all of this unfold.

Lorrie could only remember little pieces of her mother. Her long black hair, which hung in a plait as thick as her father's ropes. She remembered odd Italian words her mother would say to her such as *tesoro* and *amorino*. What they meant Lorrie didn't know. But the main thing she remembered was her mother singing as she cooked on the same range Lorrie now cooked at. Her mother always sang in Italian, even though she'd been born in London. Lorrie wished she remembered the words.

'You're not to see that man again, do you hear?' Father said, his voice no longer angry, just determined.

'But he's coming back tomorrow with a gift from my great-grandmother.' Lorrie badly wanted to see the gift, to connect in some small way with the woman who gave birth to her own mother's mother. All these faceless women who were her blood.

'You don't need anything from that family.' Father went into his bedroom and quietly closed the door.

For a long moment, Lorrie stared at the closed door. It was rare for them to have a cross word. It'd been just the two of them for so long and they always got along with each other. Only this link with the past, a past Lorrie knew nothing about, had rattled her father.

As she put away the tea things, she thought of Matteo Falcone, and although it was a betrayal to her dear father, she knew she would see him again.

* * *

The following morning, Lorrie tidied the office. Her father had a bad habit of looking for paperwork and leaving a trail of destruction in his wake. She needed to keep busy as she waited for Mr Falcone to arrive, which she hoped he would and hadn't been put off by her father's rudeness. She'd spent a restless night thinking about him and her Italian family and her mother, but mainly about him.

Matteo Falcone. Such an exotic name, at least for these parts, where there were so many common names like John, Charlie, Tom and Harry.

The office door opened, and Lorrie turned around with a welcoming smile, only for the smile to turn into a grimace on seeing Oswald Lynch enter.

'Good morning, Miss Chambers.'

'Mr Lynch.' She nodded to him and continued sorting out her piles of paperwork.

'Is your father about?'

'He'll be in the yard somewhere. They were bringing in a boat from the river.' She waved towards the small window which overlooked the yard and down to the river. 'They'll be dry-docking it for repairs.'

'Whose boat is it?'

Lorrie opened the repair ledger and scanned the list to the bottom. 'Mr Cameron's. He has sent his barge in for new caulking.'

'Good. Good. I spoke to your father about him.' Oswald rubbed his hands together. 'This is good business.'

Lorrie studied the client's details in the ledger. 'Mr Cameron is paying under the going rate Father would normally charge for caulking.'

Oswald gave her a superior look. 'In these difficult times, we must give special deals wherever we can.'

'Not to the extent of going under, surely?' Lorrie closed the ledger.

'It'll not come to that, my dear. We have plenty of business happening.'

Lorrie shuddered, disliking it when he called her *my dear*. She wasn't *his* anything. 'Business you have sent our way.'

'Indeed, what are partners for?'

'But since you have invested, our prices have been lowered.'

'And you've become busier,' he gloated.

'We are rushing through the jobs. The workmanship will suffer without the care and attention to detail Father is known for.'

'Standards are still high, Miss Chambers. Do not worry your pretty little head about that.'

She clenched her fists. How would he know about their standards? Was he a boatwright?

'I was thinking that perhaps you would enjoy a night at the theatre? Your father mentioned it is a treat you much appreciate.' His slimy smile showed his small teeth, reminding her of a rat. 'I can purchase tickets for Friday?'

'Forgive me, Mr Lynch, but that is not something I would be keen to do.'

'Why?' He blinked rapidly in surprise.

'It is hardly respectable, the two of us alone at the theatre.'

'You want a chaperone?' His beady eyes widened. 'At your age, I highly doubt that is necessary.'

Stung, she lifted her chin. 'I am only twenty-five, Mr Lynch, not in my dotage yet.'

'But time is getting away from you, Miss Chambers. Most women your age are married and have children by now. Surely, you wish for that too?'

'No, not really,' she lied. 'I am most happy caring for my father.' She'd never tell him the truth that she longed for a husband and a baby, but the scarcity of suitable men she admired had her doubting she'd ever be married with children to love.

'Come, every woman wants a wedding and a home of her own.' He waved his hands dismissively at her. 'I would, quite happily, court you, Miss Chambers. I believe I could offer you a pleasant life as my wife.'

'Thank you,' Lorrie murmured, embarrassed he'd put her in such an awkward situation. 'However, I will only marry for love, Mr Lynch.'

'You could grow to develop feelings?' he whined.

'I very much doubt it, but thank you for the offer.'

He stiffened, obviously unused to not getting what he wanted. 'Think about it, Miss Chambers. There is no rush, is there?' He bowed and walked out.

Exhaling deeply, Lorrie collapsed into the office chair by her desk. Every time Oswald was about, she felt her shoulders tighten.

The door opened and Father came in, wearing a puzzled expression. 'Was that Oswald? He didn't stay to speak to me.'

'He did come to see you, but instead asked me to marry him, or at least consider it. I've turned him down.'

'Oh dear. Poor fellow. That can't have been very nice for him.'

'You won't push me into marrying him, will you, Father?'

'Not if it's not what you want... Although he could provide you with a comfortable life, dearest.'

'No, Father. Please don't try to convince me that Mr Lynch is right for me. He isn't. He's not the man for me.' She smiled to lighten the atmosphere. 'How did the docking go?'

'Fine. As expected.' He searched through the paperwork on her desk. 'The last order from the timber merchants – did it include trenails?'

'Yes. Why?'

'Cameron's boat is carvel built, not clinker. The trenails need replacing and I don't think we have enough.'

'Why have you quoted a lower price for Mr Cameron?'

'He's a friend of Oswald's and we're doing it cheaper as a favour to Oswald.'

'Why? Surely, he wants more profits?'

'Cameron is his friend.' Father shrugged, uncaringly. 'Cameron can put more work our way. His brother works at Stanley Ferry boatyard. They can send us boats for repairs that they don't have time to do.'

'At a lower price?'

'Work is work, daughter.'

Lorrie said no more about it. She didn't trust Oswald, but Father did, and nothing would convince him otherwise.

The sound of wagon wheels crunching in the yard brought their attention to the window. A delivery of timber planks on the back of a wagon needed unloading and checking. Lorrie knew this would be the last order from this particular sawmill until they paid an outstanding invoice.

While Father went to see to it, Lorrie went up the outside stairs to their living rooms above. 'I'll make us some tea, Father.'

He turned and gave her a nod of thanks just as Matteo Falcone walked through the gates.

Lorrie's stomach swooped when Mr Falcone smiled at her. She crossed the yard to him, knowing Father watched her with a frown.

'You came?' she said unnecessarily.

'I said I would.' Dressed all in black except his snow-white shirt, Mr Falcone stood a head taller than every man working in the yard. All eyes were on him, the stranger.

'Would you like to come inside?' She gripped her hands, alarmed that they trembled slightly. No one had affected her like this before. Her senses were instantly alert and the hairs on the back of her neck rose.

'Thank you, but only for a moment, while I give you this.' He tapped the brown paper-wrapped parcel he held. 'Then perhaps we may go for a walk? If your father approves?'

Giddy at the thought of spending time alone with him, Lorrie didn't give a fig if Father approved or not. She'd always been the dutiful daughter, but instinct told her that Mr Falcone was worth the risk of her father's displeasure.

'Bring it inside and I'll make us a cup of tea.' Breathless and fizzing with excitement, she led the way over to the staircase.

Suddenly, an almighty crack echoed around the yard.

Halfway up the stairs, Lorrie stared down at the wagon as the ropes holding the tall pile of timber planks snapped one after the other. Frightened by the whip-crack sound, the two draught horses jibbed and pranced, dislodging the load.

The driver yelled, racing back to hold the head of the horses, but they shied and stomped. One plank fell off the wagon and then like a waterfall the rest followed.

'Father!' Lorrie screamed as her father tried to move out of the way, but he wasn't quick enough. The planks knocked him to the ground and then buried him.

She screamed again, slipping and tripping down the stairs. Mr Falcone grabbed her arm and lifted her down. She sprinted to the pile of wood, as did the men from the yard.

'Get him out!' Lorrie pulled at the long, heavy planks closest to her.

'Ye gods!' Jed muttered, before quickly pulling the top planks off.

Mr Falcone shrugged off his coat and began pulling at the planks, the men joining in while the wagon driver did his best to calm the horses.

It seemed to take forever before they revealed her father's head. He moaned and Lorrie fell to her knees beside him. 'Can you hear me, Father?'

He grunted in response, a spasm of pain flickering over his face.

'Jimmy, run for the doctor, hurry,' Lorrie told the youth.

Mr Falcone worked non-stop on the pile with the other men, heaving the planks away from Ernest Chambers's body.

Lorrie used her own handkerchief to wipe the dust and blood from her father's face. 'You'll be free soon, Father.'

'My legs,' he croaked. 'They feel like they're on fire.'

'It's the pain. You'll be free in a minute and then we'll get you comfortable upstairs.'

'Lorrie, dear girl...' His eyes closed.

She shook his shoulders, a scream buried in her throat. 'Father! Stay awake.'

3

Father's eyes fluttered open, the pain biting deep. 'I can't last, lass.'

'Of course you can. Look at me and don't worry about anything else, that's all you have to do.' She smiled lovingly into his face. 'Hold my hand, that's it.' She squeezed his fingers gently.

'He's free.' Mr Falcone puffed, coming to her side. 'We need to carry him upstairs and stop that bleeding.' His accent became stronger under stress.

'I'll find a flat board to put him on,' Jed said, wiping the sweat from his brow.

'No, the staircase is too steep.' Mr Falcone bent beside Lorrie. 'We'll have to carry him up ourselves.' His gaze travelled down to Ernest's legs which were bleeding through the material of his torn trousers. 'This is going to hurt him,' he warned her.

Lorrie patted her father's hand. 'Mr Falcone and Jed and the others will lift you and take you upstairs.'

'No...'

'They must get you inside.' She stepped back as the men gathered around him. Gently as they could, they picked him up off the ground, but Father still yelled out in agony and then promptly passed out.

'That's good, he's out. Let's be quick about it.' Mr Falcone took charge and the men crab-crawled sideways to the staircase with her father hanging between them.

Dashing away her tears, Lorrie raced ahead of them up the stairs and into the living room, for a moment she dithered, overcome with indecision, then she took a deep breath and focused. Her father's bed would need stripping and some old blankets placed over the mattress. She worked quickly, just managing to place newspapers and the old blankets over the mattress as the men brought father into the bedroom.

Lorrie stared at the blood spreading dark stains on his trousers. Father's face was cut and bleeding on the forehead and cheek, but it was his legs that Lorrie knew had suffered the worst.

'Warm water, Miss Chambers,' Mr Falcone said calmly. 'The doctor will need to clean his wounds. And scissors. To cut his trousers.'

'We need to stop the bleeding,' Jed mumbled. 'Towels, strips of cloth, miss?'

'Yes! I have bandages in the office, too.' She darted from the bedroom to the kitchen. In the top drawer she found scissors and then grabbed towels from a cupboard and took them into the bedroom.

Mr Falcone wrapped the towels around each leg.

Lorrie rushed back to the kitchen to put the kettle on the range to heat up. She needed more water, the bucket was empty.

'Give it to me.' Mr Falcone came across the room and took the bucket from her. 'Where is the tap?'

'Down in the yard, near the office window.'

'Here, I'll get it.' Jed led the other two men from the room, taking the bucket with him. 'I'll get the bandage box from the office, too.'

Lorrie added more coal to the range fire, cursing that she'd let it get so low.

'Go and sit with your father.' Mr Falcone took the small coal shovel from her hand. 'I'll see to the water.'

Emotion clogged her throat as she looked at him. His tender gaze made the tears burn hot behind her eyes. He gently touched her arm in comfort, and she fought the urge to step closer to him, badly needing him to embrace her. Instead, she spun on her heel and went back into the bedroom.

Her father lay grey-faced on the bed, his breathing shallow. She took a chair from under the window and placed it beside the bed. She took his hand, careful not to touch where the skin was cut. 'Hold on, Father. The doctor will be here soon and make you better.'

Jed came in with the box of bandages and a bowl of water. 'Ey, I'm that sorry, miss.' Jed gave her the box.

'Will you wait downstairs for the doctor and show him up, please?' She soaked a bandage in the water.

'Aye, miss.'

Left alone, Lorrie bent closer to her dear father. 'You're going to be fine.' She blinked away tears. 'You can't leave me. You're all I have.' Her words caught in her throat. Gently, she cleaned away the blood on his face. A deep cut on his forehead would need stitches, but his cheek was more of a graze now she could see it properly with the blood wiped away.

It seemed hours before the doctor arrived but was no more than twenty minutes.

'The doctor is here.' Mr Falcone stood in the doorway, moving aside for Doctor Carter to enter the room.

'Now, young Jimmy has informed of what's occurred, Miss

Chambers. Leave me to see to your father with just another man to help, if you please.' He kindly patted her shoulder as she stood.

She nodded. 'I'll see to the water.'

The doctor took off his coat. 'I'll need a good supply of it by the looks of it.'

'Shall I stay with your father?' Mr Falcone asked Lorrie.

'I think he would prefer Jed, if you don't mind?' She knew her father would hate to be undressed in front of Mr Falcone and he'd known Jed for twenty-five years.

'Of course.' Mr Falcone walked out with her.

Lorrie heated more water from the buckets Jed had brought up. She spilt more than she poured into the pans and jerked back in surprise when Mr Falcone took the bucket from her and finished the task.

'Sit,' he said gently. 'You've had a shock. Do you have brandy?'

'No.' Lorrie clasped her hands together and glanced worriedly at the closed bedroom door. 'He can't die on me. He is all I have,' she murmured.

Jimmy knocked and entered, carrying Mr Falcone's coat and a brown paper-wrapped parcel. 'I found these in the yard, miss.'

'Thank you, Jimmy.' Lorrie took them from him.

'Any news?'

'Not yet. Your speed at fetching the doctor was vital. Thank you.'

He flushed at the praise. 'I was lucky to find the doctor quickly. He was on Doncaster Road. The men are continuing working. We don't want to let you or Mr Chambers down by standing around doing nowt.'

Lorrie touched his arm. 'Thank them for me, will you?'

'Aye, miss.' He went out and closed the door.

She turned to Mr Falcone who was in the process of adding sugar to a teacup. 'Your coat and parcel.'

'Today has not been as I expected.' He brought over a cup of tea for her.

'No, nor me.' She sat at the table, sick with worry.

'I had plans for us to talk a great deal.' He sat opposite her, his dark eyes full of sympathy, his tone caring.

'I would have liked that.'

'There will be another opportunity. First, your father's health is more important.'

'You speak very good English.' She couldn't help saying.

He smiled. 'I was sent to this country to be educated when I was fourteen.'

Frowning, Lorrie sipped her tea. 'Father told me that my mother's family were poor. They lived in London's East End.'

'Yes, they were, my family weren't. Our great-grandmothers were cousins. That is the connection between my family and your mother's. However, my father's side of the family was not poor. We have been craftsmen for generations, but also scholars and statesmen.'

'Oh.' She tried to concentrate on what he had to say, to learn more from him. However, her brain refused to work properly.

'Would you care to know more about my family?' He gave a wry smile. 'I can stay quiet if you'd rather have some peace, or I can leave.'

'No, please stay. I would like to know more about you, and your family, and my mother's as well.' She wanted to learn more about him, and it would also take her mind off her father.

'My grandfather has eleven children. Seven of them sons. My country has been fighting for centuries and with the constant wars of independence within itself. My grandfather sent six of his sons to other parts of the world to live and raise their families, away from the fighting. My father, the eldest, he kept in La Spezia.'

'La Spezia. That is where you are from?' Despite her worry, Lorrie was interested.

'*Sì*. Yes.' He smiled.

A deep moan came from the bedroom. Lorrie jerked to her feet.

Mr Falcone stood as well. 'Do you want me to check for you?'

'I want to see for myself.' She marched to the bedroom and, without hesitating, opened the door. The smell of blood hit her first, thick and cloying. The sight of so many red-stained cloths on the floor made her reel.

Dr Carter glanced over his shoulder. 'Good, another pair of hands. Hold your father's shoulders down, Miss Chambers. You, sir, come hold his other leg.' He nodded to Mr Falcone.

Lorrie slipped to the top end of the bed. Her father's face was covered in sweat, his eyes firmly closed, his lips pressed together as he fought the pain. 'I'm here, Father.' She placed her hands on his shoulders as he writhed.

'I need to straighten these bones,' Dr Carter mumbled, his fingers coated in blood as he manipulated the left shin bone, which protruded through the skin. 'The right leg is in better shape than the left. The right leg has a sprained ankle, cuts and bruises. I fear the left leg is far more damaged. His fibula is broken. That is the snapped bone we see there,' Dr Carter murmured as if speaking to himself. 'I need to straighten it into place, close the wound and splint the leg.'

A groan escaped Father's throat. Lorrie focused on his white face, not wanting to see the doctor move skin, muscle and bone as easily as if he was a butcher cutting up a carcass.

Lorrie lost track of time as the doctor worked. Father went in and out of consciousness and when he was out, Lorrie fetched clean towels and more water.

By late afternoon, everyone was exhausted, especially Dr Carter.

After securing the final bandage, the doctor wiped his brow, his white apron streaked in red. 'That is done to the best of my skills, Miss Chambers.' He untied the strings of his filthy apron and took it off. 'Mr Chambers will no doubt get a fever from infection, for it was an open wound. I cannot rule out possible gangrene and amputation. I am preparing you.' He sighed tiredly. 'Shock may finish him yet. I am surprised his heart did not give out today. The loss of blood was considerable.'

The list of problems overwhelmed her. 'Father is strong, and I will care for him.'

'And those two things still might not be enough.' The doctor cleaned his tools in yet another bucket of water that Jimmy had been delivering to the bedroom door on a regular basis for hours.

Mr Falcone took out another bucket of red-stained water while Jed collected the soiled clothes.

'Burn them, Jed. I'll never get the stains out.'

'Aye, miss.'

'Then get yourself home. Tell everyone to go home.' She gave him a grateful smile.

'Right you are, miss.'

Dr Carter shrugged on his coat. 'I will return in the morning, early. Unless he worsens overnight, then come and fetch me, but he should sleep for a good few hours after the laudanum I gave him. I left a bottle of it beside the bed. Administer it as needed, he's going to need it.'

'Thank you, doctor.'

One by one, they left until only Mr Falcone stood in the living area tending to the fire. Lorrie scrutinised the linen cupboard and the depletion of nearly all the towels and old sheets, all cut up and used to stem the blood.

'Sit,' Mr Falcone said. 'I shall make us a drink.'

'Shouldn't you be going, too? You look as tired as I feel.'

'I am fine. My room at the inn isn't very comfortable and it's cold. I am much better here with a fire.' His half smile teased her heart.

'I can make you something to eat.' She didn't know if the bread was still fresh or if there was enough butter left. She had planned to go to the shops, to the butcher for a rabbit to stew or buy some kidneys and hearts to put in a pie.

Falcone shook his head. 'You need to rest. Shall I instead go and buy us something?'

A knock at the door had them both turning. Thinking it might be Jimmy, Lorrie opened it and stared in surprise as her dearest friend Meg stood there.

'It's you!' Lorrie burst into tears.

Meg embraced her tightly. 'I was at the brewery and heard there had been an accident. Are you all right?'

'Yes, it was Father. He was crushed by falling planks.' Lorrie tried to calm herself but seeing a friendly dear face had brought her emotions flooding out.

'How is he?'

'Terrible. One leg is terribly broken, the other sprained, he's full of deep cuts...' Lorrie couldn't speak.

Mr Falcone came closer to them. 'I shall go, Miss Chambers. Your friend is here now.'

Embarrassed, Lorrie wiped her eyes. 'Forgive me for my rudeness. Mr Falcone, this is my friend, Mrs Henderson. Meg, this is Mr Matteo Falcone, a distant relative on my mother's side.'

They shook hands and then Mr Falcone bowed slightly to Lorrie. 'I am staying at the Black Swan in Northgate. Send for me should you need me.'

Lorrie gazed at him, wanting him to stay, but simply nodded. 'You will return tomorrow?'

'I will.' He smiled and, grabbing his coat, walked out into the spring evening air.

Meg's eyes widened. 'He looks foreign and has an accent.'

'Italian,' Lorrie supplied.

'So handsome.' Meg peeled off her gloves. 'I'll put the kettle on while you tell me everything. You must be exhausted.'

Lorrie went into the bedroom and checked on her father first. He lay sleeping, drugged from the opium draught the doctor had managed to get Father to sip at. Already his leg bandages were spotted with blood seeping out from beneath. Lorrie knew she'd be sitting up beside him all night, worrying herself stupid until the doctor returned.

'Have you eaten?' Meg asked, setting out the tea things.

'Not since breakfast.'

Meg tutted. 'I'll make you some toast.'

Tears burned behind Lorrie's eyes at the kindness. Today, both Mr Falcone and Meg had considered her, wanted to take care of her, and it felt wonderful, even if the circumstances were tragic.

'It's getting late,' Lorrie murmured. 'Won't Christian be wondering where you are?'

'I just left him at the brewery. He'll collect me in an hour, or I can tell him I'll stay the night with you, if you prefer?'

'No, there is no point both of us having a disturbed night, but thank you for offering.'

Glancing at the clock, Lorrie couldn't believe it was after five. Where had the day gone? She rose to check on her father once more, but he still slept soundly. She hoped it would last some hours.

'Eat your toast.' Meg placed a plate of buttered toast before her. 'Do you have jam?'

'In the cupboard.' Lorrie sipped the tea, realising she was rather thirsty. 'How is the family? Fliss told me at church that you've brought Mabel home after her baby died. I'm so sorry to hear it.'

Meg sighed as she sat down. 'It's been so awful, I can't tell you. Freddie and me arrived in Huddersfield too late. The baby, Mabel had called her Issy, died only hours before we got there. Issy was tiny, frail from her first breath. I don't think Mabel ever wanted the baby, and was happy to give her away, yet she never expected for the child to die in her arms. Mabel was upset, of course, and in shock.'

'Naturally, she would be. It must have been dreadful for her, for you all.'

'After the funeral we brought Mabel home. She's staying with Christian and me for a bit. The whole episode has made Mabel grow up a lot. She doesn't want to go back to the mill and all the gossip.'

'What will she do instead?' Lorrie ate her toast, suddenly hungry. Listening to Meg took her mind off her father for a few minutes.

'I don't know.' Meg shrugged. 'She could live with Freddie at his pub and help him, or get another job and live with either us or Josie.'

'Josie is working well at the Bay Horse, Fliss told me. She turns up for every shift.' Lorrie spoke of the woman who had been Meg's father's other woman. Josie had thought Frank Taylor to be free to marry her, when in fact he was already married to Meg's mam and had eight children to support at home. He lived two lives while working as a narrowboat captain and died last year only weeks after Meg's mam, who never found out about her bigamist husband.

'I'm pleased Josie is reliable. She has rent and food to pay for and the responsibilities of my younger siblings.'

'Will you not take them to Meadow View House?' Lorrie asked. She knew Meg would like her brothers and sister to live with her and Christian at their manor, but it wasn't practical. They were working class and didn't fit into Meg's new world of being the wife to a wealthy brewery owner. Her siblings had stayed in the two-up two-down terraced house in Wellington Street with Josie.

'Not yet. I don't know. Just seeing Mabel in the house shows me how odd it is for her to be waited on by staff, as I know only too well. It's been eight months since I married Christian, and I still feel uncomfortable having servants to do my bidding.'

'Mabel might feel better going to stay with Freddie at his pub and help him?'

'Maybe, but it also puts her closer to men who like to flirt. You know what she's like.'

'Surely, she's learnt her lesson to not dally with any more men until she's married?'

'You'd think so, but this is Mabel...' Meg rolled her eyes. 'Anyway, I'm here to support you, not go on about my lot.'

'I'll be fine.'

'No, you won't. Your father will need full-time nursing and there's the boatyard to run. You can't do both.'

'I'm going to have to.'

'No, I'll pay for one of those home nurses to come and stay. I see lots of advertisements for young women who can be companions and such like in those awful periodicals that Maude insists I read. I think Maude made me subscribe to them because she wants to read them, not me.' Meg grinned, but everyone knew how devoted she was to her lady's maid.

'Meg, no.' Lorrie shook her head. 'I don't want a stranger here day and night and Father will not tolerate it for sure.'

'But you need help.'

'I'll manage. Thank you for the offer, but no.' Lorrie gripped Meg's hand for a moment to show her gratitude. If she was being honest with herself, the future overwhelmed her. She could run the boatyard, she didn't doubt that for she'd been working in the office all her adult life, but caring for her father on top of that would take all of her strength and courage. She knew he'd not be an easy man to nurse, he was too independent, too proud to allow her to help him. However, a stranger in the mix would be unthinkable for Father. Although the months ahead would be tough, Lorrie needed, for her own sanity, to be brave and resilient. She refused to think of the alternative; a life without Father, without them managing the boatyard together was unthinkable.

'Well then, at least you can tell me about the handsome Italian.' Meg raised her eyebrows.

'Today was only the second time I've met him, and for the poor man to be confronted by such an accident...'

'He was of help to you, though?'

'Yes. Amazing, really.' Lorrie's gaze strayed to the parcel sitting on the narrow table by the door. 'He'd come to give me a gift from my great-grandmother who recently passed.'

'That's kind of him.'

'Father was annoyed that Mr Falcone came.'

'Why?'

Lorrie shrugged. 'He wouldn't say. There was some bad blood between the families, apparently. It's the first I've heard of it, but then Father never speaks of my mother. I know so little about her life and family.'

'Mr Falcone might be able to change that, though?'

'I was hoping to ask him some questions today, but obviously that didn't happen.'

'He will return. The look he gave you was sweet.' Meg's knowing smile made Lorrie blush.

'Nonsense. He'd be feeling sorry for me.' She looked around, seeing the room from another person's eyes. They lived in a flat above a boatyard. Two small bedrooms, one main living room with a kitchen off to the side. 'Mr Falcone was sent to England for his education. I do not think he'd have his sights set on a boatman's daughter, that's for certain.'

'At least you attended a private ladies' school and could easily pass for a lady with the right clothes and house. Look at me, a lass from the waterfront, and I married Christian, a wealthy man; you're above the social standing of what I was, the humble daughter of a bigamist narrowboat captain.' Meg clicked her tongue, always annoyed whenever she mentioned her father.

'I have enough to think about without the idea of romantic notions concerning an Italian.' Lorrie tried to joke but it fell flat. Truthfully, she was scared of the future and needed Father to recover. If he didn't, she didn't know what she'd do.

4

'This is a disaster!' Oswald Lynch fumed, pacing the living room. 'How could Ernest be so foolish to injure himself like that?'

Lorrie glared at him. 'Keep your voice down. Father has been awake most of the night in terrible pain. It was an accident, Mr Lynch. The ropes snapped on the wagon.'

'When is the doctor coming? I need to speak to him regarding Ernest's recovery time. We have a yard full of orders.'

'Orders that barely pay the bills,' she snapped. 'You don't need to speak to Dr Carter about that today,' she said tiredly. She'd sat up beside her father all night as he moaned restlessly. She could do nothing but give him laudanum and wipe his forehead, offer sips of water. Finally, just before dawn, he fell into a fitful sleep, and she had nodded off in the chair, only to be woken an hour later by the factory whistles and the sounds of the town waking.

Oswald glared at her. 'This is my business, Miss Chambers, and *you'll* do well to remember that.'

'And my father's! *You* forget that!'

'And he is incapable of running it at the moment.' Oswald rubbed his head. 'I'll speak to the men.'

'There is no need. They know their tasks and work will continue as planned. You are a silent partner, Mr Lynch, did you forget that part of the deal?'

His piggy eyes narrowed. 'Do not speak to me as though I was your underling, miss. I could, at any time, demand my money back and where would you be then?'

She blinked, taking in his words.

'Yes, not so mouthy now, are we?' he taunted. 'If I wanted my money back, you'd have to sell up to release the funds and then you'd be without an income or a home. Think on that before you speak to me so disrespectfully next time!'

A wave of fear threatened to swallow her.

Oswald grabbed his hat from the table by the door and paused. He seemed to take a moment to collect himself. 'Miss Chambers, we are in this together. We need to be friends, agreed?'

She nodded, knowing that to argue with him would only make matters worse.

'Good.' He placed his top hat on his head. 'If you were to think of me kindly, to perceive me as someone who could take care of you, then perhaps we could become close friends, and possibly more...'

'I don't think so, Mr Lynch.'

'Don't be too hasty to turn me down, Miss Chambers. You may be attractive but there isn't a line of men at your door asking you to marry them. Why is that?' He tipped his hat at her and walked out.

She stood motionless for a moment. Why was that? Why had no man ever offered her marriage except Mr Lynch? She knew she had claim to some looks and was educated. She was kind and sensible. So why then was she still unmarried at twenty-five?

She didn't have the answer. Only that she wasn't going to settle for just anyone. As much as she longed for marriage and children, she'd not accept Oswald Lynch.

Entering her father's bedroom, she could smell the lingering odour of blood. Her father lay sweating, mumbling, his face flushed. Concerned at the quick deterioration since she'd left the room only ten minutes ago when Oswald arrived, Lorrie sponged cool water on her father's damp forehead.

'Father, do you want some water?'

'No. Good God... the agony...' He squirmed on the bed, his fists clenched in the sheets.

'I'll give you some more laudanum.' She took the little brown bottle from the chest of drawers and tipped some onto a spoon. Her father drank it, moaning.

'Miss Chambers?' Dr Carter stood in the doorway. 'I let myself in.'

'Doctor, he is much worse.' She rose from the chair to make way for him.

Frowning, Dr Carter examined his patient. 'His temperature is high. I don't like the look of him.' He then uncovered Father's legs and Lorrie gasped at the purple bruising and weeping wounds covering the left leg from the knee down.

'Damn it.' Dr Carter hurriedly took off his jacket. 'Boil some water, Miss Chambers, lots of it. We've got infection in his left leg which is causing the fever. It might have to come off.'

Lorrie reeled. 'No!'

'We can't risk gangrene setting in. It'll kill him.'

'But isn't there something else you can do?' Lorrie stared at the festering mess of her father's left leg.

'I'll try to save it. Hurry now. I need water. Clean cloths.'

She spun on her heel and slammed into Mr Falcone. 'Oh! Forgive me.'

He held her arms. 'What is it?'

'Father... He...' She couldn't say the words.

'You, sir, I need your assistance.' Dr Carter waved Mr Falcone into the room. 'You'll need to hold his shoulders down while I clean his wounds as it's going to be mighty painful for Mr Chambers.'

Lorrie ran to the range to heat some water. She had been soaking some of the cloth bandages, but knew she needed more. She found her purse and raced down the staircase and across the yard to find Jimmy. He was sorting in the tool shed, where all the tools needed by the men were cleaned and hung up.

'Jimmy!' She thrust her purse at him. 'Go into town, the market, anywhere and buy several sheets or as many cloths as I have money for. The doctor needs them for Father. Be as fast as you can, please.'

'Aye, miss.' Jimmy dashed from the shed and Lorrie ran back up the stairs and into the living room.

She jumped as her father's screams filled the room. She blinked back tears as she filled buckets of water, placed the kettle and pans on to heat.

Another scream rent the air.

Lorrie bit her lips to stop crying at her father's distress. She did numerous trips into the bedroom carrying bowls of warm water. The sight of blood and pus oozing out of Father's wounds turned her stomach. She kept her head down and concentrated on the job at hand. She tore up another tablecloth for the doctor to use. She now had no sheets or tablecloths left to use except what was on her bed and her mother's red damask.

A delivery of nails and paint arrived, but Jed saw to it while Lorrie kept fetching buckets of water from the pump, her arms aching as she carried them upstairs. Father's cries and wails of agony echoed across the yard. She wanted to beg the doctor to stop but knew she couldn't get involved, the man was trying to help, and she had to trust he would not let Father die.

Jimmy staggered through the door, wrapped bundles in his arms, panting for breath. 'I got as much as I could carry, miss.'

'Perfect. Thank you.' She took them from him and went straight into the bedroom. Her step faltered on seeing the blood-spattered bed, her father writhing.

Dr Carter looked up from his gruesome task of cleaning the wounds. 'Cloths? Good. Hand one to me.'

Lorrie averted her eyes from the wounds and glanced at Mr Falcone where he knelt by Father's head, holding him down by the shoulders.

Mr Falcone's tender smile calmed her a little. 'Keep looking at me if it helps,' he murmured.

She tore and cut lengths of bandages from the sheets, making a pile close to the doctor, but she would often focus on Mr Falcone's handsome face as well as wiping the sweat beading on her father's forehead and neck.

Eventually, Dr Carter cleaned his tools and washed his hands and arms. His apron was more red than white. The blankets on the bed were changed and her father given another dose of laudanum. Exhaustion had sent him to sleep.

'I shall be back in the morning, Miss Chambers, to change the dressing.' Dr Carter tiredly pulled on his coat. 'If I have missed any infection, we'll know about it tomorrow. Mr Chambers should become less feverish now. I am hoping he may be over the worst, but we just do not know. It is too soon to say.'

'Can I make you some tea?'

He patted her shoulder. 'I am away to my bed. I have not slept since yesterday. I had two births after leaving here. I fear if I sat down now, you would have me as an overnight guest.'

'You could take my bed, doctor,' she said without hesitation.

'That is generous of you, but my wife will be wanting me home.' The poor man looked fatigued. 'Thank you, Mr Falcone, for your assistance. Until tomorrow.' He gave a half-hearted wave and left.

For a fleeting moment, Lorrie worried about the hefty bill the doctor would no doubt give them, but soon dismissed it. She would pay whatever the amount was, even if it meant she ate nothing but bread and tea for a week.

'Miss Chambers?' Mr Falcone's tone was kind, gentle. He placed his hand lightly on her back to steer her away from the bedroom. 'Your father is sleeping and for the moment free of pain. You should rest also.'

'My mind won't let me rest.' She went to the range and poked at the fire before adding pieces of coal to it. 'Besides, I have work to do in the office. I need to check on the men.'

'Would you allow me to do that? To speak to the men?'

The offer surprised her. 'Why would you do that?'

'I have some knowledge of boats and repairs.'

'You do?' She was even more surprised by his announcement.

He smiled. 'I have some knowledge of a boatyard. My father builds fishing boats in La Spezia.'

'He does? How interesting.'

'Your father was apprenticed to a boat builder in London. My uncle owned the boatyard next to the one your father worked at. That is how he met your mother.'

'Yes, the small information I do know is that my mother's family had the boatyard next to where Father was apprenticed.'

'While I was in England being educated, I sometimes spent my holidays with my uncle in London when I didn't return to La Spezia.'

'La Spezia.' It sounded so exotic. Lorrie sat at the table, tired and dispirited. 'Will you tell me about it?' She didn't have time to sit and chat, but she desperately wanted to be taken away from her stressful world and into his for a few minutes.

Mr Falcone sat opposite her. Even after helping the doctor, he appeared neat and tidy, calm. Lorrie knew she was in a state of disarray, her hair falling out of the pins that held it, her apron smudged. Yet, in the careful way Mr Falcone watched her, none of that mattered. His dark eyes never wavered from her face as though he was studying each feature minutely. Under his gaze and the half smile he gave her, she felt attractive and womanly.

He leant forward, resting his elbows on the table, giving her his full attention. 'The town, La Spezia, is a port. The harbour has such blue water and dark green hills and mountains rising behind it. The people are friendly, the food delectable and the sunshine is warm on your back.'

'It sounds wonderful.'

'I wish I could take you there.'

Lorrie's heart leapt in her chest like a coiled spring. She wanted to go with him, this handsome stranger.

'Your mother's family comes from La Spezia, too,' he added softly.

'They do?' She had no idea. 'Mother was born in London, Father told me.'

'Yes, she was. But her parents came to England the same time as my uncle. Remember, your great-grandmother and my great-grandmother were distant cousins, but they also lived in the same area of La Spezia and were close friends.'

Lorrie glanced at the parcel by the door, left untouched.

Mr Falcone went to get it and brought it back to the table. 'Open it.'

Carefully, excitedly, Lorrie untied the string and pulled away the brown paper, revealing a small wooden box polished to a high shine. On the lid was painted a scene of a town in a harbour and around the scene was a border of mother-of-pearl.

'That is La Spezia,' he told her proudly.

She studied the blue of the water, the cream of the little buildings with dark green mountains behind and then more blue of the sky. 'It's beautiful.'

Opening the lid, Lorrie gasped at the braided gold necklace resting on a bed of ruby velvet. Gently, she lifted the chain out and noticed a gold pendant on it in the shape of a bent horn.

'That is the cornicello,' Mr Falcone explained. 'It is to bring good luck.'

'I can't believe my great-grandmother who I never met has given this to me.' Emotion caught in her throat.

'My nonna said that Loretta was very sad to have never seen you. The family were devastated when your mother married your father and went north to live away from her family in London. She died too young.'

'Yes, my mother did die too young. I didn't have enough time with her. My memories of her are sketchy now.'

'You should go to London and meet your family. They would welcome you.'

'London seems so far away, but yes, one day I would like to meet my mother's family.' She'd often wondered about them, but her days were full enough with looking after Father and running the office and she could never go by herself, and Father refused to speak of them.

'I could take you.' His warm smile sent shivers down her back.

'Perhaps when Father is well again,' she said vaguely, knowing it was very unlikely. Father would forbid it. 'Tell me more about them. Did my mother have brothers and sisters?'

'Yes. Two brothers, Giovani, but he goes by the name of George, and Luca, who is called Luke. They wanted to fit into the English country they were born into, so they changed their names when they became men.' Mr Falcone shrugged as though he understood the reasoning. 'When I was at school, some boys tried to tease me because I was foreign. A boy with an accent and a strange name, Matteo Falcone. My friends there called me Matt.' He shrugged again in that easy Italian way he had. 'The other boys soon stopped teasing when I became very good at boxing.'

Lorrie shivered. She hated violence of any sort but felt proud of him for standing up to those who wanted to do him harm, a lonely boy in a strange country. How alone he must have felt.

A knock on the door interrupted them. Lorrie got up to see who it was.

Jimmy stood there. 'Sorry, miss, but there's a fellow down in the yard looking for work.'

'I'm coming.' Lorrie grabbed her shawl from the hook by the door and turned to Mr Falcone, but he was already walking to join her.

The three of them went downstairs. Jimmy pointed to the man by the barrels of tar. 'That's him.'

Lorrie frowned. The man seemed interested in the goings-on inside the shed that housed a half-built narrowboat. 'Good day, Mr...?'

He sauntered over to Lorrie, giving Mr Falcone a hard stare as he did so. 'I'm here to see whoever is in charge.'

'My father is in charge, and he is unwell at the moment. I am his daughter, Miss Chambers, you can speak with me.' Lorrie didn't like the look of the man, who still had his hands in the pockets of his dirty trousers, his jaw covered in a straggly beard.

'The name is Saunders. I'm after some work, miss.'

'I'm sorry, but we don't have any.'

His expression was full of contempt. 'I'd rather talk to your father, if you please?'

Annoyed, Lorrie straightened her back. 'As I just mentioned, my father is unwell at the moment. I am in charge.'

At that moment, Oswald sauntered through the gates. Lorrie squashed a groan at the sight of him.

'What do we have here, Miss Chambers?' Oswald asked, swinging a gold-topped cane and wearing a dandy suit of silver grey with a deep purple waistcoat.

'Nothing to concern you, Mr Lynch.'

'I'm after work,' the man repeated. 'She says she has none.'

'Do you have experience in this industry?' Oswald asked the man.

'Aye, I've fixed barges at Stanley Ferry.' The man rubbed his nose.

Lorrie took a step closer to Oswald. 'We have enough men.'

'Do we?' he pondered. 'Now Ernest is abed for some time, we are down a pair of hands.'

Mr Falcone came to stand beside Lorrie. 'Then allow me to help you for a time.'

'Who is this?' Oswald peered at Mr Falcone as though he was some unsavoury character.

'Mr Lynch, this is Mr Falcone, a member of my late mother's family.'

Mr Falcone held out his hand, but Oswald ignored it. Mr Falcone's face tightened at the insult.

'Italian,' Oswald scorned. 'We'll have no Italians working in my business, thank you very much.'

Mr Falcone took a step towards Oswald, his hands clenched.

Lorrie put her hand up at Oswald. 'It is also my father's business,' Lorrie reminded him yet again. 'And may I add that I run this business at the moment. I may not actually build the boats as my father does, but I do everything else. I, more than anyone, know what we do or do not *need*.'

Oswald glared at her. 'You are being very assertive, Miss Chambers, in public. You're making a show of yourself. Let us go inside.'

He turned to Saunders. 'Return in a few days, there may be something for you then.'

Fuming, Lorrie marched away to the office. Mr Falcone and Oswald followed her.

'Really, Miss Chambers, you must get a hold of your emotions. This is why women are no good in business.' Oswald took off his hat, staring at Mr Falcone as he did so. 'And you, sir, what is your business here?'

Mr Falcone lifted his chin. He stood a good foot taller than Oswald. '*My* business is none of *your* business, sir.'

Flustered, Oswald glanced at Lorrie. 'Miss Chambers?'

She ignored his questioning stare. 'What is it that you want, Oswald? You were only here this morning.'

'I wanted to check on your father's welfare and that of the boatyard. Is that so wrong of me to be concerned?'

Her shoulders sagged. 'No, of course not. But I am handling things.' She refused to look at the pile of paperwork needing her attention and she had no idea what state each of the jobs were at in the sheds.

'We do need someone to help you, to be in charge of the men while Ernest is laid up,' Oswald said.

'I can help with that.' Mr Falcone folded his arms and leant against the desk. 'My family are in boat building, and I have some knowledge. I could spend a few weeks here.'

Lorrie's stomach somersaulted at the announcement. She liked Mr Falcone a lot, possibly too much, and to have him here every day for weeks... She was both delighted and terrified at the idea.

Oswald puffed out his chubby cheeks. 'I'd prefer a local man.'

'And I'd prefer someone experienced and trustworthy,' Lorrie replied quickly before Oswald could say anything to change Mr Falcone's mind.

'Do you trust this man?' Oswald asked her, pointing at Falcone.

'I do,' she answered without hesitation.

Mr Falcone straightened. 'Then I shall stay in Wakefield for a few weeks until Mr Chambers is well enough to leave his bed.'

'That's very generous.' Lorrie smiled. She wondered what his family would think of his decision.

Oswald sniffed with disdain. 'By the look of you, you aren't in need of money.'

Mr Falcone's eyes narrowed at another insult. 'I require no money for my services. I shall do it as a favour for Miss Chambers and our family connection.'

Oswald replaced his hat. 'Then I had better see about bringing more jobs into the yard. We cannot allow the men to be idle.' There was a gleam in his eyes. 'Yes, I can sort that out with none of Ernest's moaning that we don't have the space or the manpower to do it.'

'What are you suggesting?' Lorrie's tone showed her alarm. 'We have enough to do, and every client you send here says the cost is far cheaper than we would normally charge.'

Oswald rubbed his hands together. 'Leave it with me, my dear girl. I'm going to make money, Miss Chambers.' Chortling to himself, he exited the office.

'I do not like that rude man,' Mr Falcone stated.

'No, nor do I. Unfortunately, I have no choice but to have him in my life. He is Father's partner.'

'I feel that was unwise of your father to become involved with Lynch.'

'Do you always have such a quick perception of people, Mr Falcone?'

'Yes. Always.' He stepped closer to her, his eyes locked with hers. 'My name is Matteo.' He took her hand. 'And you are Lorrie.' Her name rolled off his tongue sensually.

Lorrie swallowed, unable to move. 'That is rather forward of you,' she whispered.

He raised her hand and kissed it. 'We have been through enough in the last few days to do away with formalities. I am Italian, we are friendly people, and we do not like to be tethered by rules and you English have so many of them.'

Her breathing quickened. His handsome face was so close, so close that she could see his eyes were the deepest chocolate brown with tiny flecks of gold in them. His eyelashes were as black as his hair.

'So, will you show me around to meet the men who work here?'

Lorrie took a step back, regaining her senses, which seemed to fly away from her whenever he was near. 'Absolutely.'

Brisk and businesslike, she led him out into the yard, and they visited the first of the two large open-sided sheds. The first shed was closer to the river and, high up on wooden chocks, a narrowboat was being de-caulked by Jimmy and another lad, Anthony.

Lorrie made the introductions and explained that the boat belonged to a local mill owner who still transported his cargo by barge and narrowboat, but for how much longer, Lorrie couldn't tell. The railways were taking the cargo trade and putting narrowboat owners out of work.

In the second shed, she showed Mr Falcone the new sailing boat that Father had been commissioned to build a year ago for a wealthy gentleman he'd known for decades and who lived near Goole. Jed was sanding the sleek wooden hull while another new employee, Roy, was inside the boat hammering.

'It has beautiful lines,' Mr Falcone said, running his hand along the curved hull.

'Father has worked on it for months, and Jed of course, but it is Father's design. The boat will be used on the River Humber mainly for private fishing trips and sailing in the summer.'

'A rich man's plaything?' Mr Falcone grinned.

Lorrie snorted. 'Exactly.'

'It reminds me a lot of the boats my grandfather and father worked on back home.'

'Do you miss La Spezia?'

'Very much. It is home.' He shrugged. 'But my fate has been that I live in England for many years. However, that is all to change.'

'You are returning to Italy?'

'In a few weeks. I want to start my own business.'

'Which is?'

'Wine.'

'Wine?' She smiled in surprise.

'My mother's family have a vineyard between the sea and the mountains. My mother's cousin who owns it is getting old and has asked me to take over.' A look of pleasure transformed his handsome features into a dreamlike state. 'It is my heart's desire to do it. I will expand the business and make it great. I have spent a good deal of time in London making contacts who will buy crates of the wine I make.'

She could hear the eagerness in his voice. How wonderful it must feel to be so passionate about something. 'I'm sure you will be very successful.'

He twitched one shoulder. 'My father is angry with me, for he wants me to be like him, a boat builder, and carry on the trade.'

'But you want to own a vineyard.'

'*Sì*. My brother will be the boat builder.' He winked mischievously. 'And I will make the wine.'

'Then you must follow your heart,' Lorrie encouraged, slightly sad at the thought he would be gone soon.

He focused back on her face. 'I will, *sì*, but first, I will help you.'

She felt flattered by his concern and attention. 'Thank you.'

His dark eyes kept her own gaze locked. 'It is easy to be in your presence. We shall enjoy our time together, I know it.'

Lorrie had trouble swallowing. His look and words took on a double meaning. 'I had best get back to Father.'

Matteo straightened, once more businesslike. 'And I will talk to the men, to Jed. He is the most senior?'

'Yes.' She turned away but paused and glanced over her shoulder. 'Come up for some tea when you're finished.'

For a long moment, their gazes held once more. A smile played about his lips and his eyes narrowed slightly. 'How could I resist such a request?'

A little breathless, Lorrie left the shed and headed across the yard. Since Mr Falcone's arrival, he had disturbed her mind, her normal way of thinking. From the moment she first met him only days ago, she'd thought of him a great deal. She was being silly, ridiculous to have such thoughts about an intriguing man such as him. A man who would soon leave and she'd never see again.

5

In the warm March sunshine, Lorrie selected vegetables from the stall in the market. Her hands moved quickly over the potatoes, turnips, carrots and onions, picking the best and handing them over to the stall owner to weigh. She'd been shopping for over an hour and was desperate to get back to Father, who had endured another agonising morning of Dr Carter cleaning his suppurating wounds. His cries of distress rang throughout the yard, causing the men to stare up at the windows and shudder.

Lorrie quickened her steps to the butchers on Kirkgate, where she bought soup bones and a rabbit to make a stew as well as kidneys and cuts of meat for a pie.

Arms laden, she hurried back towards the waterfront. She wanted to cook the pie for the evening's meal and start on the rabbit stew so it could cook slowly and be ready for tomorrow's dinner.

Matteo had taken to eating with her on an evening when the men had gone home, and the yard closed. He helped her in so many ways aside from being in the yard to oversee the men and keep everything ticking over while she concentrated on caring for her father. Matteo always made sure she had full buckets of water in the kitchen, that the ledgers were updated in the office and each evening he would come upstairs and be the company she so desperately needed.

It alarmed her how much she was coming to rely on him, and not only that, but how much she was enjoying his company. There was something about him that drew her. Attraction throbbed between them and even though she wasn't experienced in having suitors, she couldn't deny or even hide the way she felt about him. She tried, desperately, not to show him how she was feeling in his presence, but she had never felt this way about anyone before and it was overwhelming, distracting and exciting.

'Lorrie!' Fliss called from the other side of the road.

'I can't stop,' Lorrie said, giving Fliss a smile when her friend joined her. 'I've got all this and must get back.' She frowned on seeing Fliss's bandaged wrist. 'What have you done to yourself?'

'Oh, nothing.' Fliss dismissed her concerns airily. 'You know what a clumsy fool I am. I fell against a barrel in the cellar. Anyway, I was coming to you to see if you needed any help today with your father?'

'Thank you. I'm fine, though. Dr Carter has called this morning to clean Father's wounds and the pain and exhaustion Father feels afterwards drain him. I gave him a dose of laudanum before I left, and he was asleep before I had pinned my bonnet on. Matteo... er... Mr Falcone is there.'

Fliss grinned. 'Matteo is it now?'

Lorrie blushed. 'No, well, not in public... Just inside, privately...' Her words stumbled out of her mouth. 'He's been a wonderful help to me over the last week.'

'I'm pleased to hear it, and I'd like to meet him.' Fliss took one of Lorrie's full baskets with her good hand and they fell into step. 'I saw Meg yesterday at the post office and she said Mr Falcone is rather handsome, all foreign-looking and has an accent.'

'Meg says too much,' Lorrie tutted.

Fliss raised her eyebrows. 'And you say too little.'

'There's nothing to tell. Honestly. Mr Falcone is a friend. Soon, he will return to Italy.' The idea of saying goodbye to him was already something she was dreading. To never see Matteo again hung over her constantly, ready to ruin the only bit of happiness she had.

'How do you feel about that?' Fliss watched her.

Lorrie smiled brightly to hide her inner feelings. 'I will wish him well. He brought me a necklace from my great-grandmother, something I will always be grateful to him for doing, but his life belongs elsewhere.' How she wished it wasn't so.

'Unless he changes his mind. If you give him some encouragement to stay?'

'Goodness,' she laughed, 'you're making it sound as though this is some great love affair, Fliss. We are friends. He has been an enormous help to me and I will forever be thankful for it.'

'Has he never given you any inkling of wanting more?'

Lorrie thought of the strange moments when she caught him watching her when he thought she wasn't looking. The times when he held her hand and told her to call him Matteo or the snatched moments when he made her laugh with a story of what happened in the yard, or a childhood memory of Italy. He'd speak of incidents at the boarding school he attended down south when he was a foreign child in a strict and traditional country that was so alien to him. She began to know him, to understand his humour, his work ethic, his funny ways of dealing with the men to get them on his side when they didn't want to be told what to do by an Italian.

And yes, she understood the attraction between them, and she knew she had deeper emotions developing for him every day and it scared her witless. However, what did Matteo feel? Anything? Nothing? Something?

Walking into the boatyard, Lorrie sighed on seeing Oswald talking to Matteo by one of the sheds. The two men couldn't be more different, Oswald short and fat and Matteo tall and lean. One calm and the other gesturing and blowing out his plump cheeks in exasperation.

'Mr Lynch?' Lorrie addressed the annoying man first as Matteo took the basket from her.

'I was just telling Mr Falcone here that I am perfectly within my rights to give orders within this yard as I own half the business and he is a nobody.'

'Orders? What orders?' She clenched her teeth in irritation, eyeing the tight control Matteo had on his features when she guessed he wanted to knock Oswald to the ground for calling him a nobody.

'I want Jed to stop working on the sailboat and to begin showing the new fellow the ropes.'

'The new fellow?' Lorrie scowled. '*What* new fellow?'

From the side of the shed, the sallow-looking man from the week before dawdled into view, wearing a sly grin. Saunders. Lorrie remembered him.

'Shall we go into the office?' Matteo suggested.

Lorrie took a calming breath, striving for patience.

Fliss took both baskets. 'I'll go up and check on Mr Chambers.'

Once in the office, Lorrie stood behind her desk and glared at Oswald. 'You had no right to go behind my back.'

'Saunders will be working here for a time. That is my decision,' Oswald declared, staring at Lorrie, waiting for her to argue further.

Which she did. 'I told you last week, I want to cut down on wages, not increase them! We do not need more men.'

'Ah, but that is where you are wrong, my dear Miss Chambers,' Oswald gloated. 'I have acquired three more boats to be refitted. They will be arriving tomorrow.'

'Three?' Lorrie shook her head. 'We do not have the room for three. We already have Mr Bailey's boat moored in the river waiting for its rudder to be fixed.'

'These boats are owned by men who have been waiting for repairs at Stanley Ferry for months. They've had enough. I told them we could do it. I already have the deposits.' He rubbed his hands together. 'I want our men to work around the clock if they have to as I have more orders coming next week.'

'We don't have the supplies ready.' Lorrie wanted to throttle him.

'Then order them!'

'With what, Mr Lynch? We need to be paid for outstanding work before we can pay for more supplies.'

He frowned. 'Why aren't we getting paid?'

'Because Father has been unable to sign off on the finished work.'

'This is not good enough!' Spit sprang from Oswald's mouth. 'This yard is becoming a joke. Our reputation is everything.'

'My father's reputation! You do not have one within the boating community.'

'And you are a mere woman who knows nothing!'

Matteo stepped away from the door. His handsome face set like granite. 'You are starting to annoy me, Mr Lynch. You should go.'

Oswald spluttered in surprise. 'How dare you!'

'I dare.' Matteo gave a lazy one-shoulder shrug. 'Now, you will dismiss that Saunders fellow, for he looks as trustworthy as a hungry lion in a butcher's shop, and you will allow Miss Chambers to run this yard as she sees fit.'

Oswald bristled, his mouth opening and closing without saying anything.

Lorrie hid a grin.

'And,' Matteo continued, 'you will cancel the new orders until we have cleared some of the boats from the yard.'

'You have no right to tell me what to do, none whatsoever!' Oswald's eyes bulged. 'Miss Chambers, this man must remove himself from these premises. He has no say here!'

Matteo took another step towards him. 'Miss Chambers told me that you were a silent partner, Mr Lynch. I suggest you be silent now.'

'This is outrageous!' Oswald floundered, blinking rapidly as Matteo took another step closer. 'I won't stand for this.' He glowered at Matteo then at Lorrie. 'You'll be sorry for treating me this way. I was only trying to help, but not any more. I want the money I invested returned, all of it! You have two days!' He stormed from the office.

Lorrie slowly sat on her chair and rested her elbows on the desk and buried her head in her hands. She didn't need this right now.

'I'm sorry. I went too far,' Matteo murmured, coming to stand beside her.

'It's fine. Thank you for standing up for me.'

'I have made things worse.'

'I think it was inevitable that Mr Lynch would demand his money back at some point. Father should never have accepted Mr Lynch's offer to invest in the first place. He's never been a silent partner but forever giving advice to Father whether it was needed or not.'

'Why did your father accept Lynch's offer?'

'Because last year we were on our knees. We weren't doing enough work quickly enough and supply prices went up. We didn't have the manpower to repair boats fast enough and people went elsewhere, like to Stanley Ferry and places like that.' Lorrie stared out of the window. 'Mr Lynch reeled Father in with talk of money and grand ideas of making Chambers Boat Builder and Repairs a huge success. We could expand and Father could spend all his time in crafting new boats and not have to bother with smaller, dirtier jobs such as de-caulking and hull scraping as we'd have men to do those kind of tasks. Father was so excited. There is nothing he loves more than designing and crafting boats...'

'Except his beautiful daughter.' Matteo took her hands and pulled her up from the chair. 'Do not be worried about Lynch,' he said softly. 'Together we will put him back in his cage.' He grinned. 'With a gag.'

Lorrie looked up at him, her hands still in his, their bodies only inches apart. Her chest tightened. Her ribcage seemed to house a thousand butterflies dancing in her stomach.

Matteo groaned. 'Do not look at me like that, Lorrie. I am a healthy Italian male, and my natural instinct is to make love to you.'

Lorrie's knees buckled.

Matteo lowered his head until their lips nearly touched. 'But I won't. Not yet. Not until you ask me.' Abruptly, he let her go and walked out of the office.

Holding the edge of the desk for support, Lorrie panted as though she'd run up the staircase a dozen times. Her cheeks flamed. A yearning ache for him to touch her again enflamed her body. Embarrassed by her own wild longing for a man she'd only met a week ago, she took a deep breath and smoothed down her skirts. How was it that only a short time ago she thought her life to be boring and uneventful?

Flustered, she felt it would be difficult to deny Matteo Falcone anything he should ask. Not that he would, of course. He was being flirtatious. He made it clear she had control of the situation, but did she? Would she ask him to make love to her? Could she? He made it sound all so easy, so natural. But was it? He, as an Italian, might believe so, but she wasn't brought up that way.

Whatever she decided could change her life. Her mind whirled in different directions with no definite answer.

She couldn't believe that her normal sensible self was a blushing fool in Matteo's presence. One glance from him and she lost the ability to think. Instead, her body took over, demanding his touch, yearning for something from him that she'd never experienced before. For someone as intelligent and sensible as she thought herself to be, she was acting like a mindless fool.

Taking a deep breath, she left the office and went upstairs to Fliss and her father. She needed a cup of tea and to ponder on Oswald's demands.

Later that evening, she came out of her father's bedroom carrying a tray. He'd managed to eat several mouthfuls of pie and drink some tea, but he was listless and withdrawn. Lorrie had talked the whole time while she plumped up his pillows, which caused him to wince with the movement, then he'd protested he didn't want to sit up, which made eating awkward. She'd regaled him with news from the yard, without informing him of Oswald's threats. She told him about Jed finishing the sanding of the sailboat and that Jimmy had done a grand job of de-caulking the narrowboat. But no matter what she said, her father remained silent, uninterested.

'Did he eat much?' Matteo asked, clearing away their own meal.

'No.' Lorrie expected to feel uncomfortable with Matteo after the scene in the office hours ago but he acted the same as always and so she followed his lead. 'I didn't mention Oswald either.' She also felt bad for keeping things from her father. But he was in no condition to deal with any stress. She could and would handle it all and allow her father to heal and recover.

'Wise. Lynch might change his mind. His uncontrolled temper is a failing.' Matteo poured them both a cup of tea.

Lorrie wondered if Matteo had a temper or what his failings were, then quickly dismissed such thoughts. He would be gone soon.

She sat at the table, amazed to have a man serve her tea. No male had ever poured her a cup of tea before, not even her father. She glanced away, not wanting her emotions to get the better of her. She had to stay calm around Matteo and not lose her head at his every word and gesture. She was acting like a silly girl of sixteen, not a woman of twenty-five with responsibilities.

'Oswald won't let this rest,' Lorrie said, stirring a small lump of sugar into her tea. 'He'll be vengeful.'

'What can he do?' Matteo sat opposite her.

'He wants his money back and we don't have it.' The idea of explaining to Father that Oswald was pulling out of the partnership gave her a headache.

'I think he was bluffing.'

'Why do you think that?'

'He'd have not bought into the partnership unless he thought it was a good idea. Also, Lynch has gone to great trouble to find more business. He wants the business to be successful.' Matteo leaned back in the chair. 'Let him calm down and he may change his mind.'

Lorrie gazed at him, not wanting to talk of Oswald, but to learn more about this attractive man who sat at her table and who had quickly integrated himself into her life. 'Tell me more about yourself.'

'Have I not told you everything?' He laughed. 'Instead, you must share more of you. I will be asked by my family what you are like.'

'There is nothing exciting about me.'

'I do not believe it,' he said with a teasing smile.

'I have lived here all my life. Cared for Father, organised the office...' She floundered, realising just how simple her life was.

'How amazed I am that no one has married you yet,' Matteo murmured. 'You have such striking looks. Intelligent. Kind.' He raised his hands as if at a loss for words.

'The right man hasn't found me yet,' she said lightly, her heart thumping as they studied each other.

'You are ripe for loving, Lorrie.'

His words reached her slowly as if her brain needed to digest each separate word. Her skin tingled. 'You must not say such things.'

'Why? It is the truth.'

'Gentlemen do not speak like that to a woman, not one they respect.'

'I respect you, but I also speak the truth. You English are too... rigid... too strict...' He flung out his hands. 'You deny or hide your feelings because it is expected of you, but isn't life for loving? To be loved and to give love is a great joy, why be frightened of showing it?'

'Have you not spent enough time in England to understand our ways?' she joked.

'*Sì*, and it is what I miss about my home. I miss the passion. In everything people do or say they are enthusiastic. In their work, their food, their families they show their emotions. We feel alive in Italy, where everything is accepted as God's will and a gift from the hot sun to the blue sea, from the cool mountains to the narrow stone streets. We argue fervently but then we make amends passionately. We eat and drink and we sleep in the afternoon shade, and it is all about the quality of life. Isn't that a better way to live than being quiet and hiding all that we feel and being bound by rules?' He leaned back in his chair, a questioning expression on his face.

'England isn't Italy.' She didn't know how to answer him. She'd never been to Italy, she didn't know how they lived but by what Matteo said it showed a very different world to the one she knew in a small town in the north of England where everything seemed grey and it rained a great deal and the sky felt low from the smoke of thousands of chimneys. Matteo came from a port town on the edge of the sea with sandy beaches and rising mountains and clear blue skies and hot days. It sounded like heaven to a girl who'd never been out of Yorkshire.

'Lorrie!' A groan came from the bedroom.

Blinking, rising instantly, Lorrie took a step towards the bedroom.

Matteo stood as well. 'I will go. It's late. Unless you need me?'

She didn't want him to leave. 'Yes, of course, you go. I'll sit with Father for a while.'

'Good night, Lorrie.' His hand came up to touch her cheek. 'Sleep well.'

She wanted to lean into his hand, to beg him to stay a little longer, or forever, actually. She felt that he was the one person who was here for her, who saw her as someone special, not just Ernest Chambers's daughter, the spinster who worked in the office. Matteo spent time with her, talked to her and touched her so gently at every opportunity, a hand on the back or at her elbow, fingertips touching when they passed something to each other, and just now on the cheek. His presence awoke in her a longing for something she didn't even know she'd been missing. Yes, she'd wanted marriage and children, but it had been a normal dream for a woman to have. Now it had manifested into wanting Matteo to be her husband and the father of her children. But where would such thoughts, such desires lead to when he was leaving soon?

She didn't have the answers.

Instead, she gave him a half smile and turned away as her father called for her again.

6

The warm spring sunshine beckoned Lorrie out onto the landing at the top of the stairs. Dr Carter was attending to Father, and she took the moment to feel the gentle sun on her face. Below her Jimmy was helping unload some timber supplies and in the open-sided shed she could see Matteo and Jed discussing drawings of the sailboat. Roy was mixing hot tar in a barrel over the firepit, the smell wafting on the slight breeze that drifted across the river.

From this vantage point at the top of the stairs, Lorrie could see across the river to the mills and factories on the town side. Cranes worked above the boats lifting or lowering cargo onto the wharves. Narrowboats lined the moorings waiting for their loads while on the docks men scurried like ants to do their tasks.

Smoke billowed from hundreds of chimneys, pillowing up into the white clouds above. Gulls cried, swooping for any opportunity to find food. To the right, beyond the rushing weir, a tram and heavy wagons trundled over the bridge, passing the Chantry Chapel and disappearing into the throng of streets and buildings of the town.

Living on the river was never boring. She'd spent her life

watching this scene from the top of the stairs and each day it changed. Different boats came and went, the river swelled with rain or lowered in high summer. Ducks and waterfowl brought out their babies each spring and sat dejected in the snow every winter.

This small part of the waterfront belonged to her father, and her, and she knew all the neighbouring businesses, knew the people who worked along the river. It was all familiar, all a place Lorrie called home. Yet last night she had dreamt that Matteo had asked her to travel to Italy with him. She had said yes. The dream seemed so real that on waking she'd spent some minutes pondering the future, wondering if Matteo would in fact ask her such a question.

And she knew she'd go anywhere with him once her father was well enough.

'Miss Chambers.' Dr Carter came out onto the landing, placing his hat on his head as he did so.

'Can I get you some tea?' Lorrie abandoned her daydreams and focused on the doctor.

'No, thank you. I must be on my way. Your father is rather tetchy this morning. He is tired of being in that bed.'

'Yes. His patience is running thin,' she agreed. The last couple of days, Father had snapped at her each time she'd entered the bedroom.

'His legs, especially his left leg, aren't healing as fast as I would like. I know he wants to be up and about again, but he cannot put any pressure on those broken bones. He must stay in bed for another week at least, then we might be able to consider getting him to sit on a chair.'

'I understand.'

'I shall return tomorrow morning.' He doffed his hat to her and went down the stairs.

Returning inside, Lorrie went to check on her father. 'Can I get you anything?' she asked from the doorway.

'You can get Jed and Roy to come and help me down into the yard.'

'No, Father.'

'Don't tell me no, daughter.' Father's tone was cold, so unlike him.

'Please don't make this a battle.' She stepped nearer to the bed. 'Your legs aren't strong enough to carry your weight.' Though he was nothing but skin and bones since the accident.

'I'm needed in the yard.'

'Actually, you aren't. It's running very well.'

'Is the Italian still here?' Father snapped.

'Mr Falcone is being a tremendous help. I wish you would think more kindly towards him. He is doing us a great service. He changed his plans to stay here and help. Whatever happened between you and Mother's family is not Mr Falcone's fault.'

'He is still one of them.'

'What happened that was so bad?'

'You don't need to know. It is in the past.'

'Then leave it in the past, Father, and don't let it affect how you are with Mr Falcone, who has been so good to us since he arrived. He could have walked away but he didn't. He stayed and helped me when I needed the support.'

'He knows nothing about this boatyard or my business.'

'Mr Falcone comes from a family of boat builders and you know it. His uncle had the boatyard beside Mother's family yard. It's in his blood as it is in yours.'

'He needs to go, Lorrie.' Father exhaled tiredly and lay back on the three pillows that supported his back. A wire cage was positioned over his legs from the knees down. 'I need to be down there.'

'And when you're able to, then you can, and everything will be as it was.'

'Where's Oswald? I've not seen him for days.'

'He must be busy.' She bent and straightened the blanket over his waist, thankful Oswald hadn't been visiting or demanding his money back. She'd done nothing but worry he'd turn up and expect his money to be waiting for him, but of course that wasn't possible. They'd have to sell the business to give him his money back. 'Can I get you anything?'

'No.'

She turned away but he grabbed her hand to prevent her. 'I'm sorry, lass. I know I've not been the easiest of patients.'

Lorrie chuckled. 'Indeed.'

'I've spent my life in that yard. I'm not a man who can be cooped up in a room for days on end. It's driving me mad.'

'Naturally it would do. But we have no choice.' She kissed the top of his head, noticing that his sparse grey hair needed washing. 'You only have to concentrate on getting better, which means eating more to keep your strength up. The sooner you are well, the sooner you can be out of this room. However, it takes time to heal, you know that.'

He squeezed her hand. 'I'm sorry all this has fallen on your shoulders.'

'None of it is your fault, Father.'

He sighed heavily. 'Perhaps I'll have a cup of tea. Did Jimmy fetch me a newspaper?'

'He did. The *Wakefield Express*. It's on the table. I'll bring it in with your tea and I've made a lemon cake…' She winced a little. 'It didn't rise as much as I liked, but I'll cut a slice for you and see how it is.'

'Dearest, I don't know how a woman such as yourself who has numerous cookery books still can't cook.' He chuckled and she smiled in relief, for it was the first small laugh she'd heard from him in weeks.

'I do try my best!' Her failing as a good cook was a standard joke between them and she hoped this small show of humour might be the turning point he needed.

In the kitchen, she stoked the fire in the range and placed the kettle on to boil.

A knock preceded Oswald, who came in wearing an expensive-looking suit of dove grey and a gold-patterned waistcoat and a leering smile.

'Miss Chambers.' He bowed as much as his round stomach would allow.

'Mr Lynch.' She stood, aware his splendid clothes made her house dress of light brown seem dowdy. She eyed him warily. The run of Oswald-free days had come to an end.

'I have come to ask after your father.' He carried a leather satchel. 'And you, naturally.'

'He is a little better today. Frustrated at not being able to be in the yard.' Her reply was delivered coldly.

'Of course,' he simpered. 'Is he available to visitors?'

'Yes, go in. I'll bring in a tea tray in a moment.'

He paused. 'The other day... Allow me to apologise for my behaviour. It was unacceptable. My fervent nature can get the better of me, at times. I only want the best for this business, you understand?'

'What you don't seem to realise is I, too, only want the best for the business. However, you undermine me at every opportunity. You have employed a man who we do not need, and you bring work into the yard at lower prices. More work for less money is not sensible.'

'Ah, but my dear, if the turnover is quicker, we can make a

profit. Have you considered that? We must gamble a little to make money.'

'I don't wish to gamble on our livelihood.'

'You need to trust me, Miss Chambers. I know what I'm doing. All will be well and soon this boatyard will be the most sought after in all of Yorkshire, I promise you that.' His eyes narrowed and roamed over her as though sizing up a prize mare at fair. 'How delightful you are, Miss Chambers. Your ardent nature is very alluring.'

She gave him a false smile. She never knew where she stood with that man. One minute he was shouting and rude to her, then the next minute full of compliments and everything pleasant. 'So, you do not wish for your investment to be returned to you?'

He waved a hand airily. 'Not at all. I spoke in the heat of the moment.'

She left him alone with Father for ten minutes before taking in the tray. When she entered the room, Oswald was putting away some papers and an inkwell and pen.

'Ah, wonderful,' Oswald declared. 'And cake. What an honour.'

'You've not tried it yet, Oswald,' Father joked.

Lorrie noticed that Oswald didn't meet her eyes this time. What paperwork had he shown Father? The hurried way he put it into the satchel rang alarm bells in her head. What was Oswald hiding? Had Father signed something without knowing what it was?

She poured the tea while Oswald spoke of happenings in town and Lorrie made an excuse to leave the room and raced downstairs and into the yard to find Matteo in one of the sheds.

'What is it?' Matteo held a hammer and chisel, working beside Jed on the sailboat, but he put them down and walked back outside with her.

'Oswald has been sitting in with Father and he had paperwork,' she blurted out. 'I'm sure he got Father to sign something. I'm uneasy about it.'

Before Matteo could reply, Meg walked through the gates with Fliss. Although happy to see them, Lorrie's mind was in a whirl. 'What is Oswald up to?' she whispered to him while smiling a welcome to her friends.

'We'll talk later. Go to your guests.'

Lorrie embraced Meg and Fliss, both of whom gazed after Matteo as he walked back to the shed.

'My, he's incredible,' Fliss commented dreamily.

'You need a husband.' Meg nudged Fliss, chuckling. 'I agree, though, he's strikingly handsome.'

'Come up.' Lorrie steered them towards the staircase.

'I thought Mr Falcone would have left by now,' Meg said as they seated themselves at the table.

'Not until Father is on his feet again.' Lorrie filled the kettle with water. 'He said he'd stay for three weeks, which would be to the end of next week. Yet he's not mentioned leaving.'

'Perhaps something is keeping him here longer?' Meg grinned.

Lorrie busied herself at the range. Would Matteo stay longer for her?

'How is Mr Chambers?' Fliss asked.

'Fed up with being in bed.'

'And the pain?' Meg gave her an understanding look.

'It's a little more manageable, at least until the doctor comes and starts cleaning the wounds again.' Lorrie took the lemon cake to the table. 'Tell me all your news. It's been a week since I saw you both but feels like months.'

'Nothing much changes for me,' Fliss commented, her red hair peeking out from under her bonnet in wispy curls. 'I work my shifts behind the bar and spend my days at my aunt's side doing everything she says.'

'You're her servant, not her niece,' Meg declared angrily. 'She treats you like a daughter one minute and a skivvy the next.'

'Agreed.' Fliss ate some of the cake.

'Mrs Payton and Mrs Shaw both send their good wishes,' Meg told Lorrie. 'I attended an almshouse charity dinner last night that Mrs Payton hosted.'

'That is kind of them.' Lorrie enjoyed the company of the two older women who were pillars of the community and did many good deeds within the town. They'd been kind enough to invite Lorrie, Meg and Fliss along to join them in their charitable works, which they had done during the winter.

'There's a summer ball in June. Christian and me have been invited to attend. I'm terrified of making a fool of myself,' Meg said. 'The Christmas ball a few months ago was bad enough. Hours spent standing around talking to people who were only talking to me to see if I could hold a conversation... you know, the girl from the backstreets mixing it with her betters. How dare she?'

'I thought you were getting Maude to teach you some of the dances?' Fliss asked as Lorrie mashed the tea.

'She's hopeless.' Meg laughed. 'Christian is teaching me instead. The staff think it's hilarious.'

'You'll be fine then for the summer ball.' Lorrie brought the teapot to the table. 'Just dance all night instead of talking to people who bore you,' she joked.

'I thought I heard the delicious tones of female voices.' Oswald came from the bedroom, the satchel tucked under his arm. 'What a sight to behold, three beautiful women.' He bowed gallantly.

Lorrie clenched her teeth. She'd told Meg and Fliss all about Oswald. They didn't like him either.

'Mr Lynch, how nice to see you again,' Meg said, her tone cautious. Lorrie knew Meg was always ready for some barbed comment about her rise in station from a barmaid to the wife of one of the town's businessmen.

'How is your good husband, Mrs Henderson?' Oswald asked Meg.

'He is well, thank you.'

'Wonderful. And your family, Miss Atkins?' Oswald addressed Fliss.

'They are well, too, Mr Lynch.'

'Excellent. Splendid.' Oswald rubbed his hands together, grinning like a fool. 'Then I shall be on my way and allow you ladies to partake of your refreshments and talk your gossip. Good day.'

Lorrie managed not to roll her eyes at his comment. As if she had nothing better to do than sit and gossip. Is that really what he thought of her when he'd seen her busy at her desk for hours on end?

She saw him to the door, where he collected his hat and cane.

Oswald turned to her. 'Your father seems in better spirits.'

'Yes, thankfully.'

'We have spoken at some length regarding the business.'

'Oh? Such as?' Her stomach knotted.

'Just plans for the future.'

'The future? What paperwork did you bring?' She didn't trust him an inch. 'Do you wish to leave the partnership after all?'

'Ah, no. I told you earlier, I spoke rashly the other day.' Oswald rubbed his chin. 'Mr Falcone managed to get under my skin, so to speak.'

'Then there will be no more threats? I cannot live with you constantly holding that over my head.' Lorrie held her breath.

'No. At least not at this stage.' He beckoned Lorrie to step out onto the landing with him. 'You see, Miss Chambers, I am an enthusiastic man, and my desires can get the better of me at times.'

His gaze narrowed on her before he waved his hands dismissively. 'You understand how I am by now, surely?'

'I think I do.' And she did. He was infuriating. 'The paperwork you carry. Do I need to see it or store it in the safe in the office?'

'Indeed not, my dear. It was just something I needed to discuss with your father. Nothing for you to worry about or concern yourself with.' His patronising tone grated on Lorrie's nerves.

'Everything to do with this business concerns me,' she told him.

'My dear, you forget yourself. You are simply my partner's daughter, nothing more.' He paused. 'Unless you wish to become my wife? Then, as such, you would be considered someone I could trust and discuss such things with. I would make a suitable husband. Think on that.' He glanced back inside. 'Perhaps you should attend to your guests. Miss Atkins is looking delightful today, don't you think?' Chuckling, he went down the stairs.

Seething, Lorrie closed the door and returned to the table. Did he think she was jealous when he mentioned Fliss? Stupid man.

'He is loathsome,' Meg declared.

'He wants to marry me,' Lorrie blurted, rubbing a hand over her eyes.

'Gracious!' Fliss stared at her, wide-eyed. 'You wouldn't, would you? Not him.'

'Absolutely not.' Lorrie sighed. 'But he's up to something, I just know it, and he's hoodwinked Father into trusting him and he thinks that by offering to marry me I'd be so grateful I'd not care what he's up to.'

'Then he doesn't know you very well, does he?' Meg said, topping up her teacup. 'And what do you think he's up to?'

'I wish I knew. He's so secretive and has a volatile temperament. One minute he's doing his best to be charming and the next minute he's threatening to dissolve the partnership. I'm always on edge with him and he seriously believes I am considering his marriage proposal.'

'Foolish man,' Meg snorted. 'You're far too good for him.'

'Anyway, enough of Mr Lynch. Let us talk of something more pleasant instead.' Lorrie sipped her tea.

'I have some news.' Meg beamed. 'I am with child,' she announced loftily like a queen and then grinned widely and laughed.

'Fabulous news!' Lorrie rushed to embrace her, as did Fliss.

'When will we be aunts?' Lorrie asked.

'September sometime.' Meg touched her stomach, which was still flat.

'Six months to wait, then we will have a darling baby to hold,' Fliss said happily. 'I shall start knitting this very evening.'

'Me, too,' Lorrie added. 'I shall have to buy some white wool.' She wondered if she would ever knit baby clothes for a child of her own and very much doubted it. She wanted Matteo as the father of her children and that wasn't possible, unless he asked her to marry him and take her away. Only, the notion of that happening seemed unlikely for she had a life here, and his was far away in another country.

Meg sipped her tea. 'Thank you. This baby is going to be so loved. Christian is like a dog with two tails, he's so excited.'

'You must be too?' Lorrie asked, forking a small piece of cake into her mouth, and pushing her thoughts of never becoming a mother to the back of her mind.

'I am, yes... Though after last time, I'm worried as well.' A cloud of sadness entered Meg's eyes.

'Your miscarriage last time wasn't your fault,' Fliss reminded her. 'You were pushed down the stairs.'

'I know, but still...' Meg shuddered a little. 'Thankfully, my mother- and sister-in-law are coming nowhere near me this time.

Anyway, I'm very careful going up and down stairs so I don't trip and I'm lifting my skirts so high everyone can see my ankles!'

'Let them see, as long as you're safe, that's all that matters,' Lorrie declared.

'You've lovely ankles anyway,' Fliss spouted, and they laughed.

* * *

'Lorrie,' Matteo greeted her at the bottom of the steps. 'Where are you going?'

Her heart skipped a beat as it did every time she looked at him. 'To the post office and then the shops.'

He tutted with a dramatic toss of his head. 'That is indeed boring. Let us go somewhere instead.'

She smiled. 'I cannot leave Father alone for too long.'

Matteo whistled to Jimmy, who was crossing the yard carrying a basket of kemp rope. 'Jimmy, keep watch over Mr Chambers.'

'Aye, all right, Matteo.' Jimmy nodded.

'That is settled, *si*?' Matteo took her basket and placed it on the bottom step before sliding her hand through his arm. 'Now we can go.'

'Where?' she chuckled, slightly worried about leaving Father but also eager to spend time with Matteo.

'We could take the train. The first train out of the station and get off at the first stop,' he said eagerly.

'No!' She laughed. 'It could be a London-bound train and the first stop might be Sheffield!'

He rolled his eyes. 'You are no fun!'

'Let us just walk, shall we?' she suggested, annoyed with herself for disappointing him. She wanted to be light-hearted and spontaneous, but she had too many responsibilities to simply be so carefree.

'A walk it is, but not into town. I am tired of the town.'

'Very well, what if we were to cross Doncaster Road and follow the canal along to Fall Ings Lock that then joins the river on the other side of the sawmills? We'll be heading away from town and it's a nice walk along the river heading east.'

'I have not walked that before. *Sì*. It is a good idea.'

They navigated across the two busy roads that led to the bridge and town itself and followed the canal between the warehouses and mills until they were clear of buildings and the ground was open between the canal and the river. Narrowboats queued for their turn through the lock and with the sun shining the scene was pleasant. Birds dived above and sang from the trees lining the bank. Waterfowl and ducks glided across the still waters of the dark river.

'Away from town, the countryside is nice,' Matteo commented.

'Not as nice as your home, I imagine,' Lorrie joked.

'Nothing is as beautiful as La Spezia. The bay is beautiful, and the mountains flow right into the sea. There are many little beaches hidden away in coves. The sun burns the sand, and it burns your feet.' He grinned, lost to his memories. 'We eat fresh fish and juicy fruits. Ah, it is *bellissimo*.'

'You sound very homesick.' That made her sad.

'*Sì*,' he murmured softly. His eyes held a faraway look.

They stopped on a walkway bridge over the canal and watched a narrowboat leave the lock and glide into the river. The boat captain ordered his wife and children to do his bidding as they gracefully plodded along. A young boy guided a large horse along the towpath.

'I only ever read about other places in books,' Lorrie said as they walked on along the river path.

'What is wrong with that?' Matteo bent and plucked a buttercup from the grass and twirled it between his fingers.

'I would like to travel to those places and not just read about them.'

'You are a single woman. It is impossible.'

She stopped and stared at him. 'Many women travel.'

'Mostly rich women, married or widowed.'

'Then I shall have to find myself a rich husband,' she said, watching his reaction.

He shrugged in that carefree way he had. 'I hope you do.' Suddenly, he stopped and grabbed her arms. 'But he wouldn't want you as much as I want you.'

Her stomach somersaulted. His bluntness took her breath away. Before she could utter a word, he let go of her and turned back the way they'd come.

They walked back to Doncaster Road in silence. As they waited for the vehicles to clear to cross, Matteo leaned closer. 'Forgive me, I speak out of turn.'

'Do you speak the truth?' She needed to know his words weren't just flattery.

'Always.' His dark eyes held hers.

Her silly heart melted. Despite the noise of the wagons rolling by, the horses' hoofs and the people, Lorrie wanted to sink into his arms.

Matteo's hand came up to tenderly touch her cheek. Then he quickly turned on his heel and walked away.

Taking a long, deep breath, Lorrie watched him turn into a lane between two mills and disappear from sight. Although naive in many ways concerning men, she knew he was affected by her, and it tormented him. Matteo never expected his visit to Wakefield to meet her would turn out like it had. Heart heavy, she walked back to the boatyard and to her father, who needed her. She couldn't help but think she was trapped here, but such thoughts wouldn't do her any good. She had duties, responsibilities, and her own wishes had to be pushed aside.

The following day, Lorrie cleaned the kitchen and kept herself busy. Her head was full of Matteo. Nothing she did could put him from her mind. His words, his actions, every look and smile tormented and comforted her. She listened for his voice, she watched out for a glimpse of him, but he stayed out of her way all day and she didn't know whether to be annoyed or relieved. Time was running out until he would be gone and her chest tightened at the idea of never seeing him again.

As the sun set, she brought in the washing she'd hung on the line in the yard. Matteo appeared from nowhere and carried the basket of clothes upstairs for her and placed it on the floor by the table.

'Did you find out what Lynch was up to?' he asked.

'No. I haven't had the opportunity to ask Father. He has napped most of the afternoon and this morning he was with Dr Carter.' She stirred the stew heating on the range. 'Will you stay to eat?'

'No, thank you. I have letters to write. My family are asking me why I haven't returned to London or home to Italy.'

His words crushed her. 'They miss you.'

'I miss them.' He ran a hand through his ebony hair. 'I miss my home. I have been away too long.'

'Then you should go.' She turned away, not wanting him to see her sadness.

'*Sì*, I know, but you make me want to stay,' he spoke from directly behind her.

Lorrie spun around to be only inches from him. 'I want you to stay,' she whispered, gazing into his brown eyes, silently begging him to never leave her.

'Forgive me, I cannot.'

She saw the anguish in his expression. 'I would work hard every day to make you happy.'

Matteo took both her hands and kissed them.

Lorrie wanted to lean into him, desperate for his arms to hold her. She craved to be held, to be loved. She was so tired of being lonely.

'I could never be happy here, even with you, *mia bella*,' Matteo murmured.

Closing her eyes, she tried to be unaffected by him. An impossible task.

His lips softly touched hers.

Her eyes sprang open. He had kissed her! Hope flickered. 'I *could* make you happy,' she said again, determined to make him see a future together.

'Italy is my home. I could never live here. It is too cold, too grey.'

'It's nice in the summer.' She sounded pathetic and cringed. Was that what her father had said to her mother, before she had followed him north and become unhappy?

Matteo's gorgeous smile warmed his eyes. 'My family needs me at home. I am the eldest son. I have plans. I must go soon.'

'I understand.' She didn't want to understand. She wanted to cry and plead for him to stay with her. Then she had a thought. 'I could come with you!'

Turning away, Matteo swore in Italian. 'My life is complicated. I cannot ask you to leave England.'

'You're not asking. I'm offering.' She would go to the ends of the earth with him with no hesitation.

He rubbed his hands over his face and sighed deeply. He said nothing for a long time and then gave her an apologetic look. 'My family expect me to marry a girl in La Spezia. It has long been decided. Her family own a vineyard next to my cousin's. I have received many letters demanding me to return home, to do my duty.'

'Your duty,' she said dully.

'I am the eldest son. My choices affect others. It is not for me to go against my family's wishes.'

Like nails driven into her skin, Lorrie flinched with each word. Her hopes and stupid dreams of being his wife shattered. He had a girl waiting for him back home. 'I see. You have a woman waiting for you, yet you have told me that you want to make love to me. Were you lying to me?' she asked, her voice tight with disappointment. Had he been playing her for a fool all along?

'I do not want this girl, though she is good and kind.' He shrugged, as if amazed by his thoughts. 'I want *you*, Lorrie. I have since the first moment I saw you. That is the truth, believe me.'

'Then do not marry that girl.' She rushed to him, uncaring if she was being forward and unladylike. 'I will marry you and make you happy. I will move to Italy, anything.'

'If only it were that simple!' He dragged her against him and kissed her hard, demanding and seeking a response which she gave willingly. She would give him anything he asked for. The kiss was heated, passionate, giving her a taste of what joy he could give her.

Abruptly he pushed her away and again spoke in fast Italian before marching from the room and slamming the door behind him.

Dazed, Lorrie walked to the sofa and slumped onto it. Her eyes burned with tears that wouldn't fall. Matteo had been her chance to find happiness, love, a family. A tight knot of rage and disappointment curled around her heart. What a fool she'd been to think she could ever have such a man as extraordinary as Matteo. Who did she think she was? She was simply a boatman's daughter, nothing special. To believe anything different was foolish. Obviously, she was only worth the attention of ridiculous men such as Oswald. Was that her fate, to have someone lesser in every way? A moan escaped and she slapped a hand over her mouth so her father wouldn't hear.

No. If she couldn't have Matteo then she would have no one and remain a spinster. She would be a dutiful and caring daughter and help her father with the business.

Standing, Lorrie straightened her shoulders, buried her sadness, and took a deep breath. There would be no more dreams of Matteo being her husband. It was time to cast aside such fantasies and face her real future.

7

Entering the office three days later, Lorrie jerked in surprise at seeing Saunders by the desk. 'What are you doing in here?' Anger made her tone sharp.

He shrugged, his expression sly. 'Waiting for you.'

'For what purpose do you need to see me?' She kept her hand on the door handle.

'I need more work. You're only giving me a few days a week.'

'That is all we need you for,' she lied. She didn't want him here at all and by cutting down his days she hoped he'd leave altogether.

'Mr Lynch says I'm to be here all week, not three days.'

'Mr Lynch doesn't have a say in the day-to-day running of this yard, my father does.'

Saunders strolled over closer to her. 'Not you? I could've easily believed you ran this place.' He stared at her with a cunning gaze. 'I like a lady in charge.'

She stiffened. 'I have work to do, Saunders, as do you.' She opened the door wide and stepped back so he could pass through.

He paused next to her. 'I shall work here every day from now on.'

'I don't think so.' She stood her ground, trying not to show her revulsion of him. Up close, he smelt of stale sweat and his greasy hair and stained clothes added to his ragged appearance.

'We'll see what Mr Lynch has to say about that,' he sneered.

She shut the door on him and felt the need to lock it, but that was foolish. Saunders couldn't do anything other than speak empty threats.

Lorrie sat at her desk in the office, concentrating on writing in the ledgers. March was drawing to a close and she needed to tally the month's accounts. Outside the office window the men were heating tar, the acrid smell invading the yard and the office, but it was a smell she was used to, the same as the dank scent of the river.

A tap sounded on the door and Matteo walked in; his expression heavy as it had been for three days since their frank discussion and his rejection of her. '*Buongiorno.*'

'Good morning.' She ignored the rapid beat of her heart and focused on the information she was writing in each column. For three days she had done her best to not be alone with him. Instead, she spent the time with her father, helping him to hobble on one leg, the right one which was healing quicker than the left. Using her and a cane as crutches, Father had made it from the bed to a chair and the smile on his pain-filled face had been her reward.

In the next couple of days, she knew he'd want to sit at the table and invite the men up so they could inform him in their own ways what was going on in the yard.

'How are you?' Matteo asked, frowning.

'Fine.'

'We have not spoken for days.'

'I have a lot to do, and Father needs me.'

'Time is running away from us.'

She scowled. 'What are you talking about?'

'You and me. We do not have much time left together.'

'There is no you and me, is there? You made that clear.' Did he not understand how upset she was? Did he not realise he had crushed her wishes?

'Nothing is clear. Nothing is right.' His handsome face looked tormented. He ran a hand through his black hair in agitation.

'What do you want me to say?'

He shrugged and turned away slightly. 'It is difficult.'

'Not really.' She stabbed the words at him. 'You do not want me. It is quite simple, actually.'

He fell to his knees beside her chair. 'Of course I want you! You are all I think about. I want you in my bed every night.'

Her breath hitched. 'But you won't take me to Italy with you?'

'No...' He bowed his head. 'It is not possible, though it tears my heart apart.'

Lorrie lifted her head regally, hurt biting sharply. 'Then there is nothing more to be said. Now, please leave me. I have a great deal to do this morning before Dr Carter's visit.'

He bowed his head in acquiescence and went to the door. 'I came to the office to let you know that there is a man at the gates looking for work.'

'Another one?' She didn't look up. 'Send him away, please. We don't need any more labourers.'

'He says he's a skilled craftsman. A shipwright from Whitby. He would be far more useful than Saunders.'

'A craftsman would want a higher wage, too. We don't need him.' She kept writing, then made a mistake and tutted angrily.

'Lorrie.' Matteo came back to stand beside her desk. 'Look at me.'

After a slight hesitation, she stared up at him. 'Yes?' She hardened her emotions, tried to see him as just a friend, less than that. 'I am busy.'

'I will leave tomorrow.' His brown eyes locked with hers.

She felt there was no air in the office. 'I see,' she struggled to say.

'Your father will soon be on his feet, or at least able to leave his bed and oversee the men, even if it is only from the landing at first. I am not needed. So, I will go, but another man, a skilled worker, would be beneficial. Get rid of Saunders and even one of the others and employ the man at the gate. Trust me on this.' Matteo inclined his head to her and walked out.

Lorrie placed her pen in the stand. Trust him? Why should she trust him? He'd crashed into her life, turning it upside down.

Why did he have to be the one to steal her heart? Why did it have to be him who would leave her? She suddenly craved the simple life she'd had before Matteo had showed up. The life where her heart was asleep, and she felt immune to the thrills and sparks of desire and yearning. It might have been a dull life, but at least it didn't hurt, not like the gnawing pain that filled her every time she looked at Matteo.

Rising, she went out of the office and into the warm sunshine, which usually lifted her spirits, but not today. Crossing the yard, she headed for the gates, noticing the black peeling paint off them. They were another job that needed attending to, and the weeds that grew around the posts.

The man talking to Jimmy was older than Lorrie expected. Grey streaked his light brown hair, and his face had a weathered look that revealed he'd spent most of his time outdoors. She guessed him to be in his late forties. An old leather bag sat at his feet, alongside a scruffy-looking white and tan dog.

On seeing Lorrie approach, the man nodded to Jimmy, who,

realising he was shirking his duties, quickly scuttled back into the yard and to whatever tasks awaited him.

Lorrie crossed her arms. 'Good morning. I am Miss Chambers. My father owns the business. I believe you wish to be taken on?'

'Aye, miss.' He held out his hand, forcing her to shake it or appear rude. 'Jonas Bannerman.'

She quickly shook his hand and then folded her arms again. 'We have no work.'

He handed her a piece of paper.

Lorrie read the words written. A glowing reference from his previous employer and the years listed of his original apprenticeship and then his time as a master shipwright. 'You're from Whitby?'

'I am, miss.'

'And why would you not continue to work in Whitby? There are plenty of boatyards there.'

'I fancied a change.'

She glared at him. 'Are you running from trouble?'

He laughed a gentle laugh that seemed so at odds with the well-built burly man standing before her. 'I've not been in trouble since I was a foolish youth, Miss Chambers. No, I left Whitby for private reasons.'

'I don't wish to be rude, Mr Bannerman, but I have no time for games. If you are wanted by the law or by debt collectors, then you can be on your way. I'll have no trouble brought to my door.'

'Miss Chambers, believe me, I'm not in any trouble.' His honest gaze didn't waver. 'The truth is I left Whitby because the woman I have loved for twenty years died and I couldn't stay.'

Lorrie immediately felt remorseful and embarrassed that she had caused him to reveal something so intimate. 'I am sorry about your wife.'

His pewter-grey eyes dimmed. 'She wasn't my wife. She belonged to my best friend, but I loved her even though she couldn't be mine. I couldn't stay and walk the same streets she walked, not with her gone.'

Lorrie sensed his heartbreak, his pain. 'A fresh start is what you're needing?'

'Aye, miss, it is.' Bannerman took a step back. 'Thank you for your time.'

'Wait.' Lorrie thought quickly. 'I'll give you a trial until my father is recovered and able to take over the yard again. You can replace the man who is... who is leaving.'

'Right you are, miss.'

'Come back tomorrow morning. Eight o'clock sharp. My father will be awake and dressed by then. He will want to speak with you.'

'I'll be here.'

'And who is this?' She indicated to the little dog, its rough coat a mixture of white and tan colours.

'My other best mate.' Mr Bannerman grinned wryly. 'I've had him five years and couldn't part with him. He's well behaved. I've trained him properly. He's no trouble. He'll just sit and watch me work. He's a good ratter, though. So, he earns his keep.'

The little dog tilted his head and gave Lorrie an equally honest, golden-brown-eyed stare as if he knew he was being spoken about. Her silly heart melted. 'His name?'

'Rollo.'

Surprised, Lorrie smiled. 'As in the Viking warrior?'

'Yes. My father said our family descend from great Vikings. It's a family legend passed down through the generations.' Bannerman bent and scratched the dog's head. 'I can't be without him, miss.'

'The dog is welcome as long as he behaves.' She wondered what her father would say about that, but she'd deal with that when it happened.

'Thank you. I'll see you in the morning.' Bannerman doffed his flat cap at her and walked back through the lane.

Lorrie watched him go with the little dog padding along beside him, wondering why on earth she'd agreed to Bannerman working here when they had more than enough men, but his story spoke to her own ache. Tomorrow Matteo would be gone, and she'd never see him again. She understood the agony Jonas Bannerman suffered.

She wandered down to the river, the sun warm on her face. Jed and Roy were working on the sailboat, while Jimmy and Saunders caulked a narrowboat. Saunders watched her as she passed. A shiver went down her spine. She had to get rid of him, no matter what Oswald said.

Along the edge of the river, she watched Matteo fit a new steering tiller on another narrowboat. He had his back to her, bent over, focused on his mission to secure the bolts.

Her feet took her closer when her brain told her to go back to the office. The river water ebbed up the boat ramp and she was careful not to slip on the green slime coating the wooden ramp. In a graceful leap she jumped up onto the small dock her father had built when she was only a baby. Underneath it, ducks glided undisturbed. The narrowboat was painted dark blue with gold lettering and belonged to Pete Cheatle, who took coal from depots along the river to the gasworks further up the canal.

'Did you want me?' Matteo smiled as she neared.

Yes. She wished she could shout the word. Yes! She wanted him so badly it was a physical ache. 'I have taken on the man at the gates. Bannerman. He will replace you and Saunders.'

'A good decision. I spoke to him for a few minutes, and he seems a decent fellow. Experienced.' Matteo wiped his hands on a rag. 'You will get rid of Saunders no matter what Lynch says?'

'I will.'

'I do not trust Lynch. He looks as though he'd sell his own mother for a penny. You must be vigilant with him.'

She gazed over the slow-moving river to the mills and malt-houses on the other side. 'You will leave tomorrow?'

'To stay is not an option.' Matteo lifted his hands in that Italian way he had. 'My life is in Italy. I cannot lose sight of that. It is time I returned home. I have been away longer than expected.'

She strained her eyes to pick out the men loading a wagon on the wharves on the other side, anything to take her mind off what he was telling her.

'I must honour my family, Lorrie. My father and grandfather expect me home. I cannot disappoint them. My time in England is finished. I have fulfilled my duty to my great-grandmother by giving you your great-grandmother's gift. When in London I made business contacts for my father and my uncles and myself. I achieved everything I set out to do. Now I must return to La Spezia and my responsibilities there.' He leapt off the narrowboat's deck and joined her on the dock. 'I wish it were different.'

'So do I.'

'Do not despise me, I beg you.'

'Will you stay for dinner?' she asked abruptly, needing to have him with her for a few more hours despite her reasoning to let him go without a fuss.

'*Sì.*'

She nodded. 'Come upstairs once the men have gone for the day. I would like you and Father to part as friends.'

'Your father thinks very little of me.' Matteo grinned wryly.

'Father must put the past behind him.' She turned away. 'It will be a chance for him to say goodbye to all that.'

Lorrie spent the rest of the day cleaning, cooking and finally making herself presentable. She washed her hair and dried it by the fire, before brushing it up into a soft roll behind her head. She dressed with care, wearing a soft blue dress with a darker blue lace detail on the bodice and skirt hem.

With a last look in the mirror, and satisfied she appeared the best she could ever look, she left her bedroom and went to check on her father.

'Are you going out to one of your charity events?' Father asked as she entered his room and noticed her dress.

'No, not tonight. I have cooked us a meal and I thought you would like to come to the table to eat it,' she said encouragingly.

'Aye, that sounds grand.' He pulled the blankets back. 'Take the cage off for me. What will I wear? I can't sit at the table in my nightshirt.'

Lorrie lifted the cage off his legs so he could carefully swing them over the side of the bed. His long nightshirt stopped at the knees, revealing the bandages that covered his left leg from the knee to ankle. 'Let me get a vest and a shirt for you.'

'And what about the bottom half?' he frowned.

'I've cut the legs off an old pair of trousers at the knee.' She fetched the altered garment from a chair in the kitchen and showed it to him.

Father laughed. 'I'm a boy again back in short trousers.' He took them from her. 'Right. You go and leave me to get dressed.'

She hesitated. 'How will you manage?'

'I'll manage. I'll call you if I can't.'

Leaving the room, Lorrie went to the low fire and added a few pieces of coal to it. Although it wasn't cold outside, she didn't want her father to feel any chill.

When he called her back into the bedroom, he was panting with the effort of dressing himself, but he had achieved the required result and was dressed. She helped him up onto his right leg, which had healed well enough to cope with his slender weight, and passed him the cane for extra support.

'Sofa or table?'

'Table. Saves me moving twice.'

Slowly they managed to get from the bed to the table. Father's right leg took all the burden, and she knew the effort of keeping his left leg off the floor pained him by the strain on his face.

At the table, she carefully propped his left leg up on a stool. 'Comfortable?'

'Aye.' He breathed deeply. 'I ain't moving for a few hours now,' he joked.

'Do you want some laudanum?'

'No. I'll not be taking any more of that. I'm not going to be relying on it any more. I need to start clearing my head and dealing with the pain my own way. It's less and less each day.'

'Dr Carter said your left leg is healing well now.'

'Not as quickly as I would like, though.' Father glared at the offending limb. 'At least it hasn't been sawn off yet.'

'Oh, don't say that, Father.' Lorrie checked on the meal. The boiled potatoes and carrots were done. She took the leg of mutton out of the oven and placed the meat on a separate plate; the steam rising off it fogged the kitchen window. The meat was cooked and smelled delicious. Lorrie prayed that for once she'd made an excellent meal.

A knock on the door made Father frown. 'Who could that be?'

Lorrie wiped her hands on a cloth and took off her apron. She went to the door wearing a timid smile and hoped Father wouldn't rant and rave as Matteo entered.

'Good evening, Mr Chambers.' Matteo walked in carrying two bottles of red wine.

'Father, Matteo leaves for Italy tomorrow. I thought to invite him for dinner as a parting farewell.' She was proud of herself for not letting her voice wobble. She forced a bright smile to her face.

'Now, this evening is going to be a pleasant one. The past forgotten.' She aimed the words at Father.

He grunted in response.

Matteo held up one of the wine bottles. 'Glasses?'

'In the cupboard next to the window.' Lorrie pointed, praying that this evening wouldn't be a nightmare, not her last night with Matteo.

They sat at the table, with the meal before them and glasses of red wine, which to Lorrie and her father was a first. They never drank anything but a glass of sherry on Christmas Day after church.

Nervous that a wrong word could set her father into a mood, Lorrie kept the conversation light, talking of weather, of the fine spring days they'd had so far, but the subject of weather waned after a few mouthfuls of food. Silence stretched as they ate and drank the wine, which was delicious. Lorrie wished she'd tasted bottles such as this more often.

'You are definitely leaving tomorrow?' Father suddenly asked Matteo.

'Yes. I travel by train to London in the morning. I will stay one night with my uncle and his family and then I board a ship the following morning.'

'Will that ship take you to La Spezia?' Father sipped his wine, watching Matteo.

'No. We dock at Genoa. My father will collect me from there in his own boat, or my brother will.'

'Your brother is a captain?' Father's grey eyebrows rose.

Matteo grinned. 'Alfonso likes to think he is. No, he works in my father's boatyard. We can all sail.'

'And you? Will you work in your father's boatyard?' Father ate more of his meal than he had done for weeks.

Matteo held up the glass of wine ready to sip. 'My future is not in my father's boatyard. I will take over my mother's cousin's vineyard, for he has no children. His son died as a baby and there were no more. He sees me as a son and his wish, and mine, is to have the vineyard.'

'Your father agrees to this?' Father sipped more wine.

'Ah...' Matteo sighed heavily. 'It is a subject my father and I do not always agree on, but my father knows owning a vineyard is my passion and our cousin needs me. It is what families do, yes?'

'I wouldn't know.' Father poked his fork at a potato, deep in thought. 'And my daughter?'

Embarrassed, Lorrie gasped. 'Father...'

Matteo drank deeply, then refilled his and Father's glasses as they'd both drunk a glass each already while Lorrie had two sips of hers. 'I cannot take your daughter home to La Spezia.' There was sorrow in Matteo's tone.

Lorrie looked down at her plate, wishing his words didn't hurt as much as they did.

'Why?' Father frowned. 'I see the way you both look at each other. While I've been laid up in bed, you two have been thrown together to run the yard. Something has happened, I know it. My daughter has never been so happy as she has since your arrival.' Father spoke like someone condemned.

'Your daughter is very beautiful,' Matteo murmured.

'I'm aware of that.'

'And if I had the choice, I would take her home with me, but I do not.'

'Why don't you?' Father barked. 'You're a grown man, surely you can make your own decisions?'

'Do you wish for me to take her from you?' Matteo challenged.

'Of course not, but I have eyes and ears and I can tell my daughter has changed since you came here.'

'If I was another sort of man, I would take her with me, but I have commitments at home, promises to keep. If I act on my feelings, I will break many people's hearts. This way I break only my own.'

'And hers!' Father flung his arm towards Lorrie.

'I *am* sitting at this table!' Lorrie snapped, banging her hands on the table, surprising them all by her actions. She rarely lost her temper. 'I do not need for you to talk for me, Father. I am capable of sorting my own life without it being discussed at the dinner table like it was the weather!'

'Are you?' Father huffed, his expression hard. 'Not once have you shown any interest in a man for longer than a few moments. There was a fellow last year I thought you might take a shine to, but in the end, you sent him away. Now Oswald will marry you, but no, you throw your emotions at someone totally unsuitable!'

'I will never marry Oswald, or any other man...' She glanced at Matteo. 'I know my own mind, Father. Matteo has made it clear we cannot be married. He is promised to another. I accept that and I will not settle for anyone less.' She faltered, shattered that the handsome man across the table would never be hers. 'Father, you of all people should know that where a heart sets its sights, it cannot be altered.'

Father sighed deeply, his shoulders sagging. 'That is true.'

'Now, can we discuss something else, please?' Lorrie drank more of her wine, amazed that she could still sit at the table calmly when every instinct wanted to run out of the room, away from the hurt and disappointment of Matteo's rejection.

Matteo, his handsome face miserable, raised his glass to Lorrie. 'You are magnificent.'

'She is like her mother,' Father answered. 'I had never seen anyone as beautiful as Arianna. The very first moment I saw her, my world stopped and then started again with Arianna at its centre.'

Lorrie stared at her father. He never spoke like this. Never once had he spoken of his feelings about her mother in such a way. She sipped her wine, needing it to fortify her.

'You were a lucky man.' Matteo ate some meat. 'In more ways than one.'

She glanced at him. 'What do you mean?'

'He means that I should never have married someone like your mother. I was not Italian.' Father leaned back in his chair. 'He means I could have been in prison, or hanged, for what I did when courting your mother.'

'Prison? Hanged? I don't understand.' How could those two words be associated with Father? Lorrie's mind spun. Had half a glass of wine muddled her thoughts?

'Your mother's brothers, George and Luke, didn't approve of me. They didn't want their sister marrying an Englishman. They wanted her to marry an Italian. But Arianna was spirited, a woman of independent thought, which went against her strict upbringing. She refused to be told what to do.' Father's eyes softened. 'We didn't want to be without each other. My term as an apprentice was coming to an end. I'd gone to London for just a year to upgrade my knowledge and skills after studying for five years here at Moreton's Boatyard just up the river...' Father spoke quietly, sipping his wine, reliving his memories.

'And you got into trouble with the law?' Lorrie asked, hardly believing it.

'I could have, yes.' Father held his glass out for Matteo to top up. 'George and Luke followed me down an alley one night. They wanted to teach me a lesson, warn me off Arianna. They didn't realise that Arianna was waiting for me at the end of the lane in the shadows. Her brothers attacked me, but I fought back. I was quick back then, slight. They were heavier and slower, but boy could they fight. Arianna screamed at them to stop. I thought I would die at one point. I smashed a crate over George's head, knocking him to the ground. In my hand was a broken piece of wood and when Luke came at me, I stabbed at him with it out of pure instinct for survival.'

Lorrie's mouth gaped open in shock. How could any of this be real? Her quiet, gentle father, a fighter, stabbing someone?

Matteo pushed away his empty plate. 'Luke nearly died.'

'True.' Father continued to drink. 'George and me dragged him back to their flat above their boatyard. Arianna stood full of rage at what had happened, that three men she loved had turned on each other so viciously. When her parents saw what happened, her father wanted to kill me himself. I thought I would have to fight him, too.'

Father rubbed a hand over his eyes.

'I told Arianna I was going home to Wakefield. She could come with me or stay. She chose to come with me, though her father begged and pleaded and forbid her. He said he'd go to the police, have me sent to jail.' Father looked down into his glass. 'He would have done it, but Arianna said she'd never forgive him if he did that, and she would never see him again or contact them. Her mother was hysterical, Luke bleeding. We all thought he would die. A doctor came and stitched him up and while he did so, Arianna and me fled into the night.'

Lorrie stared at her father, seeing a different side to him. The man she thought she knew had a past she had no idea about. 'Did Luke survive?'

'He did,' Matteo answered. 'But your father is hated by the family, not only for the incident with Luke but for taking Arianna away from them.'

'I killed her.' Father bowed his head. 'I brought her here away from her family to a place unfamiliar. I should have left Arianna in London where she was happy.'

'She loved you,' Lorrie murmured. 'You didn't force her.'

'No, I didn't, but losing contact with her family changed her. She became sad, especially when you were born. Arianna had no family women around her to give her advice or comfort. She was lonely. Her father never forgave her for leaving.'

'That is why we have had nothing to do with them.' Lorrie finally understood.

'Until now.' Father finished the glass of wine, glaring at Matteo.

Lorrie held her glass out for Matteo to refill. 'Well, I'm pleased Matteo has come here, Father. His arrival gave me something of my mother's family, and it's made you speak about something which has always been taboo.'

Father grunted.

Annoyed, Lorrie picked at her food. 'To have some questions finally answered after all these years is actually quite a relief.'

'Then if you are agreeable, I will return to my bed.' Father reached for his cane, his movements slow.

Lorrie and Matteo quickly stood to assist him back to the bedroom.

'Goodbye, Mr Falcone,' Father said from the bed.

At the door, Matteo bowed his head. 'Goodbye, Mr Chambers.' He walked out.

Lorrie fussed with the pillows, her mind whirling with all that had been said.

'Leave them.' Father took her hand. 'Forgive me for not talking of your mother more. I should have.'

'I wish you had. You loved her. Mother should be spoken of, not buried away. I want to know all about her. We should celebrate that she was alive, that she was here as your wife and my mother.'

Father sighed deeply. 'You are right. We should speak of her. I haven't done because it was so painful, but that wasn't fair to you.'

'From now on, we do not shy away from mentioning Mother's name.'

'No.' He squeezed her hands. 'I will make amends, Lorrie. Anything you want to know about Arianna, I will tell you.'

'Thank you.'

He kept hold of her hand when she went to move away. 'You will forget Falcone in time. His memory will fade, and the sting of his rejection will not pain you. If Falcone loved you enough, he'd marry you and take you to Italy.'

She knew he was right, but her heart was too full to speak. She kissed her father's head and left the room, mentally preparing herself to say goodbye to the man she'd grown to love.

8

Lorrie watched Matteo clear the table for a moment, amazed that he did so. She liked that he helped her in so many small ways. She would miss that.

He looked up as she approached, his smile wry, his gaze tender. 'Do you wish for me to go?'

'No.' She took the bucket and filled the kettle to heat water to wash the plates.

'Leave that,' Matteo said from near her shoulder. 'Let us take a walk.'

'At this time of night?' she chuckled, stacking the pots.

'It is warm out. We can go down by the river.' He took the wash-cloth from her. 'There will be time enough tomorrow to clean.'

She stared into his eyes, hating that there would be no tomorrow for them. She followed him to the door, noticing that he grabbed the other bottle of red wine and two glasses from the table as he walked by.

A full moon shone in the clear April night sky. No breeze ruffled the river. A stillness calmed the warm night air. Somewhere an owl hooted, but for once the waterfront was quiet. No boat whistles blew, no factory horns blared, no men shouted and hollered.

They walked through the yard and to the little dock. By the water's edge, Lorrie watched the moon shimmer over the black surface. It had its own beauty, the waterfront, harsh, noisy and smelly by day, but at night the industrial ugliness was muted in blacks and greys with pinpricks of yellow light twinkling from gaslights.

'You are quiet,' Matteo whispered.

'After tonight we will never see each other again, will we?'

He took a long time to answer. 'No. I shall not return to England again. I need to concentrate on my future now.'

A future without her. Lorrie should have felt slighted, and she did in a small way, but overriding that was thankfulness that she had met him. He had changed her life in a month. Even if she never experienced it again, she now knew the feeling of desire. She had fallen in love for the first time, and it had been with a handsome Italian, which was so unique, so highly improbable in her small world, but it had happened, and she was grateful to have met him, even if she would miss him terribly.

'Shall we have that wine?' she asked.

He poured the wine into two glasses and softly clinked his glass against hers. '*Salute.*'

'*Salute,*' she whispered, emotions high.

They sipped their wine and were silent, each with their own thoughts.

Lorrie didn't want the night to end. She didn't want to say goodbye. How do you say farewell to the one person you never want to let go? Tears burned behind her eyes, but she blinked them away and thought of something to say. 'What does *tesoro* and *amorino* or *amorina* mean?'

'*Tesoro* means treasure and *amorina* means sweetheart.' He spoke the words properly in Italian, which reminded Lorrie of how her mother spoke them. A flood of sentiment surged for her long-dead mother.

'My mother used to say those words to me.'

'You were her treasure.'

It comforted Lorrie to know that her mother used to call her those special words. Her mother had loved and cared for her but was gone too soon, before Lorrie could make more memories with her.

Matteo turned his back on the water and gazed at the yard. 'I have enjoyed my time here. Although unexpected, it was worth the journey.'

'Then you will take away fond memories?'

He touched her cheek. 'Many fond memories.'

A frisson of desire ran through her.

He took her hand and they strolled into the shed that held the sailboat. In the dark shadows, he gently pulled her to him and kissed her.

Lorrie didn't resist. She wanted his kiss more than anything in life.

'Another memory to take with me,' he murmured against her lips.

She couldn't step away. She couldn't reprimand him for taking liberties because she wanted the same as he did.

Matteo kissed her again and then moved away, closer to the boat. He glided his hand across the hull's smooth carved timber. 'Such beauty. Such talent. Apart from you, I will think of this boat often.'

She smiled. A short ladder stood beside the hull to allow the workers to climb up onto the deck. With one hand holding her wine glass and the other holding the ladder, Lorrie climbed up onto the deck. The shed was open at one end to the river, letting in a grey light of the moon, enough for her to see her way to the bow. She heard Matteo climb up behind her.

Drinking the last of the wine, Lorrie stared at the inky river, the stars and the moon. Matteo's hands came around her waist and she leaned back into his chest, shivering with delight at the contact.

'I cannot stop myself from touching you. My time here has been a sweet torture seeing you every day but not able to hold you.'

When his lips nibbled her neck, she stifled a moan and closed her eyes, enjoying the sensation. She felt light-headed, unused to drinking wine and having a male's attention, and not just any male, but Matteo's attention. Turning in his arms, she reached up to run her fingers through his black hair, lost to his mouth as they kissed deeply.

Matteo shrugged off his coat and laid it on the deck, then took her shawl and did the same. Lorrie had no objections when he eased her down onto the makeshift bed. She had only a few hours left with him, and she wanted, *needed* his love to sustain her for when he was long gone.

Matteo undressed her slowly, reverently, taking his time to expose each inch of skin in the moonlight. Every touch, every kiss was drummed into her mind, capturing the moment for her to keep and savour when she would be alone and aching for him.

Matteo pulled off his clothes before joining her naked on the coat. He murmured words in Italian as he kissed her, his hands caressing every part of her. 'You want me?' he asked, sucking a nipple.

Lorrie arched into him, her senses leaping, her mind a melting pot of thoughts, but the overriding thing was for him to never stop. Later, she would judge her actions, but right now, she flung all caution to the wind and made love to the man who made her body sing and her heart soar.

She took his lead, and when he encouraged her to touch his

2 ANNEMARIE BREAR

most intimate parts, she did so with an amazing lack of shyness. She had this one night with him, to learn about a man's body, to kiss and stroke Matteo's beautiful physique. All her wonderings, all her fantasies of what it was to have a man love her came forth and she absorbed the heat, the urgency, the curiosity of it all with a thirst that surprised her.

When he laid her down and knelt between her legs, she was more than ready for him. Eagerly she reached for him.

'Do you want to change your mind?' he murmured, stroking her inner thighs.

She sucked in a breath. This was the time to get up and walk away. He was giving her the option to keep her virginity, her reputation, something she prided herself on. But none of it mattered, not in the heat of the moment, not when he was kneeling before her, driving her near mad with desire. 'I want you,' she said on an intake of breath.

His gorgeous smile shone in the moonlight as he moved over her, coming closer to kiss her thoroughly as he entered her.

Lorrie closed her eyes, her breath caught in her chest, until he moved slowly, bringing her out of her own mind.

'Feel your body,' he whispered, 'feel mine... *amore mio...*'

Another kiss and she gripped his back, focusing on the rhythm, the building of sensations. Matteo kissed her, his tongue speaking a language of its own. Lorrie clasped him tightly as he moved quicker, his moans joining hers, until suddenly her body hit such a pinnacle that she felt suspended, Matteo forgotten, the hard wood beneath her back forgotten, everything was centred on the core of her body and the amazing high she was floating down from.

Matteo slumped against her, heavy and panting. Lorrie lightly stroked his back with her fingertips. Her mind whirled. She'd become a woman in the true sense and was fascinated by it.

'Do not feel ashamed,' Matteo whispered against her ear. 'It is natural.'

'I'm not ashamed.' And she wasn't. As he said, it was a natural occurrence for a man and woman to mate. She should have been horrified that she had allowed her body to rule her head and utterly ashamed to have given away her self-respect. But she wasn't. How could she be when she loved Matteo? She would marry him tomorrow if she could. It wasn't as if she was a woman of the night selling her body for coins. No. She adored him and no doubt he would be the only man she would ever be with. How could spending a few hours alone with him be wrong?

No one would ever know. It was their secret. Their magical special hidden delight. She would never regret this night. Her feelings for him were true. This one night of love would have to sustain her for a bleak future without him.

'I wish we had more wine.' He grinned, kissing her neck as he wrapped her shawl around them both.

'I could make us a cup of tea?' But she was loathe to move from the cocoon of his arms.

'No. Stay here with me.' He held her tightly. Matteo leaned his head back against the side of the boat, pulling her against him. 'This was unexpected. I did not plan to seduce you tonight. I do not wish for you to think I have used you.'

'I don't think that.'

'Regrets?' he murmured.

'None.'

'Good.' He sighed heavily. 'I wish things could be different.'

'Me too.'

'I will never forget you.'

She glanced up at him. 'I hope you don't.'

'It will be a night I can cherish in my mind and heart and when

I am an old man watching the sea or strolling along my vines, I will think of you.'

Lorrie threaded her fingers through his. She liked the idea of that, of this night being remembered when they were old.

His finger tilted her chin up for another kiss. 'Look for love again, Lorrie. You are too passionate to waste your years on this one memory,' he said as though reading her mind. 'You deserve so much more.' His lips touched hers softly, like the gentle wings of a butterfly.

Lorrie suddenly held his head, demanding a stronger kiss, needing to feel and touch him again. Tears burned behind her eyes, but she closed her eyes and wouldn't let them fall. She didn't have time to weep now, that would come later when he was gone. They still had a few hours before dawn, and she would wring every last wonderful second out of them... with him.

* * *

Lorrie woke to a gull screeching. She blinked, disorientated and cold. It took her a moment to realise she was on the deck of the sailboat in the shed and gasped in surprise. A part of her believed last night had all been a dream. Yet her state of undress and the noise of the waterfront awaking to a new day quickly confirmed the truth.

In a panic, knowing the men would be arriving any moment, she quickly dressed. Of Matteo there was no sign, only his empty glass next to hers.

A wave of acute heartbreak washed over her. She clutched the side of the boat, wanting to cry out her pain, her sense of loss.

'Miss Chambers?' Jed stood at the opening of the shed, a look of utter shock on his face.

'Jed.' She stared back guiltily, aware that her hair was falling around her shoulders. She bent and pulled on her shoes, flustered.

'Can I help you down, miss?' Jed asked kindly, standing at the bottom of the ladder.

'Yes, er... I was... You see, I...' She couldn't meet his eyes and she stumbled over to the ladder, her shoes unlaced, her shawl hanging off her shoulders. She was mortified he'd seen her. Not Jed, the man was like an uncle to her. She'd known him all her life. He'd been the first man Father hired when he took over the boatyard.

'I'll not be telling a soul, lass,' he whispered as she came down the ladder.

She had no words to say. How could she explain herself to the old man?

A factory whistle blew, shattering the quiet morning. Lorrie jumped, her mind a mess. From outside the shed she heard Jimmy chatting to Roy. 'I'd best go...' She gathered her shawl about her. 'Thank you, Jed.'

'Right you are, miss.' His tender smile brought tears to her eyes.

She hurried across the yard, abruptly concerned that she'd left Father alone all night. What if he'd called out to her needing help? Guilt carried her upstairs as fast as she could go. She ran into her room and quickly brushed her hair and tied it up in a ribbon before washing her face. No sound came from the bedroom next door. She hurriedly went to her father's bedroom door and listened. Opening it slightly, she sagged in relief on seeing Father start to stir from sleep. He'd not woken early for once.

She was all fingers and thumbs as she raked out the cold ashes and reset the fire with twists of newspaper and kindling. A match caught on the second strike, and she watched the newspaper burn and curl, licking the sticks until finally it held, and a small blaze grew.

Filling the kettle, she left it on the hob to boil and then added more wood to the fire before gathering the buckets and going downstairs to the tap in the yard.

The sun rose over the rooftops and the noise of mills and factories and hundreds of people walking on the cobbles joined the clatter of horses and carts, the groan of the dockyard cranes and the boat horns. Another day was starting just like all the rest, but for Lorrie it wasn't simply another day. It was the first day of the rest of her life. A life without Matteo in it.

'Shall I take these up, miss, and see if your father needs a hand to get washed and dressed?' Jed held the two wine glasses.

Lorrie felt the blood rush to her cheeks, and she looked away to change the buckets over and fill the next one. 'Yes, thank you, Jed.'

Jed took the full bucket in his other hand and carried it upstairs for her.

Humiliated that Jed knew she'd been with someone on the boat, she had to brazen it out. The old man knew her as a good person. She wasn't a hussy. No doubt he would guess who she'd been with, but Lorrie had no compulsion to ever speak of it, not to Jed, not to anyone.

Somehow, she managed to cook breakfast, ham and eggs for her and Father. They spoke little at the table, her father reading the newspaper that Jimmy had brought up for him, and Lorrie's head was too full of the events of the night before.

Matteo had gone. The three words rang like a doom bell in her brain. How would she stand it? To never see him again? To never see his cheeky smile that made her toes curl in desire. Last night had been such a delightful experience. They had shared something special, intimate. She'd given him everything she had, yet still, he had left.

A searing pain clamped her chest. She bowed her head, not

trusting herself to look up in case her father saw her despair. In a fit of activity, she cleared the table and cleaned the kitchen, needing to keep busy, occupied and to not think or feel about anything.

The little gold clock on the mantel chimed eight times and at the same time a knock came at the door.

Lorrie opened it and blinked in surprise at Jonas Bannerman.

'Good morning, Miss Chambers.' His warm greeting matched the kindness in his grey eyes.

She'd forgotten all about him. 'Mr Bannerman. Do come in.'

She waved him inside, then saw Rollo sitting on the mat and opened the door wider for him to come in too.

'Father, this is Mr Jonas Bannerman. A shipwright from Whitby. I mentioned him yesterday.'

'Ah, yes. Welcome, Mr Bannerman.' Father folded away his newspaper and was all interest. 'Come, sit. Have some tea.'

The men shook hands and Mr Bannerman sat at the table, Rollo by his feet.

Lorrie fetched a cup and saucer and poured out the tea for Bannerman. Rollo eyed her as she did so, and she deftly gave him some ham fat she had on a scrap plate. His shaggy tail wagged, and she swore he grinned.

'I've brought you a selection of my design drawings, Mr Chambers.' Bannerman took a rolled-up tube of paper that stuck out of his satchel. He spread the papers on the table for Father and Lorrie to study.

'My, they are impressive.' Father lifted one of the boat designs for a closer inspection.

'It's been my life's work,' Bannerman said, matter-of-factly. The man had no false sense of pride, nor boasted.

Lorrie warmed to him immediately. He seemed genuine, a solid character. Being an older man, she didn't have to worry about him messing about like Jimmy and Roy tended to do when no one was looking.

'You'll want a decent wage,' Father murmured. 'Your ability and years of knowledge demand it.'

'Only what I believe I'm worth.'

'We don't have much call for designing boats. I have one in the shed now, a sailboat for a gentleman who lives near Goole. Other than that, we are lucky to handcraft more than one boat a year. Our bread and butter comes from repairs.'

Lorrie blushed at the mention of the sailboat.

'I'm happy to do repairs, too.' Bannerman rolled up the designs. 'I simply need to work and settle down somewhere new.'

'And you didn't fancy staying on the east coast?'

'No.' Bannerman shook his head. 'I thought to try along the rivers and canals first and make my way west to Liverpool if nothing came available.'

Father glanced at Lorrie, and she nodded slightly, giving him her approval. 'Well, we could certainly do with your expertise. I'm laid up, and Jed, my leading hand, is older than me. His hands are full of arthritis and in another year or two he'll struggle to hold a chisel. We have a young apprentice, a lad of fifteen, Jimmy, and then two labourers, Roy and Saunders. We had more men, but had to let them go, times are lean.'

'But Saunders is to be given his marching orders,' Lorrie put in quickly. 'I, we, don't feel we can trust him.'

Father sipped from his teacup. 'Saunders was hired by my partner, Oswald Lynch, when I first had my accident. Oswald thought he was doing a good thing bringing another man to help in the yard, but Saunders has no experience.'

Lorrie wanted to add that the man was shifty and leered at her at every opportunity.

'Right.' Bannerman nodded, his expression thoughtful. 'And

the Italian?'

'He's gone,' Lorrie managed to mumble, inwardly wincing at the stab of agony those words brought.

'I don't know when I'll be able to work again,' Father said, tapping his left leg. 'Recovery has been slow. It'll be a few more months yet before I can stand on these legs for an entire day. I need someone in the yard who can do the same work as me and Jed. Someone to teach Jimmy and Roy.'

'You can count on me,' Bannerman said firmly. 'I work hard and keep to myself. I don't make trouble or nosy about in other people's business. I want a quiet life.'

'Sounds good to me.' Father held out his hand. 'Welcome to Chambers Boat Builder and Repairs.'

Bannerman shook Father's hand and then nodded to Lorrie.

She still hadn't seen the man smile. 'Shall I show you around?' She led him out and down the stairs and across to the largest shed, which held the sailboat. She introduced Bannerman to Jed, bending to scratch Rollo's ears while the two men talked.

'Who is this then?' Oswald appeared at the shed door, behind him stood Saunders.

Lorrie silently groaned. She didn't want to deal with Oswald today. 'This is Mr Bannerman, a shipwright from Whitby. He has come to work here.' She turned to Bannerman. 'This is Mr Oswald Lynch, my father's partner.'

The two men shook hands, but Oswald's tight expression showed his displeasure. 'A word, Miss Chambers, if you please?'

Lorrie followed him outside where Oswald stood and glared at her. 'You hire another man, yet Saunders tells me his hours are reduced to just three days?'

'Mr Bannerman is highly qualified. Saunders is not. We don't need another labourer. Saunders has to go.'

'Then dismiss Jimmy or Roy. Saunders stays.'

'Jimmy and Roy are apprentices,' she argued. 'Despite their younger years they seem to know more than Saunders, who spends most of his time lazing about pretending to look busy.'

'Saunders will buck up his ways.' Oswald's face reddened as he glanced at the offending man, who had followed them outside. 'Won't you, Saunders?'

'Aye.' Saunders shrugged, not caring in the least to look contrite.

Lorrie wondered why Oswald was so keen to keep Saunders around.

Suddenly Oswald clapped his hands and smirked. 'Shall we have a cup of tea? I will see your father if he is available for a visit?'

'Father is upstairs at the table. Go on up. I shall finish showing Mr Bannerman the yard.' Lorrie turned away from him, knowing she was being rude and didn't care. The man made her blood boil.

With Oswald in the living quarters, Lorrie took her time showing Bannerman the whole yard and at the edge of the river she pointed out the various other buildings and businesses that stretched along both banks. A narrowboat captain waved to her as he went by on his long vessel, and she waved back.

'This is a busy river and dockside,' Bannerman said in surprise.

'The waterfront is a hive of activity,' she agreed before turning to stroll back amongst the small boats that were in dry dock.

'What is that shed over there?' Bannerman gestured towards a long narrow shed situated at the end of the property and behind the dry dock area.

'It once was another repair shed, but Father deemed it too narrow and so now it's a storage shed that rarely gets used as we have other storage areas closer to where the men work.' Lorrie walked over to the double doors and struggled to pull one open, the other door wouldn't budge. 'They aren't even locked. So, there's nothing of any worth inside or Father would lock it.'

Peering into the dim, dusty interior, Lorrie could make out pieces of timber, a broken window frame, a wooden bucket with no handle. Beyond that, into the back of the shed, stood tins of old paint, a rusted rake and various crates, plus a set of wooden drawers. Cobwebs decorated the ceiling joists like ancient lace and the one window was so dirty you couldn't see out of it. Dead flies from summers long past littered the windowsill.

While Rollo darted inside, sniffing eagerly between the timbers stacked along one wall, Bannerman gave the place a considerate amount of scrutiny. 'If I cleaned this place out, could I live here? I'd pay rent, of course.'

'Here?' Lorrie's eyes widened. 'Really?'

'It's bigger than the room I rent at the hotel I'm staying at.' He stepped further inside. 'I could partition the back area off and have a bed in there and this front bit I could have some chairs, a table, maybe a small range to cook on.'

Lorrie tried to imagine the old shed cleared of rubbish and turned into some kind of living quarters. 'It would be a lot of work.'

'I could start clearing it at the end of each day. The evenings are lighter and longer now, which would give me more time.' He walked around the side of the shed that edged closest to the water. 'It looks solid enough.'

'The roof might leak.' Lorrie stood back to search the bit of roof that she could see for any holes.

'Would your father and yourself be willing to let me live here?' Bannerman asked, clicking his fingers for Rollo to return to him.

'I don't see why not. The shed is not really of any use to us in the state it's in.'

'No, and with my rent, it will be an income asset instead of a place to dump rubbish.' He closed the door and turned to her with an inscrutable expression. 'I'll give you time to discuss it with your father.'

'I'm sure Father will agree to it, but I must ask him before I say yes.'

Bannerman nodded. 'Thank you. I'll go and find Jed and start work.'

Lorrie watched him walk away and then glanced back at the shed. The rent would be welcome, not that she would consider charging him a lot for it. It made sense to turn the shed into a useful building. She thought more about it as she walked back to the office. It would be strange to have someone else living in the yard. She was used to only her and Father living here. Yet Bannerman didn't seem the kind of man who would be demanding or noisy or forever knocking on their door wanting company. Actually, he seemed a bit of a loner. She doubted he would cause any trouble. The man had a quiet, reserved manner about him.

Going upstairs, she could hear Oswald's voice before she walked through the door.

'Ah, there she is. The delight of the entire waterfront,' Oswald crooned.

Lorrie grimaced at his false platitudes and went to the fire to add more coal to it. 'Tea?'

'Not for me, my dear Miss Chambers,' Oswald declared, standing. 'I am a busy man and must be about my business.'

'Good to see you again, Oswald,' Father said, reaching for his cane. 'And have those papers drawn up.'

'Indeed, Ernest. I'll call again tomorrow.' Oswald put on his top hat and bowed to Lorrie, who stood frozen by the fire.

Once Oswald had left, Lorrie rushed to her father's side. 'What papers? What's happening?'

'Help me up, dear. I shall lie down for an hour.' He eased himself up on his good leg.

'But what are these papers you speak of?' She took his weight on his left side.

'Oswald has decided that he'll invest more money into the business.'

'Why?' Lorrie didn't understand it.

'Oswald sees great potential in us.' Father hopped along to the bedroom.

'Does he want a higher percentage of the business? He holds 35 per cent already. What more does he want?'

'An equal 50 per cent,' Father said, dropping down onto the bed with a wince.

'No, not half, Father. It's too much.' She was aghast at the idea.

'My dear, we must think of the future. When I am gone, you will need someone to help you or at least someone we know who will buy the other half of the business from you. Oswald is fully prepared to buy you out once I'm dead. He will be generous. I have his word.'

'And you trust him?' Lorrie couldn't believe what she was hearing.

'Have you thought about the future without me?' Father asked, leaning back against the pillows. 'You will be alone with no one to take care of you.'

'I don't need taking care of, and it definitely won't be Oswald Lynch I'd turn to.'

'Well, you can at least run the business with Oswald and likely stay here in your home, or if he buys you out, you can find a nice little cottage somewhere.'

'I can do that without him having a 50 per cent share!' she huffed.

'Can you?' Father frowned. 'Without me, and with Jed close to retiring, who can you rely on?'

'You talk as if you're dying. You could live for years yet, you're not ancient.'

'No, but we have to be prepared. I trust Oswald to do the right thing and take care of you if something should happen to me.'

'I don't need him to take care of me,' she repeated, trying to make him understand. 'I could run the business without Oswald, without you if need be.'

Father's face softened. 'Dearest, you would have to sell. Boat captains wouldn't want to deal with you, a woman, without qualifications or a team of qualified tradesmen.'

'I would work it out, trust me to know what to do, please, Father. You mustn't sign away any more of the boatyard to Oswald. I don't trust him.'

'Why? Because he's not Matteo Falcone?' Father snapped. 'Oswald has told me how Falcone treated him with contempt. What has Falcone been saying to you?'

The mention of Matteo brought emotions to the surface that she'd been burying all day. 'This has nothing to do with Matteo.'

'Doesn't it? Oswald has offered to marry you, but you've turned him down and set your heart on someone who you'll never see again! If you married Oswald, your future would be safe. Your children could carry on the tradition of working in this yard. It would be a Chambers legacy.'

'I don't love him!'

'What has that got to do with it? Oswald is security.'

'I didn't trust Oswald long before Matteo arrived, but you seem blind to him and his sly ways and his eagerness to take control over the business.' She glared at her father, tears burning hot behind her eyes. 'You married for love, yet you want me to marry a man who turns my stomach just to save this boatyard!'

She ran from the bedroom and into her own room to fall on the bed. Her heart wept at the loss of Matteo, wishing he'd never left her, and she sobbed for the grim future stretching out before her.

9

Lorrie tucked her arm through Meg's as they strolled through the sweeping gardens of Meadow View House, Meg and Christian's splendid home. In the May sunshine, swallows ducked and dived above their heads, some seeking the safety of the high branches of the chestnut trees at the edge of the garden while others gathered on the fence separating the fields beyond.

'What a glorious day. This is my first spring here at Meadow View and I have such plans for the garden, though I know nothing of growing plants, but the head gardener here has taken me under his wing, and we plan to design more garden beds over the summer,' Meg announced happily as they wandered past a stone birdbath surrounded by flowering roses of pink and yellow.

'It's a lovely change for me to get away from the yard and be amongst greenery.' Lorrie paused by a lavender bush and picked a stem, the scent strong as she sniffed it. 'It's so nice to smell flowers instead of tar and sawdust.' She gazed up at the cloudless blue sky. 'To see the sky without a cover of smoke haze.'

Meg squeezed her arm. 'Come here whenever you want to

escape, whether I'm at home or not. You've been tied to that boat-yard since your father's accident without a break.'

Sighing deeply, Lorrie strolled on. 'Apart from going to the market, I've not left the yard or Father, but he's much better now. This morning he insisted I take myself off for the day, but I feel guilty for leaving him.'

'You said the men will look in on him every hour, he'll be fine.'

'I know...'

'And he's able to hobble about with the cane.'

'Yes...'

'So, what's the real problem?' Meg tilted her head at her, placing one hand on her small pregnant stomach. 'Out with it.'

'I don't know, and that's the truth.'

'You've been low since Matteo left.'

Lorrie paused at the fence gate and leaned on the top rail to watch the cows grazing, their calves close. Matteo was never far from her mind. She fell asleep at night thinking of him, crying silent tears for what could have been. She relived their lovemaking, tormenting herself with memories of his kisses.

Meg stood beside her. 'I know the ache of loving someone who you think can never be yours. Loving Christian and knowing he was above my station and unattainable was torture.'

'But you got your man in the end,' Lorrie murmured.

'And there is a possibility that Matteo may change his mind and return for you.'

'I thought that, too. For weeks since he left, I keep expecting him to walk through the yard and whisk me away to his homeland where we eat food in the sun and walk through his vines.' She stared into the distance. 'Those expectations are dimming more each day.'

'I'm so sad that he did this to you.' Meg placed her arm around

Lorrie's waist. 'My hope is that he comes to his senses and realises what he left behind.'

'Why should he when he has a woman already there?' Lorrie straightened, tired of the low moods that held her in such a tight grip. 'I must stop this maudlin. It'll do me no good to continually think of him, to wish for things to be different. They won't be.'

'How can I help?' Meg asked, her tone kind but determined.

'Talk to me of other things. How are your brothers and sisters?'

Turning to lean on the fence, Meg gave a wry smile. 'At the moment, they are all behaving!' She laughed. 'Freddie has taken Mabel to live with him at the pub. She's thriving and staying away from boys. Mabel's learning to work in the kitchen, she has a surprising knack for cooking. Who would have thought? She never once lifted a pot when we lived in Wellington Street.'

Lorrie grinned, Meg always lifted her spirits. 'And the others?'

'Susie is still at the mill, she's a good girl and is no trouble. I can say the same for Betsy, who is learning a great deal. It was the best thing we did getting her that apprenticeship at the milliners. She made me a hat for summer, it's straw dyed blue with white roses and feathers sewn into the upturned brim at the side. Very stylish.'

'I should go to the shop and request one myself,' Lorrie said with a smile. 'And Nell and Nicky?'

'Nell says she wants to be a teacher when she leaves school. Christian says we should get her a place at a training college as soon as she is of age to go.'

'A teacher, now that is a good profession for her.'

'Yes, and such a skill would get her away from working in the mills or factories,' Meg added. 'Nicky... Nicky has suffered another episode of weakness last week. Josie kept him home from school and sent for us immediately.'

'Why didn't you tell me?' Lorrie felt ashamed she hadn't

known. She'd been too wrapped up in her own misery to think of others.

'It was all very sudden. We took him to London again to see the heart doctor, that specialist Christian found, but there is nothing to be done, apparently. It's the same story I've been told since he was born. Even with Christian's money and taking Nicky to the best London doctors, there is nothing to be done. His heart is weak, the same as my mam's heart was.'

'Poor sweet boy.' Lorrie was sorry that Meg's youngest brother was ill. She knew how worried Meg was about him.

'I want Nicky to come and live with us, but he won't leave Josie.' Meg pushed away from the gate irritably. 'Josie cares for him devotedly, but I wish he was here away from the dampness of Wellington Street.'

'Maybe he will come here when he's a little older?'

'Christian says he should go to a school that will foster his drawing skills, but Nicky is too weak to board away.'

'Shame, for he has such talent with his art,' Lorrie said as they started to stroll back towards the house.

Meg rubbed her stomach. 'I hope I don't pass that condition on to this little one.'

'I'm sure you won't. You don't have it and it's only Nicky out of all your brothers and sisters who developed the weak heart. Take strength from that.' Lorrie injected a positive note to her voice and changed the subject. 'Have you heard from Arthur?'

'A card from Spain. His ship docked there last month, and he finally sent a message, so I know that he is safe. My brother is enjoying the seaman's life.'

'Who could blame him? He's seeing the world.' For a fleeting second, she thought of Matteo and Italy. If things had been different, she'd be seeing some of the world, too.

'Oh, there's Christian.' Meg waved as her husband came out

onto the terrace. A maid followed him with a tray of cakes and sandwiches and Titmus, the butler, wheeled a trolley out with tea and coffee.

'This is a delightful surprise,' Christian said, kissing Meg's cheek before doing the same to Lorrie. 'I thought I'd come home to an empty house.' He looked at Meg. 'Weren't you visiting your seamstress this morning?'

Meg sat on one of the cushioned wrought-iron chairs. 'I cancelled. Lorrie arrived.'

'Oh!' Lorrie blushed, embarrassed. 'You should have said you had an appointment.'

'Nonsense.' Meg waved away her concerns. 'I can go to the seamstress any time. Getting measured for this ever-growing bump isn't as important as spending time with you.'

Lorrie squeezed Meg's hand. 'Thank you, but you still should have told me.'

'Eat,' Meg commanded. 'You're as thin as a sparrow.'

Lorrie had lost her appetite when Matteo left and only ate enough to give her enough energy to get through the day. But because Meg was watching, she ate a triangle of egg and cress sandwich and actually enjoyed it. She ate more as Christian spoke of the brewery and the new equipment he'd bought.

Meg handed Lorrie a slice of fruit cake on a plate but spoke to Christian. 'Did you call on Freddie?'

'Yes.' Christian crossed one leg over the other. 'Mabel was out the back in the kitchen. Freddie says she is keen to learn more cooking skills. To give the customers the option for simple, yet good, food while they have their beer. Freddie says the men will drink more and stay longer if they can have food, too. It's a good business plan.'

'I'm happy Mabel is throwing herself into the cooking and has settled down at the pub.' Meg's worried frown lifted.

'This might be exactly what she needs,' Lorrie added. 'Being in charge of the pub's kitchen will keep her focused and give her responsibility.'

Meg nodded. 'I certainly hope so.'

'Freddie told me something interesting,' Christian said, reaching for his teacup and saucer. 'About Oswald Lynch.'

'Mr Lynch?' Lorrie tensed.

'It seems Mr Lynch has got himself into some kind of trouble. Apparently, he owes some rather nasty people money. How much, Freddie didn't know. But Lynch was in the pub last night and paid extra to have the snug to himself. He ordered Freddie to not tell a soul he was in there. It seems he wasn't keen to go home at closing time either. Freddie said Lynch basically ran up Westgate as fast as he could go.'

'Someone is after him then,' Meg judged.

Lorrie shivered. That was all she needed, Oswald in trouble.

Christian forked a piece of fruit cake. 'Lynch is a slimy eel for sure. It's not the first time he's been in trouble with the wrong type.'

'Is he gambling?' Meg wondered.

'Either that or investments gone bad.'

Lorrie shifted on the chair. 'He's asked Father to sell more of the business to him, be an equal partner. How can he do that if he has money problems?'

'The man has many irons in many fires.' Christian shrugged. 'Knowing Lynch, I'm guessing he's running from men who he's taken money from for investments, and he owes them. That's not to say he doesn't have other money stashed away.'

'I was surprised he wanted to pour more money into the boat-yard. His returns are minimal. It will take years for him to get his money back. The yard is busy, yes, but we only make enough money to cover expenditures because Oswald has lowered our prices.' Lorrie rubbed her forehead, her head aching with this news.

'I expect Lynch has a plan, what it is, who knows?' Christian gave Lorrie a comforting pat on the hand. 'But keep a watch on him.'

Declining Meg's offer to be taken home in the carriage, Lorrie strolled the country lanes from Meadow View House back towards the waterfront. With the river on her left, she could see it between farms and buildings, spotting narrowboats gliding by until the farms were replaced with mills and malthouses, factories and houses.

Walking gave her time to feel the sun on her face, to watch the birds flying above in the clear sky. She didn't have to think of the business or her father. She simply strolled along, enjoying being away from the yard.

Naturally, her mind wandered to Matteo. It had been four weeks since he left. Four weeks. It surprised her that she'd managed to get through them with her sanity intact. He had not written to her and that hurt. She expected something, anything to show her that he cared, that she meant something to him. What they shared had meant the world to her, but obviously not to him. Tears burnt behind her eyes, but she didn't give in to them, not this time. She didn't want to arrive home with red eyes and cause her father concern. He worried about her, often asking if she wanted to talk to him, which was impossible. How could she tell him she'd lost her virginity to a man she'd never see again? Father would be so disappointed and shocked, and she couldn't bear to see that in his face.

Entering the yard, she was pleased it was Saturday afternoon and the men had gone, except Jimmy who sat at the top of the stairs, reading the newspaper.

'How's Father?' she asked him with a smile, climbing the staircase.

'He's fine and talking to Mr Lynch. That's why I'm out here in case Mr Chambers needs me. Besides, I'd rather be sitting in the sun than inside on such a lovely day,' the youth replied, folding the newspaper and standing up.

Lorrie's shoulders sagged at the thought of Oswald being here. 'When did Mr Lynch arrive?'

'About ten minutes ago. I made them both tea and then Mr Chambers said to have one myself, so I brought it out with me.' He picked up the teacup from the landing. 'I was going to help Mr Bannerman, but I wouldn't be able to hear Mr Chambers if he shouted for me.'

'Thank you for staying, Jimmy.' She took the teacup from him and in return gave him a few pence for looking after her father. 'See you on Monday morning.'

'Ta-ra, Miss Chambers.' Jimmy dashed down the stairs and out of the gates with all the energy of youth.

Lorrie hesitated at the door, not wanting to go inside and be polite to Oswald. The less she saw of him the better. She worried what he might be saying to Father, though worrying about it got her nowhere, for Father always brushed off her concerns and thought Oswald could do no wrong. They wouldn't discuss their conversations with her, which was extremely frustrating. In their eyes she was a mere woman with no place in their talks concerning the boatyard. To be dismissed made her angry and frustrated. She only hoped Father wasn't making a big mistake trusting Oswald.

Annoyed that her father didn't confide in her enough, Lorrie placed the teacup back on the landing and went down the stairs. She strolled across the yard with the idea to sit on the dock in the sun until Oswald had left.

Rounding the end of a boat in dry dock, she heard banging

coming from the storage shed Bannerman was turning into a home. Her steps altered and she walked towards the sound of industry.

'Good afternoon, Mr Bannerman.' Lorrie slowed and gave him a smile as he turned from the saw bench.

'Good day to you, Miss Chambers.' Bannerman wiped the sweat from his brow. He wore old clothes and was covered in sawdust.

Lorrie bent to scratch Rollo's ears where he sat near the pile of timber. 'Who's a sweet boy?' she asked the dog, who quickly rolled over for his tummy to be rubbed.

Bannerman shook his head at the dog and rolled his eyes. 'He'll have you doing that for hours, miss.'

'I don't mind.'

'Did you have a nice morning out visiting?'

'I did. It's always a treat to visit Meg at Meadow View.' She straightened and peered in through the open door.

'You can go inside if you want.' Bannerman dusted his hands and indicated for her to go before him.

Inside, the old shed had been transformed. Cleared of all the rotten pieces of wood, the broken window frame and numerous other accumulated rubbish, the shed looked much larger. The one window the shed boasted had been cleaned and sunlight streamed through to brighten the floor space, highlighting the bareness of it.

Over the weeks, Bannerman had built a partitioned wall at the back, and Lorrie spied a bed roll on the wooden floor. Shocked, she stared at him. 'You're sleeping on the floor?'

'For now. It's no bother now the nights are getting warmer.'

'Oh, Mr Bannerman, you can't sleep on the hard floor and then work all day. Your poor back will be broken.'

His soft laughter filled the shed. 'I confess, it's a bit difficult to

get up on a morning. I'm no longer twenty, even if my mind some-
times thinks I am.'

Lorrie gazed at him. It was the first time she'd heard him laugh
or seen him properly smile and the transformation was incredible.
Dimples appeared in his cheeks, banishing the sad expression he
always wore, and his grey eyes turned a soft blue.

'We must get you a bed.' She stopped staring at him and
focused on the open space. 'And everything, really. For this to
become your home, you need furniture.'

'Don't worry about it, miss. I'll get things in time. The main
concern is getting the roof watertight. There was a leak in the back
corner.' He pointed to a new piece of boarding that stood out
amongst the older ceiling. 'I'm surprised a shed has a ceiling, it's
usually open to the rafters, but I noticed when I was up in there
that it has more storage space.'

'What did you find? Treasure?' Lorrie laughed.

'I wish. No, only old bird nests and dead mice.'

'Nice.' She grimaced.

'Still, having a ceiling suits my purpose better. It'll be warmer
in winter.'

'You need a fire in here.' She started to imagine how the place
could look with some effort.

'Aye, I've bought an old stove, it's around the side. It's a bit
rusted but a good clean and some blackleading will soon have it
looking new again. I've got to put the chimney through the roof,
which is my task for this afternoon.'

'May I help?' she asked impulsively, not knowing why, only that
she liked his company. In the four weeks since he started working
in the yard, he spent at least an hour a day with her father talking
of designs and the craft of boat building. She half listened to their
talk as she made them tea or went about her household chores,
but she was aware of Bannerman's intellect. He read widely and

had travelled up and down the east coast from Scotland to Kent. His stories were interesting yet not boastful. Sometimes when she was busy in the office, she noticed Bannerman and Jed working in the yard, each respectful of the other's knowledge and opinions. The two of them with their skills and knowledge were soon accomplishing a lot in the yard. Jobs were getting finished, boats were returned to their owners, and this allowed Lorrie to finalise invoices and see more income trickle in faster than before.

She liked Bannerman. He had a trusting manner, a kind face. The man was a perfect addition to the yard.

'I'm not sure there's anything you can do, miss.' Bannerman frowned in thought. 'You could hold the ladder for me while I'm up on the roof perhaps?'

'I will. First, let me go and change. I'll be right back.' Lorrie hurried to the living quarters, helping Bannerman would be a nice way to spend the afternoon. The weather was too glorious to be inside.

'Ah, my dear.' Father held out his hand to her as she entered. 'You have returned. How was your visit to Meg's?'

'Lovely.' Lorrie kissed her father's cheek and inclined her head in acknowledgement to Oswald. 'Mr Lynch,' she said stiffly. After hearing about his problems from Christian, she'd grown even colder towards the man.

'You look most animated, Miss Chambers. Your visit must have lifted your low spirits of late,' Oswald patronised.

She clenched her teeth, but ignored his comments and turned to Father. 'Do you need me at all?'

'No, dearest.'

'I need to change and then I said I would help Mr Bannerman. He needs a ladder holding for him.'

'Surely he can't ask you to do that?' Oswald was aghast. 'You are his employer's daughter.'

'I am perfectly capable of holding a ladder, Mr Lynch. I am stronger than you think.'

'Ernest, you must not allow this,' Oswald protested in shock. 'It is hardly dignified for your daughter to be assisting in building work.'

Lorrie burst out laughing. 'Mr Lynch, what a thing to say. I'm holding a ladder, so a man doesn't fall and break a bone, not constructing a house in Westgate.'

Her father chuckled.

In her bedroom, she changed into a dark brown dress that she used for washing days. She paused to tuck her great-grandmother's necklace under the collar. She'd worn it every day. Having the necklace against her skin comforted her.

A wave of relief washed over her when she emerged from her room to find Oswald gone.

'Father, Christian told me that Oswald is in debt.' She had to tell him. 'He's wanted by some nasty characters.'

'A bad investment, yes, I know. Oswald told me today.'

Lorrie sat abruptly on a chair. 'He told you?'

'That's why he called. He can no longer buy a larger percentage of the business. I agreed to cancel the deal.'

She sagged in relief. 'I'm so pleased.'

'Don't be,' he warned, looking anxious. 'Oswald has asked to borrow some money from me, but the amount he wants I haven't got.' Father rubbed his head. 'Oswald mentioned he might have to sell his stake in the boatyard. But we can't afford to buy him out.' Father tapped his fingers on the table. 'Oswald could sell his share of the boatyard to someone else. This is not a good development, my dear.'

'So, either Oswald wants to sell to a stranger or have us return all his money?' Lorrie fumed. Not this again. The horrid man was forever threatening to take back his investment, but now she knew they weren't empty threats. Oswald needed money and fast and wouldn't care how he got it.

'It's looking that way, yes.'

'How will we do that?' Fear gripped her insides.

'A bank loan perhaps? I'd hate for Oswald to sell his part to someone else.'

'Perhaps I can speak to Christian? He may wish to invest in us?'

'It wouldn't hurt to try. I'd rather Christian than a stranger. However, I do have some other people we can speak to. I'll give it some thought. Help me down the stairs, dearest. I will come and sit out in the sun while you help Bannerman.'

'Can you manage the stairs?'

He nodded. 'It's time I tried. Everything has changed today, lass. I need to take control of this business again. So, help me get downstairs so I can talk to Bannerman. He's an intelligent man, he might have some ideas.'

Surprisingly, her father managed the staircase with little problem. Once he was sitting comfortably in a chair in the sun, Rollo sitting beside him, Lorrie held the ladder for Bannerman, who needed to be on the roof to insert the stove's chimney pipe into place.

'Do we not have any copper leading to put around it?' Father called up to Bannerman.

'No, but I did find some small sheets of tin, which will do the job for now,' Bannerman called back down.

After the chimney was in place and Bannerman safely on the ground, Lorrie set about scrubbing the stove while Bannerman assembled the chimney inside the shed.

Father snoozed as they worked, and the sunny afternoon was perfect. Lorrie lost herself in the scrubbing of the pot-bellied stove. She used her own blackleading to give it a lustrous black shine and was proud of her efforts after an hour's toil.

'That looks super, miss. Thank you, though I feel guilty that you did it,' Bannerman said in his gentle manner.

'Nonsense. I was happy to help.' Lorrie washed her hands in a bucket of water. 'Let's get it into place and light it, then you'll be able to have some warmth tonight and can boil water.'

In the shed they manoeuvred the stove into place and Bannerman attached the chimney to meet the part coming down through the roof. While he worked, Lorrie searched through the other sheds and found a can of white paint and a couple of brushes.

'What this?' Bannerman asked as she returned.

'The walls need painting. We might as well do it while the sun is shining.'

'I can't ask you to do more, miss.'

She grinned. 'You're not asking. I'm offering. There's an hour or two of sunlight left. I can make a start.' She paused. 'Perhaps, later you could join us for supper? Father has something to discuss with you.'

'I would be honoured to.' He gave her a half smile.

For a while they painted in silence until Lorrie felt the need to find out more about this man who'd slipped quietly and efficiently into their lives.

'Are you an only child, Mr Bannerman?' she asked, her hand moving the brush in smooth strokes across the wall.

'I wasn't, no. I had a sister. She died aged eighteen. There were other babies my mother had when I was young, but they died within days of birth, about four of them, I think, but I was too young to remember much of it. My mother died about five years ago. I had looked after her since my father went. He was lost at sea in a storm ten years ago. A typical tale amongst seafaring families.' Bannerman dipped his brush into the paint. 'Having no family left made it easier to leave Whitby...'

She nodded, and didn't comment, knowing he would be thinking of the woman he had loved and lost.

'I am grateful to have come across this yard.' Bannerman glanced at her. 'You and your father have given me a chance to begin again, and I thank you for it.'

'Your expertise would have aided you in getting work anywhere. We were the lucky ones that you chose to call on.'

'Fate can be a mystery, don't you think?'

'It can. Fate or the will of God as some would call it.'

'I'm not a praying man...' He didn't look at her and kept painting.

'A non-believer?'

'Indeed. No God could be so cruel.' He quickly raised his hand. 'Forgive me. This is not a discussion that ever ends well, so I will keep my mouth shut.'

She nodded. 'I pass no judgement.'

'Lorrie,' her father called from his chair outside.

Downing their brushes, they went out to him. 'Do you want to go up, Father?' Lorrie asked.

'Aye, I do.' He grabbed his cane and Lorrie and Bannerman helped him to stand and together they assisted him slowly up the stairs and into the living quarters.

'Do you want to lie down on your bed for a bit, while I cook us a meal?'

'No, I've been sitting about all day.' Father looked to Bannerman. 'I thought perhaps we could have a talk while Lorrie prepares supper?'

The two men sat at the table talking quietly, Rollo lying on the floor by their feet, as Lorrie made a salad and fried some pieces of chicken she'd bought that morning. The snippets of conversation she heard were about advertising with the focus on boat design. Her father was keen to return to designing and with Bannerman's experience and skills they could make a great team. Boat design and building would generate a higher income.

'What are your thoughts of these plans, Miss Chambers?' Bannerman asked as she placed their plates in front of them and sat down.

'The repairs are important for quick turnarounds to keep the money coming in, whereas boat design and builds are longer projects,' she mulled. 'However, yours and Father's talents should be exercised more, and our reputation could benefit from offering more than just repairs. I think we should advertise in newspapers further afield than just Wakefield.'

'Where are you thinking?' Father asked.

'People who can afford to have leisure vessels will prefer to have custom-made boats. We need to target the rich.'

'That's an excellent idea,' Bannerman agreed, eating his meal. 'We could advertise in *The Times*.'

'It's a start.' Father nodded, relaxing. 'I shall draft the wording tomorrow for the advertisement.'

Lorrie was so pleased to see the spirit enter her father's manner again. A few months ago, she truly doubted he'd ever have been the man he once was.

She began to clear away the table and Father asked Bannerman to help him to the bedroom.

'May I help you tidy away?' Bannerman asked Lorrie, coming out of the bedroom.

'Thank you for the offer, but I suspect you'd rather get back to working on the living quarters.' She smiled, giving Rollo the scraps to eat.

Bannerman paused by the door. 'I appreciate your help today.'

'I enjoyed it.' Surprisingly she had. For a few hours she hadn't thought of Matteo and that was a nice change. 'Will you allow me to go shopping for you on Monday?'

'Shopping for me?'

She gave him a superior woman's look. 'Mr Bannerman, you need a great deal to make that shed a home. With your agreement, I'd like to purchase a few things for you. Nothing fancy, just some pieces from the market to make your living arrangements more comfortable.'

He didn't answer her for a long moment. 'Very well. I will give you some money and let you pick whatever you want, but not a penny of your own will you spend. Deal?'

She nodded happily. 'Deal.'

Bannerman gazed at her for a moment. 'Good night, Miss Chambers.'

'Good night, Mr Bannerman.'

When he and Rollo had gone, Lorrie finished cleaning and for the first time in weeks felt a little lighter in spirit. She *had* to get back to her normal self and put the affair with Matteo away into the past where it belonged. No good would come of her pining for a man who did not love her enough. She had her father, a business to run and good friends. It would be sufficient.

10

───────

'Morning, Father.' Leaving her bedroom, Lorrie glanced at the clock on the mantle, it had just gone seven. She wanted to be away to the market to shop for Bannerman's shed, but she also had wages to prepare and delivery invoices to tally.

'Good morning, dearest.' Father sat at the kitchen table, reading the newspaper Jimmy had brought up along with a bucket of water. Father had shaven this morning, though since his accident he'd started growing a moustache, which suited him very well.

From the meat box in the larder, she brought out a marble slab that held the paper-wrapped kidneys she planned to fry for breakfast along with some eggs. Opening the parcel, the smell of the kidneys hit her nose and she gagged. 'Oh!'

'Lorrie?'

'They must be bad.' She hurriedly wrapped the paper over the kidneys and continued to gag. 'I'm sorry.'

'Nay, it's not your fault.'

Lorrie heaved over the sink, eyes watering.

'Let me help you,' Father said, grabbing his cane to rise.

'No, no, I'm fine.' Blinking rapidly, Lorrie straightened and wiped her eyes. She took a deep breath, feeling ridiculous.

'You ought to take them back to the butcher where you bought them and demand your money back,' Father scoffed.

'We've never had bad meat from Smyth's Butchers before.' Lorrie couldn't understand it. Giving the paper parcel the side-eye, she buried it in the bin she'd take downstairs to empty into the incinerator in the yard.

'Can you manage an egg, lass? I'll be fine with that.' Father shook out his newspaper and continued to read.

Stomach still quivering, Lorrie tentatively fried two eggs and toasted some bread for him and made a pot of tea.

'Feeling better?' Father gave her a smile as she placed his plate before him.

'Yes.' As quickly as it came, the sick feeling had left her, but she wasn't going to chance it by eating and so sipped a cup of tea for a few minutes. 'I'm away to the shops and when I get back, there's work I need to do in the office.'

'I'll shout for Jimmy to come and help me down the stairs.' Father cut up his egg. 'I'm going to be in the yard every day from now on.'

'Don't overdo it, please?'

'I won't. A couple of hours won't hurt. Bannerman and Jed have it all under control, anyway.'

'They do, so don't push yourself too hard.' She cleaned up the kitchen and then donned her hat and gloves.

On the landing, she stood to feel the morning's warmth. The smoke from the numerous factory chimneys couldn't hide the blaze of the sun.

'Miss Chambers,' Bannerman called from below. 'My money

purse.' He handed her a small leather pouch when she joined him at the bottom of the stairs. 'Spend it wisely,' he joked.

'All of it?' She laughed.

'The bare necessities. I'm a simple man.' Humour lightened his grey eyes.

'I'll do my best,' she replied, walking to the gates.

Saunders came into the yard, late as usual.

His presence irritated Lorrie. 'You're late!'

'My time is my own,' he slurred, the smell of alcohol on his breath.

'And you're drunk!' She was disgusted by him. 'Get out. You're not working here today. In fact, you're not working here at all any more.' She turned to shout for Bannerman but found he'd not gone more than a few steps behind her. 'Mr Bannerman, see that Saunders never sets foot in this yard again.'

'You can't do that!' Saunders lunged forward. 'I'm Lynch's man.'

'You're nothing, mate.' Bannerman leapt in front of Lorrie and grabbed Saunders by the front of his shirt. Bannerman marched him outside of the gates and pushed him away. 'Now get going and don't ever come back.'

'I'm owed wages!' Saunders spat, stumbling.

'Speak to Oswald Lynch about it,' Lorrie told him, both angry and annoyed at the confrontation.

They watched Saunders loiter about the lane for a few minutes before he finally walked off.

'How are you feeling?' Bannerman asked.

Although a little shaken, she was fine and smiled at him. 'I'm so pleased to see Saunders gone finally.'

'Don't walk into town the normal way across the bridge. Take the ferry across or hail a hansom.' Bannerman gave her a telling look. 'Just to be safe until that fool has gone to drown his sorrows in some pub.'

'I'll hail a hansom. I'm glad you are here looking out for me.' She smiled and walked up the lane.

Although she had much to do in the office, Lorrie strolled the streets towards the market. She gazed at window displays and waved to Betsy, Meg's younger sister, who swept the front step of the milliners.

In the market, she spied the stall she wanted and headed for it, determined to make Bannerman's shed more of a home. She spent some time selecting cooking items and crockery, a frying pan and utensils, creating a pile of items at the end of the stall.

'That's a load to carry, miss,' the stallholder commented, adding it up with a pencil and paper. 'Do you want me lad to take it home for you? I'll not charge you for delivery.'

'That would be wonderful, thank you. Chambers Boat Builder and Repairs.'

'Aye, I know it.' He accepted the money she gave him. 'If you want owt else, just let me know.'

Lorrie nodded her thanks and kept going. A stall close by sold blankets and sheets. Lorrie bought a set and two thick blue blankets and a pillow. Arms and basket full, she left the market and walked to a second-hand furniture shop on Kirkgate. In there she spent Bannerman's last coins on a single bed and mattress and a padded wooden chair in orange velvet. She dipped into her own money to pay for delivery, but she wouldn't tell Bannerman that.

Now suddenly hungry, she caught the omnibus at the end of Kirkgate which took her over the river and back to her side of the waterfront. Jimmy came rushing up to help her when he saw her coming through the gates with arms laden.

'You've had a successful trip by the looks of it, miss.' He took the bundle of blankets from her and the basket of sheets.

'I have, Jimmy. We'll take these to Mr Bannerman's new sleeping quarters.' She carried the pillow. 'Where is he?'

'He's taken Jackson's barge down the river to check the tiller. Mr Jackson brought it in an hour ago and asked if we could have a look at it,' Jimmy told her as they walked through the yard.

'And my father?'

'He's in the big shed working on the sailing boat. He and Jed have been sanding. Don't worry, Mr Chambers has been sitting down the whole time.'

'Good.' Lorrie hadn't been near the sailboat since the night with Matteo and had no intention of doing so now. Instead, she opened the door to Bannerman's shed and placed the items she'd bought on the floor.

Sending Jimmy back to work, she went upstairs and made herself a cup of tea, wishing she had some cake to eat, too. She'd have to do some baking this afternoon.

From downstairs she heard the tinkle of a bell and Mr Make-peace call out. The baker and his lads walked the streets with his horse and cart, filled with bread, and called out for trade.

Lorrie grabbed her purse and went down to the yard and bought two loaves of bread from him. The fresh bread smelt divine, and she could have torn into a loaf with her teeth, she was so hungry.

With a wave to the baker, she went back upstairs and cut slices from the loaf. She spread them with butter and honey and, loading them on a plate and taking her cup of tea, she went down to the office and, with a sigh of tiredness, collapsed onto the chair.

She ate while she worked, counting money into piles for each man's wage. Outside she heard the men talking, the rhythmic sound of saws and mallets. It was the familiar background noise she'd always known.

Father hobbled in, leaning heavily on his cane. 'Word has just reached us that Bannerman is drifting on the river, Jackson's tiller has completely broken off. Jed and Roy are taking the rowboat out to tow him back.'

'Oh dear.' Lorrie helped him to the other chair in the office. 'You look tired.'

He grimaced and rubbed his left leg, which always pained him, more so when he'd been on it for too long. 'I can handle the pain, it's the restricted movement that drives me mad. To not be able to simply walk about as easily as I did is difficult to come to terms with.'

'Can I make you some tea, or something to eat?'

'I'm fine. I had a cup with the men. Jimmy's quite good at making tea on the camp stove in the shed.'

The shout from the yard sent Lorrie to the door. The furniture cart had arrived. 'It's Mr Bannerman's furniture. For the shed.' She darted out before he could ask questions as to why she was shopping for Bannerman and directed the driver past the office and to the other side of the yard.

With the driver's help, they brought in the bed and mattress and placed it behind the partition wall. The chair she asked him to place near the stove. She decided to make the bed with sheets and blankets so that Bannerman wouldn't have to do it when he returned. She hoped he wouldn't mind her forwardness.

She noticed he'd put up two shelves on the painted walls. One shelf held two books and a candle, the other held a small round of bread wrapped in muslin, a jar of jam and a tin of tea leaves.

Lorrie studied the books, both on seafaring. It didn't surprise her that Bannerman enjoyed reading. He'd arrived with only one bag and yet in that bag he carried two books, so they must mean something to him. By the stove, he'd placed an upturned crate to use as a makeshift table. On this Lorrie placed the crockery, then remembered the old bookshelf in the back of the office.

Returning to the office, Lorrie saw that her father had gone back to the sheds, or probably to the ramp to watch the return of the boats.

The old bookshelf stood on the far wall where the light from the window didn't reach sufficiently to be useful. It was full of ancient ledgers and piles of paperwork she'd been meaning to get rid of or properly organise into drawers. The bookshelf was only waist high and built of light wood. Though in need of a good clean, she first wanted it carried to Bannerman's living quarters.

With Jimmy's help, they carried it between them to Bannerman's and placed it against the wall near the stove and under the window.

'This is going to look nice when it's done,' Jimmy said, looking around.

'Yes, it will.' Lorrie wiped the shelves clean with a cloth and then filled them with the crockery she'd bought at the market.

Making several trips upstairs, she raided her own stock of candles, found a spare rug she no longer used, a water jug, a kettle, a cushion for the chair and several books she thought he might like to read by Charles Dickens and Anthony Trollope.

She arranged the cushion on the chair before the stove, placed the books and supply of candles on the bookshelf and sat the kettle and jug on the crate. The rug she spread between the stove and chair, knowing Rollo would love that position near the fire and his master.

Giving the place a final glance over, she smiled at how welcoming the shed had become. It was turning into a home.

It was late, the sun already sunk low into the horizon when the boats returned to their little dock.

Lorrie stood with her father and Jimmy as Jed and Roy rowed the small rowboat, pulling the sailing barge behind them with Bannerman using a long pole to keep the barge on course.

'I was starting to worry,' Father said as Jed and Roy docked.

'He was downriver a fair way,' Jed said. The old man looked exhausted. 'We should have taken Jimmy with us for extra strength, but luckily, we had a horse towing for part of the way. Donny King was nearby and lent us his horse to tow the barge until we got to Harry's ferry, then we had to row from there.'

Bannerman struggled to bring the barge to a halt beside the dock, and Jimmy and Roy threw him ropes to hang on to as they hauled him in, slowing him down enough for them to tie the ropes to the dock.

Once the barge was secured, Bannerman hopped off with Rollo beside him, for the man went nowhere without the little dog. The men slapped each other on the back for a hard job done well.

'I thought at one point I'd ram a narrowboat,' Bannerman said, shaking his head. 'We were fortunate.'

'Let's call it a day,' Father declared. 'My daughter has your wages in the office. Collect them and get yourselves away home to rest.'

Lorrie led the way to the office, and seated behind her desk, she doled out wages to each man, striking a tick beside their name as they collected the money. Jimmy helped her father up the staircase as she finished off in the office.

She was locking the office door when Bannerman came around the corner of the building.

'Miss Chambers.'

'Yes?' She held the bunch of keys and waited, hoping he'd not be unhappy at her interference in his home.

'What you've done...' Bannerman paused, frowning.

'You don't like it?' She sagged in disappointment. 'Or did I spend too much?'

'No, no. It's great, truly, all of it.' His eyes clouded for a moment as he brushed his hand over his grey-streaked hair. 'You went out of your way to make a home for me.' He shrugged, lost for words.

'You need to be comfortable, Mr Bannerman, you work hard. I didn't do much. A few things to help you out.' She smiled shyly, embarrassed now.

'That is an understatement, Miss Chambers. I have a bed, a chair, things to cook and eat with, books, candles, a rug that Rollo has claimed as his...'

She laughed gently. 'You have little food, though, he may complain about that.'

'Ah, yes. I shall visit the market to rectify that.'

'I'm going into town in the morning, let me know what you want, and I'll get it for you. I don't know if you've noticed while you've been here, but the baker calls at the yard every day at about ten o'clock and the butcher at three. Every second day is the milkman, he stops by about six or six thirty. You can purchase from them. Father and I won't mind you stopping work to do so. Keeping the milk fresh is a problem. I usually pour it into a bottle with a stopper and suspend it from a rope on the dock to keep it cool in the water...' She abruptly stopped talking, knowing she was rambling, and heat flushed her cheeks.

His gaze held hers. 'I'll never forget your kindness.'

'Well, I consider you a friend, Mr Bannerman, and I enjoy helping my friends.'

He nodded, the twilight casting shadows over his face. 'Thank you.' He walked away, Rollo trudging at his heels.

Lorrie turned for the staircase, feeling tired and a little out of sorts, but pleased she had made a small difference to another person's life.

It'd been a long day, and she was ready for bed, but first she'd have to make a meal for her father and then clean the kitchen, bring up water and heat it for their nightly wash, likely the coal bin was low too. Jobs her father would have done but ones she'd taken over since his accident.

Tomorrow she'd have to go shopping for food, visit the post office, start soaking clothes ready for wash day, and change the sheets on her and Father's beds. As well as all that she had work in the office, meals to cook and she was meant to be calling in on Fliss for afternoon tea and had promised Father to speak to Christian about investing. She felt exhausted just thinking about it. Yet keeping busy kept her from thinking about Matteo. Most nights she was so weary she fell into bed and slept without dreaming of him and for that she was grateful.

Walking through the door, she found her father on the floor near the sofa, struggling to get up. 'Father!' She rushed to his side, her heart in her mouth. 'What happened? Are you hurt?'

'I tried to put some coal on the embers, get the fire going a bit, but I overbalanced on one leg and fell.' He grimaced. 'I'm not hurt.'

In the dim light, Lorrie scanned his trousers for bleeding. 'Are you sure?'

'Yes, I'm fine. Get me to the table, lass.'

Holding on to furniture, they made it to the table where she eased him onto a chair. 'Are you sure there isn't any pain?'

'No more than usual, my dear. My left leg just isn't very strong, and I forget that sometimes. Most frustrating.' He unbuttoned his jacket. 'A nice cup of tea and some bread and butter will see me right.'

'Is that all you want to eat?' she said, surprised.

'Aye, don't bother yourself with doing anything more, I'm too tired to eat.'

Her hands shook a little as she struck a match to light the gas wall lights, illuminating the living areas in golden light. Lorrie quickly placed the kettle on to boil and sliced the bread and buttered it, her mind troubled. She didn't think she could cope with another accident. Although Father had progressed a lot, tonight showed he was still fragile in many ways, and she needed to keep a closer eye on him.

She set the table and added a jar of strawberry jam in case he chose to have that on his bread. He ate while she mashed the tea and brought it to the table. She sat opposite him and poured them each a cup, adding sugar and milk. Her appetite had gone, but she nibbled at a slice of bread, knowing her father would comment if she didn't eat.

'Have you heard from the Italian?'

She jerked at the mention of Matteo. 'No, nothing.'

'He didn't deserve you.'

Lorrie didn't want to discuss Matteo and sipped her tea. 'I will visit Christian tomorrow at the brewery and speak to him about investing.'

Father nodded. 'I don't know what I would have done if you'd gone to Italy.'

She stared at him and then sighed. 'Don't think of it, Father. It hasn't happened nor will it.'

'Since he left, your spirit has left too.' Father took her hand. 'I'm sorry you're hurting.'

'I'm fine,' she whispered, feeling quite the opposite. She was exhausted by the end of each day, both mentally and physically.

'Time heals. The pain becomes less raw.'

She didn't fully believe him for she still saw the haunting in his eyes whenever he spoke of her mother, which was rare. 'I'm sure it will.'

'The thing is you must keep busy. No time for maudlin.'

'Lucky for me I'm always busy.' She kept her tone light.

Father drank the last of his tea. 'Help me to my bed, dearest. I'm done in for today.'

'Of course.' She heaved him up, having gained more upper strength since his accident from lifting him. Together they hobbled into the bedroom and Lorrie gently helped him onto the bed and took off his boots.

'Goodnight, Father.' She kissed his cheek and left him to undress and don his nightshirt.

As she tidied the kitchen and banked the range fire down for the night, she wiped away the silent tears that fell.

11

Lorrie opened her eyes and a wave of nausea rose in her throat. She sat up and gagged. Staggering over to the washbowl, she splashed cold water on her face from the jug and took a deep breath. Outside her window, the sun climbed above the rooftops on another clear day. She concentrated on listening for the boat horns to take her mind off her roiling stomach. What had she eaten that had upset her? She tried to think past the bread and butter from last night. Was the butter rancid? She didn't think so.

Noise from the next room indicated Father was also awake and dressing. Lorrie splashed her face again and sucked in a large breath. Opening her window, she felt better as a slight whisper of a breeze touched her skin.

She completed her toilet and dressed in a deep blue skirt and bodice before pulling on her black boots. She brushed her hair and plaited it, twirling the plait into a coil at the back of her head.

Leaving the bedroom, her stomach surged again, but she fought it as Father came out of his room, leaning heavily on his cane. 'Good morning.'

'Good morning, dearest.'

'Did you sleep well?' She gently held his elbow as they headed for the table.

'Like a baby, my dear girl.' His smile was honest and wide. 'Today is a new day.'

'What would you like for breakfast?'

'Eggs if we have any?'

Making breakfast became a battle of fighting against the urge to be sick all over the floor. She moved slowly, each task an endeavour to complete.

'You look a little pale,' Father said as she brought over a plate of toast.

'I feel slightly unwell,' she lied.

'Go downstairs for some fresh air.' Father frowned. 'Have you eaten something that didn't agree with you?'

'I must have.' Though she couldn't think what. 'A cup of tea will set me right.'

'Leave the eggs. The toast will do with some jam.' His concerned expression made her feel guilty.

'I can cook some eggs.' Her stomach churned even as she said the words.

'No. Go outside, I insist.'

Needing no more encouragement, Lorrie fled the room and raced down the staircase to throw up beside a water barrel.

'Miss?' Jimmy dashed to her, her father's newspaper tucked under his arm.

'I'm good...' Another lie. She leant against the wall of the office, gulping air.

'Can I get you anything?'

'No, thank you. I shall rest a minute.'

The bell of the baker's cart came through the lane to the yard's gates. Lorrie pushed herself from the wall and waved to signal she needed to buy something.

'I'll go up and get your purse, miss?' Jimmy asked. 'It's on the dresser?'

'What would I do without you, Jimmy?' Lorrie squeezed his arm in thanks.

She bought two loaves of bread and a half loaf for Mr Bannerman which she told Jimmy to go and take to him.

Once upstairs, she made a cup of black sweet tea and sat at the table.

'The colour has come back to your face,' Father said, looking over his newspaper.

'I'm fine now.' This time she wasn't lying. The tea had revived her. 'I have a busy day ahead.'

'I'll go down and spend the morning in the sheds with the men.'

'Don't overtire yourself,' she warned, clearing away the breakfast things. His fall last night was still fresh in her mind.

Pinning on her hat and pulling on her black lace gloves, Lorrie collected her purse and basket.

At the bottom of the steps, she let go of her father's arm and watched him hobble slowly towards the larger of the sheds where the sailboat rested.

Mr Bannerman waved to her as he joined him, and she waved back.

Feeling much better, Lorrie left the yard and headed to the brewery on the next street.

Despite the early hour, Christian's horse was in the stable and also the Hendersons' carriage was in the yard. Meg stood near it talking to Christian.

'Lorrie!' Meg clasped her hands as Lorrie reached the couple. 'This is a lovely surprise.'

'You're looking well.' Lorrie kissed Meg's cheek.

Meg patted her small round stomach. 'We're both doing nicely. What are you doing here?'

'I've come to speak to Christian about business.'

'Is everything all right?' Meg's forehead creased.

'Yes, for the moment. But I do need to ask for some advice.'

Christian nodded. 'Come into my office.'

Once seated in Christian's wood-panelled office and declining some tea, Lorrie explained her concerns about Oswald. 'I don't trust him. I never have. He told Father that he owes money to some people. He wants to sell his shares in the boatyard, but we don't have the money to buy him out. We need another investor who is willing to buy Oswald's shares.'

'If Lynch is desperate and it sounds as if he is, then he'll probably sell to the first person who makes an offer. Your next partner could be someone wholly unsuitable, or someone who wishes to have a lot of say in how everything is done in the yard.' Christian steepled his fingers, seated behind his desk opposite Lorrie and Meg. 'Unfortunately, I'm not in the position to invest. I'm sorry.'

'Christian!' Meg held out her hands. 'Surely you can?'

'Darling, no. I've already invested heavily in new machinery for the brewery, plus I bought the public house in Westgate that Freddie manages for me, and the pub needed a complete refurbishment. I simply do not have the spare capital to invest in the boatyard.'

'I understand,' Lorrie murmured, deflated.

Christian's handsome face looked sad. 'I am sorry. However, I will speak with friends and acquaintances and perhaps I can find you some other gentleman who is willing to purchase Lynch's share. If you wish me to?'

'Yes, I would, thank you.'

'Until then, I would watch Lynch very closely. He is not a trustworthy man.'

Heavy of heart, Lorrie rose from the chair. 'Thank you, Christian. Ideally, Father and I would like you as a business partner, but I fully understand your position. Any help in finding someone else is appreciated.'

'I'll walk out with you,' Meg said after kissing her husband goodbye. 'Are you going into town or back to the boatyard?'

'Into town. I've to visit the post office and buy some vegetables and a dozen other things.'

'Let me take you in the carriage, it'll save you the walk.' Meg smiled. 'I can drop you off on my way to see Josie. Nicky has been in bed for two days. I'm going to try and convince him to come and stay with us for a little while to give Josie a break.'

'Is Josie not coping?'

Meg climbed into the carriage. 'Honestly, I don't know. Fliss says she turns up for her shifts each night at the pub. Susie minds Nicky, Nell and Dolly, but apparently Josie has been quiet and not her usual self. I worry she's exhausted from looking after Nicky and the others. I remember the feeling so well.'

'Josie has it easier than you did,' Lorrie said, sitting beside her. 'You had no money and couldn't pay the rent and you had your mother to care for, too. Josie has less people to look after than you did, and you send her food baskets every week and you pay her rent. I fail to see how Josie has it so bad in comparison.'

'Well, I'll find out today what the problem might be, if there is one. Fliss might have got it wrong.'

'I haven't seen Fliss in a while. I am a terrible friend,' Lorrie said ruefully.

Meg clasped Lorrie's hand as the carriage joined the vehicles crossing the bridge. 'You've had a lot on your plate since the accident. Fliss understands that.'

'I know but I still feel as though I'm neglecting my friends.'

'Nonsense.' Meg shook her head. 'Why don't you and your

father come to us on Sunday afternoon after church? You'll enjoy it more if your father comes because you won't be worried about him being left alone at home. I'll invite Fliss, too, and we'll have tea on the terrace. I'll send the carriage for you.'

'I'm not sure. Father isn't one for entertaining.'

'No, but sometimes, it wouldn't hurt for him to realise that you need to do something other than be in that yard. You've run it by yourself for months. I'll send the carriage at two.'

The carriage dropped Lorrie off near the cathedral. Lorrie waved Meg goodbye and headed along Teall Street to the market. At the beginning of the outside stalls, Lorrie caught a waft of sourness, the smell of rotten vegetables. Her stomach churned. A wave of nausea rose, and she swayed, knowing she was going to be sick. Dashing to the side of the street, she slipped in between two carts and threw up the contents of her stomach into the gutter. She heaved until her eyes watered.

'Nay, lass,' a kind voice came from behind her.

Wiping her mouth, feeling wretched, Lorrie straightened.

'Feeling better, miss?' The man stepped closer, holding out a clean handkerchief.

'I have one, thank you,' Lorrie mumbled, groping for her reticule to pull out a folded square of linen. She dabbed her mouth, trying not to retch again.

'Would you like to come to my stall and sit down?' He pointed to a stall on the other side that sold gardening tools.

'The smell...' She gagged as the breeze picked up the stench of rotten fruit.

'Ah, yes, it can be a bit unbearable at times. Old Gordon needs to clear the drain near his stall. He only does it once a week as he can't bend too well these days. He sometimes hires a lad to help him.'

Lorrie didn't care about Old Gordon or his lad or his stall. She just knew she needed to get away from the market and its multitude of aromas.

'Being in the family way is hard on a woman when the sickness is upon her.' The man nodded wisely. 'My missus was sick morning, noon and night, she was. Poor lass. With all four she couldn't keep a thing down. Some women grow enormous with their babies, not my missus, she was rake thin, she was.'

Lorrie had stopped listening to him. The words *in the family way* ricocheted around her brain. She promptly vomited again into the gutter, half crying as she did so. No, no, no!

She stumbled from the market, the handkerchief against her face, the tears running freely as she dodged people needing to get away, away from the man's words, but they followed her, pounding in her head. *Family way, family way.*

There was no peace from her thoughts. She walked aimlessly. Her mind whirled and fluttered like a trapped bird in a net. Nothing made sense yet everything did. She knew women were sometimes sick when with child. Meg had told her that. Meg had felt ill a few weeks ago from the smell of fried bacon, which upset her severely as she loved bacon.

Matteo.

Had they made a baby?

Her heart ached. Why couldn't he have taken her with him?

She sobbed into her handkerchief, turning away from the people passing by. By a shop door, she leant against the wall, too shaken to take another step.

'Lorrie?' Fliss was suddenly in front of her, grabbing her shoulders, her face full of concern. 'Lorrie! What's happened? I saw you from across the street, I was running an errand for my aunt.'

Lorrie leaned her head into Fliss's narrow shoulder and cried broken-heartedly.

'Goodness! Lorrie, you're frightening me.' Fliss held her tight, even though she was inches smaller than Lorrie.

'Excuse me, ladies. May I be of assistance?' A man stopped beside them.

Lorrie covered her face, forcing herself to calm down.

'Thank you, sir,' Fliss said. 'Could you find us a hansom cab, please?'

'No, Fliss. Let us walk,' Lorrie mumbled.

'Very well.' Fliss took her elbow and turned to the man. 'Thank you, sir. Your kindness is appreciated, but we shall be fine now.'

He nodded and went on his way.

'You do not have to tell me what's wrong if you don't want to,' Fliss said, slipping Lorrie's arm through hers as they circled around the cathedral and headed towards the river.

Feeling drained of emotion, Lorrie stared ahead, her thoughts jumbled, her heart thudding in her chest. 'I might be with child, Fliss,' she whispered, hardly believing the words she spoke.

Fliss misstepped, paused, then continued walking. 'Are you certain?'

'Not completely.'

'You have... been with a man?' Fliss stared ahead.

'Matteo.'

'Then it is likely?'

'Yes...'

'Did he force you?'

'No.' Lorrie stopped. She'd never seen Fliss so rigid, so cold. 'I love him.'

'But you are not his wife, Lorrie. What you've done is wrong.' Fliss's blue eyes narrowed. 'You willingly went with a man with whom you are not united by God.'

'Gracious, you sound like your aunt!' Lorrie snapped. Fliss's condemnation was hard to bear.

'It was selfish, Lorrie. Don't you see? You have now ruined your life. You're unmarried and with child. You're bringing a bastard into this world, an innocent who will live with the stain of illegitimacy all its life. How is that fair?'

'Keep your voice down.' Lorrie glanced around them at the people walking.

'Why? You won't be able to keep this a secret for long,' Fliss scoffed.

Lorrie strode away, hurt by Fliss's unsympathetic reaction.

Fliss marched alongside. 'Your father, how will he cope with this tragedy, the shame?'

Lorrie rounded on her friend. 'Hopefully better than you have!'

'What did you expect? Embraces and congratulations?' Fliss held her hands up in despair. 'This is shocking, Lorrie, not something to be pleased about.'

Tears welled in Lorrie's eyes. 'Do you honestly think I don't know that?'

Fliss took a step back. 'I never thought you would be so foolish.' She turned and walked away.

For a long moment, Lorrie stood still, blind to the people walking by, the horse and carts, the shrill of a train's whistle. She felt so alone. Wounded. Hollow.

A tiny voice inside told her this could all be a mistake. There was no child. Life couldn't be that cruel to make her an unwed mother. The shame. The guilt. Her father's reaction...

Somehow, she made it home, did the tasks required of her throughout the day. She even behaved as close to normal as she could during the evening until she could escape to her bed where she cried into her pillow and begged for her monthly show to appear and save her from humiliation.

12

In the July heat, Lorrie hung out the sheets on the line strung between Bannerman's shed and a large oak tree that had managed to survive in an industrial area. Lorrie was fond of the tree, one she remembered climbing as a child and being proud that in a world of buildings and cobbles, coal smut and smoke from a thousand chimneys, the boatyard had a beacon of greenery. The oak tree provided shade as the sun arched across the clear blue sky, but nearer to Bannerman's shed was a sunny spot where the washing could dry away from the smell of burning tar.

'There you are.' Oswald pushed away a damp sheet to stand closer to her. 'I've been looking for your father.'

'He's on the river.'

'On the river?' Oswald's eyebrows rose in surprise.

'Yes. It's the first time since his accident. They've taken the sail-boat out to test how she sits in the water.' Lorrie half turned from him to peg out a pillowcase. 'He'll be back in an hour or so if you wish to return then?'

'Or I could wait with you?' His sly expression made her grimace.

'I'm rather busy.'

'I feel you are avoiding me, Miss Chambers. It's been weeks since we have had a decent conversation. I told you I had forgiven you for getting rid of Saunders.'

Lorrie ignored that last comment. When Oswald found out about her sacking Saunders he'd ranted and raved in the office, only calming down when Bannerman came in.

Looking at the horrid man now, Lorrie wished he was as easy to get rid of. 'I believe you have been away?' Father had told her Oswald had left Wakefield last month. Creditors were after him or so Father had heard from not only Christian but clients who came for their boats to be repaired.

'Business took me from home.' Oswald studied his fingernails.

'Successful business, I hope?'

Oswald's gaze drifted away. 'Indeed.'

'Excellent. We have been busy as well.' She hung another pillowcase on the line.

It was true that the boatyard had picked up more work, which was wonderful, but she had also kept herself fully occupied from the moment she opened her eyes until she closed them again, not wanting to think about Matteo or the possible future of there being a child. She woke at dawn each morning, vomiting into the chamber pot by the bed, trying not to make a noise and wake her father. The morning sickness didn't ease, and her monthly show hadn't arrived. In fact, the last one she'd had was in March and she and Matteo had shared that night together in April and now it was July. Her breasts were tender, and she ate raw cabbage at a furious rate. It was all adding up to a conclusion that terrified her.

'Shall we indulge in a cup of tea, and you can tell me what keeps you so busy each day?' His patronising tone matched his stupid grin.

Lorrie picked up the empty basket. 'I really don't have the time, forgive me.' She stepped towards the lean-to behind the office where she did the washing in the big copper pot.

Oswald grabbed her arm, preventing her from taking another step. 'I do not appreciate your rudeness. I could make your life very difficult.'

She glared at his offending hand on her arm. 'Do not threaten me,' she growled.

'I don't know what I ever saw in you,' he sneered. 'You're nothing but a pathetic boatman's daughter, not worth my time.'

'And you're not worth my time!' She walked away, not caring she had caused offence.

Oswald sauntered about the yard as she continued to do the washing. For an hour he poked about the sheds, inspecting the boats the men were working on, he spoke to Jimmy and Roy before finally standing on the dock as Father returned with Bannerman.

The washing finished, Lorrie went into the office and began working on invoices and writing in the account ledger. She was counting out the wages when her father and Oswald walked in.

'My dear, the sailboat is a triumph.' Father beamed, easing onto a stool to rest his leg. 'Mr Baird will be delighted.'

'I'm glad.'

'She rode in the water like an angel. Could you write to Mr Baird and inform him he can come for an inspection of the boat at his convenience?'

'I'll do it now and you should stay off your leg for a bit.' She searched through a drawer of client files and found Mr Baird's address in Goole. She had mixed emotions of the sailboat leaving. It was a reminder of Matteo and the night they shared, but it also gave her pain in the chest whenever she saw it.

Oswald stood by the open door, looking out at the yard. 'The yard is full, Ernest.'

Father rubbed his hands together. 'A beautiful sight indeed, isn't it?'

'Yes...' Oswald murmured, before turning back to them. 'I'd best be away. I have an appointment and this afternoon I must catch a train to London. Good day.'

Lorrie sighed in relief when he left. 'What did he want?'

'He asked if I had found the money to pay him out. He wasn't happy with the answer I gave him.' Father frowned, watching Oswald leave the yard. 'For a man who has debts, it's not stopping him from travelling about, is it?'

'As long as he isn't here, I don't care where he goes.' Lorrie took out a fresh piece of paper with the boatyard's letterhead at the top. 'I'm getting low on these. I need to visit the printers and order some more.'

Father placed his hand over hers. 'Dearest girl, you do too much. You're pale and so thin. You're working yourself to the bone. You must ease up.'

'I'm fine, Father,' she lied.

'I'm not blind, daughter. You've not been the same since that Italian left you. I wish to God he'd never come here. You've lost your bloom. I see the way you pick at your food and how you can't sit still for a minute. You've shadows under your eyes and I'm worried, love.'

His gentleness brought tears to her eyes. 'I won't deny that I have struggled since Matteo left. I miss him.'

'Then write to him. Do you have an address for him in Italy?'

'No.'

Father grunted disparagingly. 'That's likely because he didn't want you to follow him, the cad.'

'Don't, Father, don't be cruel. He was honest with me.' She took a deep breath. 'As painful as it is, if Matteo was missing me and wanted me in his life, he'd write. He knows *this* address.'

'You could always write to your mother's family in London. Your uncles are still there even if your grandparents have died.'

'My uncles? The family that have never once come to visit me or even written a letter?' She shook her head. 'No. My great-grandmother sent me the necklace, but she is gone, and the others don't matter.'

'Well, promise me you'll return to the daughter I used to know. The one who talked to me and baked terrible cakes and who laughed. I miss *that* Lorrie.'

'I will try. I promise.'

He nodded and left the office, limping across the yard and back to the larger shed that seemed so empty now the sailboat was in the river.

Lorrie wrote the letter to Mr Baird and sealed it in an envelope ready to post. She looked up as a shadow crossed the doorway and smiled at Bannerman. Rollo came straight to her for a pat, which she instantly gave him.

'I'm away into town and your father said that you might have a letter I could post for you?'

'Oh, yes. That is kind of you.' Lorrie stood quickly, too quickly for the room spun and she had to grip the edge of the desk to stay upright.

'Miss Chambers!' Bannerman leapt to her side and held her. 'You are unwell?'

'No, no. I'm fine.' She frowned at the sudden dizziness. 'I must have stood up too fast.'

'Sit back down.' He eased her into the chair. 'Your father mentioned to me his concerns over you. The weight you've lost.'

'He shouldn't have.' She gazed up into his pewter-grey eyes and saw the concern in them.

He went and closed the office door and came back to hunker

down before her. 'I saw you, the other day when you were sick behind the lean-to.'

She stared at him, mortified.

'You can tell me to mind my own business, of course, but I see you as a friend. So, if you want to confide in me, anything you say won't be repeated, you have my word.'

Lorrie clasped her hands in her lap, tempted to spill her sorry story out to him, but she held back, because once she spoke of the matter it would become real, and having done that with Fliss and lost her friendship, she was reluctant to lose Bannerman's. 'It is nothing, honestly.'

'You aren't ill?' His tone told her he didn't believe her.

'I am not ill, no.' That at least was the truth. A baby wasn't an illness. She scratched Rollo's ears, needing his comfort.

'You do know you can trust me, don't you?' he said softly.

'I do, yes, thank you.'

'Very well.' He stood and clicked his fingers to Rollo and stepped to the door. 'I'll go and post this letter for you. Is there anything else I can do for you while I'm in town?'

'Could you...' she faltered.

'Whatever it is, I can do it,' he promised with a gentle smile.

'Could you stop by the butchers and collect my order, please? It's paid for.'

'Consider it done.'

She sagged against the chair after he'd closed the door behind him. Not having to visit the butcher was such a relief, for the smell inside the shop made her gag and she had to hold her breath for long lengths of time while she was being served.

Bannerman's kindness meant a lot to her. Over the months since he'd moved into his shed, she had helped him in small ways to make it more comfortable. On Sunday afternoons, when the sun was shining, she and her father would sit with Bannerman outside his front door and chat and drink elderberry cordial.

Those few hours on Sunday afternoons were becoming her favourite time of the week. She'd sit with Rollo by her side, sometimes she would be on the chair and other times she'd sit on a blanket and simply listen to Father and Bannerman talk of building and designing boats.

Bannerman's quiet ways soothed her nerves, and she enjoyed seeing her father open up about his past, something they had rarely spoken about before. She learnt a lot about her father's boyhood and his parents, memories he'd not shared with her, but relaxed and sitting in the shade of the oak tree, his tongue loosened and she listened to his tales. Bannerman coming to work and live at the boatyard had done that. The two men had become great friends, and she knew her father relied on Bannerman's knowledge and intellect to help him with the business.

Bannerman had become a friend to them both, but sharing her secret with him would ruin that friendship. She thought of Fliss. Since the day in town when she'd told Fliss she thought she was with child, Lorrie had only seen her at church. Each time they were meant to meet up for afternoon tea, as she, Meg and Fliss had done each week for over a year now, Fliss found an excuse not to attend.

The hurt of losing Fliss was more acute than Lorrie expected. She'd come to depend on both Meg and Fliss as her true friends and to lose one or both because of spending one night with Matteo hurt deeply.

Had that one night been worth all this pain? And worse was yet to come when she could no longer hide her condition, and everyone would know of her shame.

* * *

Something woke Lorrie. She lay still in the darkness, only a pale streak of light showed around the edge of the closed curtains. In summer the room didn't get fully dark. She waited for the nausea to rise as it often did the minute she opened her eyes, but as the seconds ticked by, there were no symptoms, and she was grateful. Perhaps she could sleep for a bit longer, it was Sunday, after all.

She nestled into the pillows, deliberately closing her mind to the anxious thoughts that constantly plagued her night and day. How much longer could she hide her condition? Bannerman had seen her being sick. He was a clever man and wouldn't take long to grasp the situation. Losing his good opinion saddened her more than she thought it would. And then there was Father... To confess to him her wicked behaviour seemed impossible. He'd be ashamed. Would he send her away as Meg had sent her sister away when she was with child and unmarried? Where would she go? She'd be alone. Would Father have nothing more to do with her and never want to see her again? How would she cope in the world alone and without support?

She tossed about in the bed, knowing she'd not get back to sleep. Her problems appeared insurmountable. For a second, Oswald came to mind. Marrying him would solve one of her problems, but could she do it? Could she lie for the rest of her life to a man she disliked and say the child was his and born early? Could she tolerate being his wife? She shuddered at the very idea. To have him touch her... control her... No, she couldn't do it. She'd rather be on the streets begging or give the child away.

A muffled crack sounded outside her window. Tiredly, Lorrie rolled over, hoping the wind wouldn't be too severe and toss things about in the yard. She hated the wind. She didn't fancy walking to church in a gale, either.

A loud bang jolted Lorrie upright in bed. She stared about the room, shrouded in the murky grey light of predawn. She listened intently, wondering if it was Father bumping into something. No sound came from the other side of the wall. Had something fallen in the yard?

A yell came from outside. A dog barked. Rollo? What was he doing out so early?

Scrambling out of bed, Lorrie went to the window, rubbing the sleep from her eyes. Opening the curtains, she faced a blanket of white instead of the yard below. Fog? She couldn't see out of the window for a moment. Then the fog shifted, but it wasn't fog. It was smoke. She could smell it now. The breeze blew the smoke away from the window to reveal the horror below.

Lorrie froze, not believing her eyes. Angry red and orange flames engulfed each shed from the large open-sided one to the smaller tool shed. Flames reached as high as her bedroom. Smoke billowed even higher up into the grey sky. She blinked, her breath catching. Was she dreaming?

Below, Bannerman came into view, racing about like a madman with buckets of water, Rollo barking crazily, spinning in circles. Suddenly, a ball of flame belched from the large open-sided shed, pushing Bannerman back.

Lorrie grabbed her dressing gown and ran from the room. 'Father! Father!' She flung open his bedroom door.

He was half out of bed, scowling. 'What is that noise?'

'Fire!' Lorrie yelled at him, before running through the sitting room and wrenching open the door at the top of the staircase.

On the landing, the smell of smoke hit her like a physical force. 'Bannerman!' she shouted down to him.

She ran down the staircase, ignorant of her bare feet, and flew to his side where he used a damp sack to extinguish the flames closest to him.

'They're all on fire, all the sheds and outbuildings and most of the boats too,' he panted, his shirt hanging out of his trousers.

'Run for help!' she begged him, taking the sack from him to continue slapping at the flames, which was an impossible task.

'I'll knock on every door.' He sprinted away but the gates were closed and chained.

Lorrie raced back upstairs for the keys as her father hobbled out on the landing with his cane.

'No, God, no!' Father stared, gaping at the scene before sliding and tripping down the stairs to help put out the flames.

Lorrie didn't have time to warn Father to be careful of his bad leg. She threw the keys to Bannerman and turned back to the inferno. She grabbed the sack and whacked at the flames eating the tool shed. She had to save the tools of their trade.

Her father limped badly, the cane thrown away, collecting buckets and scooping water from the rain barrels to throw on the fire. Their efforts were useless. The raging blaze found more items to consume, pots of oil, buckets of tar, piles of kemp and old caulking. The buildings themselves were made from old dry timbers and perfect fodder for the ever-growing fire.

The heat buffeted Lorrie as the fires grew out of control, but she kept slapping the sack against the flames, eyes watering. The roar of the blaze thundered in her ears. She winced as she trod in bare feet on the rough cobbles, but there was no time for finding boots.

'The boats!' Father yelled, pointing to those in the sheds.

'It's too dangerous to go in,' she called back, wiping her hair out of her eyes.

A terrible crack ricocheted like a gunshot. A beam in one of the sheds fell, crashing into the narrowboat below. The heat grew intense.

'I've got to get to the sailboat,' Father shouted, arms up against the bulging flames.

Lorrie squinted through the thick smoke to see the beautiful sailboat alight where it was moored next to the dock. How could a fire start on the sailboat? Other vessels were on fire too and she stood in stunned shock at the enormity of what they were facing.

'Lorrie, help me save it!' Father made a dash for the sailboat, staggering between two burning sheds. 'We've got to reach the sailboat, cut it free and let it drift into the river.'

'No, Father!' she cried out to him as smoke billowed between them obstructing her view. 'Father!'

She ran closer, the heat hitting her face. Smoke choked her throat, every breath scraped raw.

In horror, she glimpsed her father hobbling between fallen debris. Abruptly he landed on his knees, staggered up, then fell again.

'Father! I'm coming.' She darted forward just as a loud crack came from her right. The roof of each shed was made out of slate tiles. They were growing too heavy for the weakened timber structures and slowly the tiles began to slide off the collapsing frames. The tiles rained down on the narrow path between both sheds.

'Father!' Lorrie ran forward, flames leapt out, devouring everything in their path. Coughing from the smoke, Lorrie stumbled towards her father, but flames criss-crossed in front of her.

'Lorrie!' Bannerman suddenly pulled her back. 'It's not safe.'

'Father is trying to get to the sailboat,' she spluttered, eyes weeping from the sting of smoke.

'I'll get him. You go back, men are coming to help.' Bannerman pushed her back. 'Find more buckets.'

'I'll help you.' She grabbed his arms to stop him from leaving her behind.

Before he could answer, an explosion blasted out from the fire and sent them flying through the air.

Lorrie landed with a thud on her back, her fall broken by a

large coil of rope. A pain shot through her shoulder where she'd landed on it. She lay for a moment, dazed.

Bannerman lay a few feet away, eyes closed.

'Bannerman...' Lorrie moaned. She rolled off the rope and crawled towards him. 'Oh, God, help me,' she whimpered, shaking his shoulders. 'Jonas!'

'I'm all right. Winded.' He wheezed, opening his eyes. He groaned and swore.

A thunderous roar shattered the air as two of the sheds could stand no longer and fell into themselves like a stack of cards. Smoke billowed up, blocking out the sky.

'Father!' Lorrie screamed. Where was he? Had he made it through and down by the river? 'We have to find him.'

Bannerman got up onto his knees, swaying slightly. 'You must stay here.'

Flooding through the gates, men abruptly seemed to come from everywhere, running and yelling to each other, giving orders to anyone who'd listen.

Bannerman scrambled to his feet, then helped Lorrie up. 'Stay here. I mean it,' he demanded as she went to rush towards the fire.

'Father!' she cried, staring at the collapsed buildings, the flames and smoke still rising. 'I can't see him.'

'I'll find him, but I don't want to have to search for you too.' He ran over to the men who were getting into a line to pass buckets of water to each other to put out the largest shed. Its sides and roof trusses were on fire and looked ready to collapse.

Bannerman took a few men with him, and they ran around to the far side of the yard towards the river.

Lorrie couldn't do nothing. She looked around for the sack, but it was gone. She grabbed a broom from beside the office and started to whack at the flames on the crumpled tool shed. Her efforts were in vain for the tool shed was lost, devoured by the flames, but she wouldn't give up. Her arms ached as she fought the fire, the pain in her shoulder throbbing. Her chest felt tight with smoke and her eyes constantly watered.

The town's only fire brigade, a brightly painted water wagon drawn by a team of horses, came down the lane, bell clanging. Men jumped off the wagon with shouts and yells which filled the air, competing with the crackling of the flames and the snapping of fallen timbers.

The sun rose higher, brightening the devastation, but also giving the newly arrived firemen a clearer view of where they needed to concentrate their efforts.

Lorrie searched through the smoke for any sign of her father or Bannerman.

'Here, lass, come sit down.' A kindly older woman, as round as she was short, took Lorrie's elbow and led her over to the staircase and gently eased her down on the bottom step. 'I've brought tea and some cups. Looks like you need it.'

Lorrie vaguely recognised her as one of the tenants living in the terraced houses near the bridge. 'Thank you but I need to find my father.' Lorrie used the railing to heave herself up, coughing as she did so.

'Nay, lass. You've done enough. Let the men do the grafting now. I'm Mrs Cronin, by the way.' The woman glanced up at the staircase. 'Shall I go up and get you a coat or something to cover you?'

Lorrie didn't reply as she watched the men, neighbours and nightwatchmen of the surrounding factories, work hard at dousing the flames of so many individual fires.

Mrs Cronin came down the stairs behind her and wrapped Lorrie's coat over her shoulders. 'There, that's better. Now I'll make you some tea.'

Lorrie strained her sore eyes to see beyond the ruined buildings for any movement. She prayed for Bannerman to appear with Father.

More people came to help as word spread of the fire. Her hand was taken by Freddie, Meg's brother, and she turned to lean her head on his shoulder.

'I'm right sorry this has happened, Lorrie,' he murmured.

'How did you know?'

'A young lad ran past the pub when I was outside swilling the cobbles. He said a boatyard was on fire and when I looked above the rooftops, I saw the plume of dark smoke coming from the direction of your place. I came as fast as I could, and I've sent word to Meg and Christian.'

Lorrie stood on shaking legs, needing to do something. 'Help me find my father. He's on the other side of the fire.'

Before they could take a step, the last of the sheds collapsed. Everyone paused for a moment as smoke and ash rose like a cloud. Suddenly, there was an open view of the river where there had never been one. All the buildings that blocked the river from the office had disintegrated into burning, smouldering ruins.

Once the smoke and ash cleared enough from the collapse, Lorrie could see straight to the dock. There, Bannerman knelt beside a form lying down. Two men were gathered around them.

She sprinted for the dock, her coat falling from her shoulders, her bloodied and black feet treading through hot embers, but she didn't care.

Bannerman caught her before she fell down beside her father's body. 'Cover him!' he barked at the two men.

'No! No, let me see.' She tore away from Bannerman and gently knelt beside her dear father's head. One side of his face was cut and seared as though hit by an iron. Blood seeped from the back of his head.

'I'm sorry, Lorrie. I think it was instant,' Bannerman whispered, crouching next to her. 'A blow to the head, it seems.'

It took several moments to take in what he said. 'Are – are you certain he's dead, not unconscious?'

'There's no pulse, no breathing. I've checked, but I've sent a man for Dr Carter. We won't move him until the doctor comes.'

Sorrow and shock clogged her brain. She tenderly stroked her father's cheek on the side not damaged. 'He's been through so much and now this... It's not fair.'

'No, it's not.'

Someone placed her coat around her, but she focused on stroking Father's cheek, rough from the need of a shave. She memorised his features, his bushy eyebrows that he'd wiggle at her to make her laugh when she was salty about something. His mouth that always smiled for her, his intelligent eyes of dusky blue. No more would she hear his voice.

Bowing her head, she couldn't breathe. Bannerman held her tight, but it didn't matter, for she was numb and cold. What had been left of her heart, broken by Matteo, now shattered into oblivion.

13

A narrowboat in drydock was saved, the damage light. Other boats in the sheds were lost and the sailboat had burned down to the water level and sunk. The yard was a blackened ruin of charred broken structures and even hours later still smouldered.

Lorrie sat on a chair at the table, still wearing her filthy nightgown and dressing gown. Meg, large with child, bustled about her, making tea and plates of food for her that she couldn't eat and so were sent downstairs to the men lingering in the yard.

Dr Carter came and, shaking his head sorrowfully, told Lorrie her father had indeed gone. He sent for the undertakers to take Father's body away. Lorrie hated the idea of her father lying on a cold slab in the dark recess of a damp cellar beneath the doctor's rooms. He should be in a coffin and placed on the table here where she could sit with him, but Dr Carter said he needed to do an examination to establish the cause of death. Lorrie thought that would be obvious, but had simply nodded and allowed Meg to take her upstairs away from the scene.

'Will you not come home with me?' Meg said, easing down into a chair. 'You can't stay here by yourself.'

'There's so much to do,' Lorrie murmured, the stench of smoke thick in the air.

'You need looking after,' Meg persisted. 'And don't say you're fine because I know you're not.'

Lorrie rubbed her sore eyes, wanting this all to be a bad dream. None of this could be real. How could she have lost not only her father but the boatyard as well? It was too much to comprehend.

Meg leaned forward and took her hand. 'For one thing you need a proper bath and to sleep in a bedroom that doesn't smell of smoke.'

Lorrie nodded, knowing she needed to be sensible. Yet the thought of moving from this chair seemed an insurmountable task at the moment. To move, to leave the yard would make this nightmare all so tangible.

Commotion at the door had them turning to see Fliss dash into the room and gasp with horror at the state of Lorrie before falling to her knees beside Lorrie's chair.

'I'm so very sorry, Lorrie,' Fliss sobbed. 'Someone told me there had been a fire and a death and I nearly fainted thinking it was you. I've been the worst friend, please forgive me,' she cried harder, burying her face into Lorrie's lap.

'There's nothing to forgive,' Lorrie murmured. Fliss's emotions were too confronting when Lorrie couldn't summon a tear.

Fliss gripped Lorrie's soot-covered hands tighter. 'I had no right to condemn you, to judge you.'

'You were acting on your feelings. I understand that.' Lorrie pulled her hands free and took a sip of water to ease her burning throat.

'Well, I wish someone would tell me what this is all about,' Meg puffed. 'I've not seen you two in the same room for months and Fliss would change the conversation every time I mentioned you, and now she is asking for forgiveness?' Meg's eyes narrowed. 'Out with it!'

Lorrie sighed. 'Can I tell you later? Now isn't the time.'

Meg raised her eyebrows. 'Very well.'

Fliss rose to her feet and took another chair at the table, still weeping. 'Who died?'

Lorrie went to speak but no words came out.

'It was Mr Chambers,' Meg whispered.

Like a hammer hitting her in the chest, Lorrie finally absorbed the truth, her father was gone. He had left her alone. Her dear father dead, like her mother. She had lost them both. How would she go on? She gulped for air, the pain too much to bear. A strangled wail escaped her raw throat.

'Lorrie!' Fliss returned beside her in a second, Meg a little slower due to her girth.

'I-I...' She couldn't speak. The enormity of it all overwhelmed her.

'Get her some more water, Fliss,' Meg commanded, gently holding Lorrie to her. 'Cry if you want. There's only the three of us.'

Lorrie shook her head, forcing herself to calm down. Later she would grieve and face the devastating loss.

A knock on the door heralded a policeman with Bannerman behind him.

Bannerman gave the policeman a filthy glare. 'Miss Chambers, Senior Constable Abbott is here to speak to you. I asked him to come back when you are more... composed, but—'

The older policeman stepped forward. 'Forgive me, Miss Chambers, but I need to do my duty. I'm Senior Constable Abbott from Wakefield Borough Police and I'm here to investigate the fire and the death of your father,' he told her, his tone gentle. 'I understand this is an extremely difficult time but the sooner I start asking my questions, the sooner I can leave you in peace.'

'Please take a seat. What do you need to know?' Lorrie asked, taking a deep breath, wiping her eyes with the back of her hand. She was in a state, filthy and stinking of smoke.

'Can you tell me in your own words the events of this morning?' Abbott asked, pulling a chair from the table and sitting down. Abbott placed a notebook on the table. He wrote down everything Lorrie said. She went through the whole event from the moment she woke up until they found her father.

'Have you seen anyone acting suspiciously in the last few days?' he asked.

'No.' She looked at Bannerman, who stood by the door. 'Have you?'

'Mr Bannerman has given us his version of the events,' Abbott said before Bannerman could reply. 'I believe there is a partner to this business?'

'Yes, Oswald Lynch.' Her voice became husky from talking with a sore throat.

'Where does Mr Lynch live? He will need to be informed of what's happened.'

Lorrie paused. She really couldn't deal with Oswald should he arrive now. 'He lives in Northgate. I believe he is currently in London.' She hoped he still was. She needed time to come to terms with it all before Oswald turned up wanting answers.

'Is that so?' Abbot wrote more in his notebook. 'Did your father have any enemies, Miss Chambers?'

'Enemies?' Lorrie stared at him in shock. 'No, none. Why would he have enemies? He is... was well respected. He's never done anything wrong.' Her throat convulsed.

'Is there anything else, senior constable?' Meg stood, indicating that it was time he should go. 'My friend is in need of some care, as you can see. It has been a traumatic day for her.'

'I shall return tomorrow, Miss Chambers. Do not leave town.'

'Leave town?' Lorrie frowned, not understanding. 'Why would I leave town?'

'My early conclusion and from yours and Mr Bannerman's reports, I deem this fire as highly suspicious.'

Lorrie blinked rapidly, not wanting to accept that. 'Suspicious.' Had she heard him correctly?

'Someone did this on purpose?' Meg was as shocked as Lorrie.

Abbott replaced his hat on his head. 'One fire, an accidental one, would take some time to spread to all the other buildings. Both Miss Chambers and Mr Bannerman have stated that all the buildings were alight, including the boats in dry dock, which were nowhere near the buildings and a sailboat in the water. It is obvious that multiple fires were deliberately lit at the same time for all those fires to be burning at once, and if that is so, then that is arson, which has led to a death.'

Lorrie felt faint. She swayed and Bannerman was instantly beside her, as Fliss and Meg came to her aid. A deliberate act? Why? Who? She shivered. Why would anyone want to do that to them? Father had died because someone had purposely lit those fires. Tears burned hot behind her eyes, but she couldn't give in to her grief, not yet.

'I shall take my leave now, Miss Chambers, but I will return tomorrow to speak with all of your staff. Thank you for your time and I'm sorry for your loss.' He bowed his head and left.

'Deliberate!' Meg fumed. 'Whoever has done this needs to swing from a rope.'

'Shush, Meg,' Fliss whispered, 'that is hardly helpful right now.'

'But who could it possibly be?' Meg demanded to know.

Lorrie couldn't think straight. All she could smell was smoke on her clothes and body. She needed to wash, to plan and she couldn't do any of that in her filthy nightclothes.

'Tell me what you need me to do, Miss Chambers,' Bannerman said quietly, his hand still on her elbow.

She found a small smile for him from somewhere. 'I'm going to go with Mrs Henderson and bathe, but I'll be back before nightfall. Can you make sure all the fires are out, please, and, well, just keep a watch on things here until I return?'

'Of course.'

Lorrie took a step, wincing at the pain in her feet from running about all morning with no shoes on, treading on embers and rough cobbles.

'Let me get you some clothes to take to Meg's house,' Fliss said, hurrying to the bedroom.

Meg gathered her things, pulling on her gloves. 'You don't have to come back here this evening. You can stay with us.'

'I do have to come, Meg. I need to find answers.' The idea of staying here without her father was a sobering thought, but she shook it from her mind.

'Surely that can wait a day or two? Let the police do their job.'

Shaking her head, Lorrie slipped her feet into a black pair of shoes. 'I owe it to Father.'

Fliss came out of the bedroom carrying a large case. 'I've packed what I feel you'll need and the only black dress I could find...'

Jolted that she'd be wearing mourning now, Lorrie nodded her thanks. 'I shall need to visit a seamstress to order a new dress for the funeral.'

Meg embraced her. 'I'll have my seamstress come to the house.'

Lorrie sighed, her secret would soon be out in the open. Her stomach would soon become difficult to hide. She would have to tell Meg. Would she disown her as Fliss had done? She glanced at Fliss, who smiled shyly.

'Allow us to help you,' Fliss said, her cheeks reddening. 'I'll do anything you need me to do.'

With Bannerman carrying the case, they went down the stairs to Meg's carriage waiting in the lane.

'Thank you, Mr Bannerman,' Meg said as he helped all three ladies into the carriage.

'I'll be back soon,' Lorrie called to him as the carriage pulled away.

It felt wrong to Lorrie to leave the boatyard. It was as though she was betraying her father somehow. She took a long look at the smoking ruins of what was once her father's pride and joy and a lump rose in her throat. She would find whoever had done this and make them pay.

* * *

Jonas watched the carriage until it had disappeared up the lane between two mills. He turned and surveyed the damage and sighed deeply. The fire, the devastation, Ernest Chambers's death floored him. He couldn't believe it had only happened this morning.

At dawn, he'd woken to Rollo barking. Cursing, Jonas had climbed from his warm bed and let him out, thinking he needed to pee, but on opening the door he'd been faced with a yard alight, smoke and flames and the crackle of splintering timber.

Instinct urged him to run and put it out, common sense told him it was futile. He'd done his best, doubling his efforts when

Miss Chambers came running down the stairs in her nightwear, hair loose, barefooted. Her spirited fight against the inferno impressed him. She rose higher in his esteem. Lorrie hadn't wilted at the sight of danger. She hadn't fainted, screamed and wailed in despair, not willing to help, not terrified getting close to the flames, or worried about getting dirty as so many other women would have been. Her courage awed him.

In the months he'd been living and working here, he'd felt, for the first time ever in his life, rested in mind and heart. In this yard he was able to work freely as someone who was respected, but more than that, he'd been able to live his life without hiding his secret. At home in Whitby, he'd always been on alert to not accidentally reveal his true feelings in front of his best friend. Loving your best friend's wife was a dreadful thing. He'd spent years living a half-life. However, here, he felt that guilt lifted from him, and he was happy. True, he missed Whitby and his friends, but the fresh start had been exactly what he needed.

The fire had ruined all that now.

The thought of moving on filled him with sorrow. He didn't want to leave the boatyard where he'd managed to find solace from a broken heart. He hadn't expected to find happiness. Contentment would have been enough. If he was honest with himself, he would acknowledge he was happy because of Ernest and Lorrie Chambers.

In this yard, he'd found a kindred spirit in Ernest Chambers, a boat builder like himself. Someone who enjoyed discussing designs and techniques of creating beautiful vessels.

Both Ernest and Lorrie had given him work instead of turning him away. He truly believed the Italian had something to do with it, but hadn't mentioned it to Lorrie, for he knew she'd been smitten with the foreigner, and he'd left her.

Still, Ernest and Lorrie had seen his qualities and respected them. They'd given him somewhere to live and, best of all, they'd given him friendship when he thought he'd never have a friend again.

Walking down towards the river, Jonas picked his way through the ruins of the large shed, grey ash thick beneath his boots. He kicked at a blackened timber. Gone. All of it gone. A nice little business it was, too.

What was he to do now?

Go back to Whitby? No. Immediately he dismissed that idea.

Whitby held only bittersweet memories for him. Years of living on the edge of another family. His best mate Samuel had married the only woman Jonas wanted. He'd hid his love for Jeanie ever since he first spotted her as a young lad working as an apprentice for her uncle. He and Samuel had been best friends since they were in short trousers, but whereas he wanted to be a boat builder, Samuel worked with his father on a fishing boat.

He smiled now, looking out over the dark silver river as his memories surfaced. The years melted away and he was a silly youth racing through the narrow streets of Whitby, hollering as he chased Samuel, who'd taken his cap. They'd rounded a corner and knocked a girl flying through the air.

Samuel had laughed and apologised, but Jonas had hurried to help her up. One look at her pretty face and he'd been lost. Jeanie had given them such a tongue-lashing, he'd been mortified, while Samuel laughed even more, teasing her. Jeanie was soon giggling with him. She'd only ever had eyes for Samuel.

Squatting down on the dock, Jonas rubbed Rollo's neck. 'I should have left them then,' he murmured. 'Instead, I was a fool and stayed around.'

He'd been Samuel's best man on their wedding day, the godfather to all their four children. Jonas had sat with Jeanie when

Samuel was fishing out at sea and storms rolled in and she'd worry and pray for his safe return.

So many times, he'd brought Samuel back to Jeanie when her husband had drunk too much at the pub. So many times, he'd bounced their children on his knee, wishing they were his own. So many times, he'd turned away from other women's advances because they weren't Jeanie.

And where had it got him?

A lifetime of loneliness.

At the age of forty-five, he should have his own home with a wife and children, working in his own boat design business. He had none of that. Now he didn't even have a job. He'd have to leave and start again somewhere else.

Bowing his head, he walked toward his hut, miserable and dejected. Ash and dirt were ingrained into his skin. He smelt of smoke and his clothes were filthy.

He glanced up at the flat above the office. Sadness filled him again. No more would he sit with Ernest and talk of boat designs. No more would Lorrie ask him to stay and share a meal with them.

Perhaps it was a blessing. Over the last few months, he'd seen Miss Chambers as a good friend. Her little ways of making the hut more comfortable, her friendly face, her interesting conversations were all becoming too comforting. He'd noticed that he'd started to look for her in the yard or in the office. It made his day when she smiled at him.

No. He couldn't do it again. He refused to care for a woman who would never be his. Miss Chambers loved the Italian. He realised that from the first day he stepped into the yard. Although the Italian had left her, at any time he could return, and Jonas wasn't inclined to have his heart broken all over again.

'Shall we have a wash, boy?' Jonas asked Rollo. 'We stink. Let's heat up some water.' He went into the wash house next to the office and took down the tin tub hanging on the wall that Lorrie had said for him to use whenever he wished.

'We need to look presentable when we leave, don't we, boy? We've got to find a new job and a new home.' The concept depressed him more than he could say.

14

In the well-appointed rose bedroom at Meadow View House, Lorrie relaxed in the bath that two maids had filled with warm scented water. Rain clouds filled the sky outside the window and Meg had insisted on a fire being lit and towels warmed on a rack in front of it.

With her hair washed and a cake of lavender soap used to scrub away the smoke and grime, Lorrie felt cleaner, but the bath had also relaxed her, and she was sleepy.

A knock on the door sounded before Meg strode in with a maid behind, carrying a tea tray. 'I thought you might like some tea and something to eat.'

'Thank you,' she replied, her voice still husky.

'Fliss has gone home. She has a shift in the bar and has to open up. She said she'll come and see you tomorrow.'

Lorrie waited until the maid had left, before asking Meg to hold out the towel for her. When she stood, she noticed the small swell of her stomach and wondered if Meg took any notice.

'Once you're dressed, I'll dry your hair in front of the fire,' Meg said. 'I used to do that for my sisters,' she added wistfully.

'If you have a little girl, you'll be doing it again.' Lorrie dried her body and donned clean undergarments.

Meg poured them a cup of tea and placed shortbread biscuits on a plate for Lorrie. 'I doubt it. Christian is adamant there will be nursery maids and nannies. I'll hardly get a look-in. It'll be so different to when my mam had our lot. I was involved in everything, especially with Nicky. He was like my own child.'

'Remember, you are the mistress here and if you want to do more with your own baby then that's your right. Don't let some stiff and starched nanny order you about.' Lorrie found it easier to concentrate on Meg's issues than deal with her own.

'Some of the nannies we have interviewed have scared me witless. They seemed more suitable to the army than a nursery. One woman told us that she would allow us to view the baby between ten and eleven in the morning and again between three and four in the afternoon for thirty minutes.' Meg's astonished tone matched her expression. 'Can you imagine such a thing? I laughed in her face, I did. I could only *view* my baby? View! Was the woman mad?' Meg shook her head and chuckled. 'Christian soon had her shown to the door.'

Lorrie smiled. Meg was the tonic she needed to push away the misery, if only for a minute or two.

'So, the search for a suitable nanny continues. I know I must have one, for Christian is an important man and as his wife I need to be his hostess and I have my charities, as you know, so I can't act as though I'm still living in Wellington Street and strap the baby to my chest as I scrub the front step.'

'Definitely not,' Lorrie agreed. She pulled on the black skirt and shuddered. She hated black. The black bodice with black cord edging only just buttoned up. Her breasts had grown and strained at the material.

Suddenly the sight of herself in the mirror on the other side of the room was too much. Her cheeks were gaunt and any claim she once hoped to own of being pretty had vanished. A sob escaped, then another and suddenly she couldn't stop crying.

'Come here.' Meg embraced her and led her to the chair by the fire. 'Cry all you want. Your father was a good man and deserves tears.'

Lorrie knew she was upset for more than just her father and felt guilty. She was carrying a child to a man who didn't want her. She was alone and in trouble and then there were all the responsibilities of the boatyard. It was all such a huge, torrid mess. How could she go on?

Meg handed her a handkerchief and she blew her nose and tried to stem the flow of tears.

'We will find out who lit those fires, Lorrie,' Meg murmured, taking a warm towel and gently drying Lorrie's long black hair. 'Christian is already speaking with the police and the men who work in the neighbouring businesses, for if someone could do that to your father's boatyard, then who's to say they won't try it somewhere else? The businessmen of the waterfront are concerned.'

'But why did it happen? None of it makes any sense.' Lorrie blew her nose.

'Maybe it was young lads and it got out of control?' Meg brushed Lorrie's hair.

'Since Abbott mentioned it being deliberately lit, it's all I can think about. Why would lads light several fires? One fire would have been enough for them, they would have run the minute it became a blaze.'

'I agree with you. This seems planned...' Meg paused in her rhythmic brushstrokes.

'Why would anyone do that to us?'

'I don't know. Let's hope the police find out. But you mustn't worry yourself too much or you'll become ill.'

Sipping her tea in front of the fire, Lorrie enjoyed the rarity of someone brushing her hair. 'No one has done this for me since my mother died when I was a child.'

Meg squeezed Lorrie's shoulders. 'That is a great shame.'

'I have something to tell you...' Lorrie whispered, her voice unsteady.

'That you are with child?' Meg said, continuing to brush her hair in long strokes.

'You guessed?' Lorrie's cheeks reddened and she was glad Meg stood behind her.

'This is my second pregnancy and I saw my own mother with child many times. I know what a woman looks like when she is growing a child.'

Tears flowed over Lorrie's cheeks. 'Do you hate me?'

'How could I?' Meg came around and knelt in front of Lorrie. 'My own sister got herself into trouble. I didn't hate her. You are my very dear friend who I love. I couldn't turn my back on you. Babies happen. Women are tempted and who am I to criticise anyone? My father was a bigamist. I have no right to judge you or anyone.'

'But you must have an opinion?' she murmured sadly.

Meg smiled softly. 'You loved Matteo.'

'I did, I do. I thought the world of him. I would have gone to Italy with him, or anywhere. But does that excuse my behaviour?'

'If I'd have been given only one night with Christian, I would have taken it and hung the consequences.' Meg shrugged. 'Desire, love, passion, all of it makes us feel alive, and it makes us do things we wouldn't normally do.'

'But he wasn't mine to have.' Lorrie wiped away the tears. 'Women are meant to keep themselves chaste until marriage.'

'Do men?' Meg scoffed. 'No, they have as many women as they want. I feel it is wrong that we must take all the blame and punishment if we give in to desire.'

'I will be shunned once I can no longer hide my stomach.'

'Yes, sadly you will, but not by those who love you. Christian and I will never abandon you.'

'Fliss did.'

'Now I understand why you two were so distant with one another.'

'Yes, she found me being sick in the street...' Lorrie rubbed her aching forehead, a headache building. 'Fliss was horrified when I told her.'

'I'm sure Fliss is sorry for it. Remember, she has her aunt's godly words in her head. The Bible is read each night by her aunt.' Meg drank some of her tea. 'Fliss loves you as I do. Why else would she come running to the yard thinking something horrible had happened to you when she'd heard the news?'

'I still cannot believe any of it,' Lorrie said softly. 'The baby, the fire, Father gone...'

'What will you do? About the baby? Give it away?'

'I honestly don't know.' Lorrie stared into her tea, unable to answer the question that had been haunting her for months.

'The decision is yours. You have time to consider what you want to do.' Meg continued to brush Lorrie's hair. The warmth of the fire after a bath relaxed Lorrie. She could happily have stayed like that for hours, but the pressing sadness of her father no longer being alive weighed on her mind.

'Please eat something,' Meg murmured. 'You'll need your strength for what lies ahead.'

They sat quietly for some moments before Lorrie placed her empty cup and saucer back on the tray. 'I should go.'

'There's no need to go back to the yard now. It's gone five o'clock. Come downstairs with me and we'll talk while we wait for Christian to return and then we'll have dinner.'

'I can't rest, Meg. I need to go home.' Lorrie plaited her hair and rolled it into a knot behind her head and secured it with combs.

Meg nodded. 'Go for an hour or two and then come back and stay here tonight. I don't like the thought of you being there on your own.'

'Bannerman is in the yard.'

'Why not wait until the morning?'

Lorrie kissed Meg's cheeks. 'I need to go.'

'Very well, you stubborn mule,' Meg scoffed gently. 'This room is yours if you change your mind.'

'Thank you.'

The rain fell harder as Lorrie travelled back to the yard in the Hendersons' carriage. The grey evening twilight matched the greyness of the coal-stained buildings on the waterfront and turned the river into a bleak strip of pewter. People hurried home as the factory whistles shrilled.

Lorrie thanked the driver as she descended from the carriage and told him not to wait. She knew she wouldn't return to Meg tonight.

Lifting her skirts high off the wet cobbles, Lorrie stepped through the gates. Awed by the wide gap that showed the river so clearly where before it had been blocked by the boat sheds, she stared at the charred ruins. The rain had put out the smoking embers and made channels in the ashes. It was all so ugly. It was difficult to accept the change.

She couldn't bear to look at it, the destruction, the ruin of her father's business, the emptiness after so many years of hard work.

Tiredly, Lorrie climbed the stairs, the rain soaking the cloak Meg had given her to wear. Yet despite the wet weather, she was hesitant to open the door and walk in, knowing her father would never be there again to greet her.

Drawing in a deep breath, she turned the handle and walked

inside. Warmth and light hit her. The fire in the living area crackled behind the screen and a glow emanated from the range fire. Lamps were lit, one in the kitchen and the other on the small table beside the sofa, cocooning the flat in golden light. All the windows were open to allow the smoke smell to dissipate, replacing it with the damp smell of rain.

She took off her cloak and went to the fireplace and held her hands out to it. She recognised the irony of enjoying this blaze where earlier fire had killed her father and destroyed their business.

Behind her the door opened, and Bannerman walked in, only to check his step on seeing her. He held two buckets of water. Rollo ran to her, wagging his shaggy tail. She bent to pat him as she always did.

'I didn't expect you back tonight.' Bannerman's hair was damp, he'd washed and changed his clothes. 'But I thought in case you did, I'd open all the windows for an hour or so to get rid of the smell of smoke, but then it rained...' He shrugged. 'It became cold in here, so I lit the fires to keep the place warm and make it welcoming.'

'That was very thoughtful of you.' Tears stung her eyes at his kindness.

'I thought you'd need water, too.' He placed the buckets beside the stone sink.

'Father mentioned only the other day we should look into getting taps plumbed up here. No more water buckets...' Her voice broke. No more would she have conversations with him, no more plans would be made, no more visits to the theatre, or walks into town or to church.

'How do you feel?' Bannerman's eyes softened at the question.

'Exhausted.' It was the truth. Fatigue plagued her body.

'It's been a very long day.'

'One to forget.'

'Have you eaten?'

'I've had a cup of tea. I couldn't face anything else.' She glanced around the flat and shivered at the cold air creeping in.

Bannerman started to close the windows. 'I've some stew simmering in the hut. You're welcome to join me.'

'Thank you, but no. I think I might go to bed.'

'Probably the best thing to do. Get warm and try to sleep.'

'And tomorrow will be a different day, this one will be over.'

He nodded, his expression gentle. 'I'll bank the fires and leave you in peace.'

Her fingers rubbed Rollo's ears while she watched Bannerman place lumps of coal on each fire and then place the fireguard on the hearth.

Task complete, Bannerman walked to the door and paused. 'I'm just across the yard. You shout for me should you need anything, understand?'

'Yes, I will.'

'It doesn't matter what time.' He clicked his fingers to Rollo.

'Thank you for everything,' Lorrie said, wishing Rollo could stay with her for comfort. 'For what you did today, for caring...'

'I wish I could have done more.' Bannerman seemed hesitant to leave. 'Will you be all right?'

'Absolutely.'

'Goodnight, Miss Chambers.'

'Goodnight, Mr Bannerman.'

Once he'd closed the door behind him, Lorrie stumbled into her room and collapsed on the bed as a fresh wave of grief shook her body. She cried for her father, for everything she'd lost, and she cried in fear of her bleak future.

* * *

The Dock Girl's Shame 187

Lorrie woke cold and hungry just before dawn. As miserable as she felt, she knew she'd have to face the day. No doubt the police would call, and she had to visit the undertakers and arrange Father's funeral.

Poking the range fire, she added twists of newspaper to the winking embers and small slivers of kindling. Once the fire was caught, she placed the kettle on to heat and a frying pan. The bread loaf was stale, so she sliced it for toast and fried an egg. Sitting at the table, she watched the sun rise through the window. The rain clouds from yesterday had gone, replaced by a clear blue sky.

With breakfast eaten, she felt better, pleased that the nausea she'd suffered from for so many months had disappeared in recent days. After a wash and tidy up, Lorrie left her bedroom and, taking a deep breath, opened the door to her father's bedroom.

A faint waft of smoke lingered, and she opened the window to air the room. On the dresser she gently touched her father's hairbrush and shaving tools. A framed sketch of her mother stood in front of the oval mirror. It had always been there for as long as Lorrie could remember. It was the only picture she had seen of her mother. Part of her knew she should put it in the coffin with Father but the selfish part of her wanted to keep it. She had no drawings of her father and that saddened her. Would she forget what he looked like one day?

Going to the wardrobe, she opened it and took out a dark brown suit, her father's best. She could smell his shaving soap in the material and tears gathered ready to fall. Quickly, fighting the sorrow, she took the items the undertaker would need to dress Father and left the room.

She heard shouting on the stairs outside before the door was flung open and Oswald stood there, his round face florid with anger, his barrel chest puffing as if he'd run a mile.

'What in God's name happened?' he demanded, jabbing his gold-topped cane in Lorrie's direction.

Pushing past him, Bannerman glared at him, placing himself between Lorrie and Oswald. 'You have no right to barge into Miss Chambers's home.'

'No right!' Oswald fumed. 'My whole business has been burnt to the ground; I have every right to know what has happened.'

'The police are investigating,' Lorrie said calmly, her anger simmering.

'Investigating! I want more than that. I want the culprits caught!' He pounded the cane on the floor. 'Imagine my horror to arrive at the train station this morning to see this in the newspaper!' He flung the *Wakefield Express* newspaper onto the table. The headlines were large:

Waterfront Fire. Man Dead.

Lorrie's stomach churned. She looked away.

'Get out!' Bannerman snarled. 'How dare you confront Miss Chambers this way? She has lost her father!'

Suddenly, Oswald bowed his head. 'Forgive me. Ernest was a good man. He did not deserve this.'

Lorrie forced her legs to work and walked over to the range to make tea.

'Let me.' Bannerman took the kettle from her. 'Go and sit down.'

'Oh, no, I...'

'Please.' His tender look was enough for her to do as he asked.

Both she and Oswald sat at the table in silence. She couldn't look at him and she had no desire to talk to him.

'Do the police have any idea who did this?' Oswald asked eventually when Bannerman brought across the teapot and cups.

'No, not yet,' Lorrie murmured, pouring the tea.

'Young lads?' Oswald muttered.

'Too sophisticated for lads messing about.' Bannerman sniffed the milk. 'This has gone off. I didn't hear the milkman this morning.'

'I'll make do with no milk,' Lorrie said. It was no hardship to drink black tea.

'What do you mean it was too sophisticated for lads?' Oswald glared at Bannerman.

'Multiple fires were lit around the yard.'

'Lads could have done that,' Oswald insisted.

'If there had been a bunch of lads messing about in the yard, I would have heard them and definitely Rollo would have.' He indicated Rollo lying at his feet.

Oswald huffed. 'So, we are to believe the non-barking of a mutt as to whether lads were involved or not? How ridiculous.'

'He's not a mutt, and he's a good guard dog,' Bannerman defended.

'Obviously not good enough!' Oswald snapped.

'Enough!' Lorrie stood, irritated by Oswald's voice. 'I must go to the undertakers before Senior Constable Abbott arrives.'

Both men stood, but Oswald frowned. 'The police are coming back?'

'Yes, to update me on any information, or lack of.' She gently folded Father's suit into a large canvas bag.

'Would you like for me to come with you?' Bannerman asked.

'Thank you, but no. I shall be fine on my own.'

'What of the business?' Oswald tapped his fingers together. 'Word will have spread, and the boat owners will descend on us demanding answers, compensation.'

'Then, as you are a partner, perhaps you can stay here and deal with that until I return?' Lorrie pinned on her hat.

'I have things to do.' Oswald took his cane and collected his hat. 'I shall be back this afternoon.' He paused. 'Forgive me. I am being a cad. Please, allow me to escort you to the undertaker. Your father was a dear friend to me.'

Surprised by Oswald's sincerity, Lorrie found herself taking his arm. She gave Bannerman a small smile of thanks as she passed him.

Oswald didn't speak until they were crossing the bridge, the river gushing over the weir below. 'I am sorry this has happened, Miss Chambers. Ernest didn't deserve to meet his end in such a way.'

'No.'

'You must not be afraid. You are not alone. I am here for you.' He guided her across Ings Road and under the railway bridge, which had a train going over it and the thundering noise gave her time to think before replying.

Once they were walking along Kirkgate, she waited for a carriage to rumble by before speaking. 'That is kind of you to say, Oswald.'

He halted and placed his hand over hers where it rested on his arm. 'I know now is not the time to talk of marriage, but my offer is still there. I can provide you with a good life. You will want for nothing. I'll buy you a house in the country, if you want?'

With the rumours of his debts, she doubted he could afford to, but she preferred the nice Oswald to the harsh one. 'As you say, now is not the time to think of such things,' she parried to humour him. She placed a hand on her stomach. Marriage to Oswald would solve her problem of being an unwed mother...

Inside the funeral parlour of Richardson's Undertakers, Oswald was attentive to her, and she let him speak for her. Handing over Father's suit wrenched at her heart and tears welled. She couldn't trust herself to not break down in front of them all.

'I insist on paying for everything,' Oswald said to her as they sat on red velvet chairs in a sitting room with dark panelling and vases of flowers on every surface.

'Really?' She stared at him in shock.

'Definitely.' He stood as the funeral director and a woman came in, the woman smiling kindly, and Lorrie thought her to be the man's wife.

'We shall collect your father from Dr Carter's office as soon as he informs us he has finished his examination,' Mr Richardson told her.

She didn't understand why she left everything to Oswald. She should have made more of a stand to organise the funeral, but she didn't have the energy. A date was selected, a coffin, too, and the transport and newspaper notices, and Lorrie simply nodded to it all.

Once outside again, Oswald looked up and down the street as if expecting someone. 'I must go, my dear.'

'Yes, of course.'

'I shall be at the yard by two o'clock to hear what the police have to say.' Oswald scuttled away and Lorrie watched him, trying to decide whether to visit the shops for food or not. As Oswald ducked into a side lane, she thought she saw Saunders join him, but was distracted by a man standing in front of her and dipping his hat.

'Miss Chambers, how sorry I am to hear of your poor father's fate in that terrible fire.'

'Thank you, Mr Armstrong,' Lorrie replied to the owner of a textile mill further along the river.

'Many of the businessmen in the area would wish to attend the funeral, if that pleases you?'

'My father would be honoured. A notice is going into the *Wake-*

field Express newspaper tomorrow and the day after. The funeral is to be Friday at eleven.'

'I shall spread the word, Miss Chambers. Good day, and again, my condolences.' He tipped his hat again and carried on.

Lorrie entered the grocers and waited in line to be served. In front, two older women were chatting to Mr and Mrs Hynde, the shop owners. Lorrie glanced around the displays of fruit and vegetables absent-mindedly until Mr Hynde came over to her.

'Miss Chambers, what a terrible tragedy. My wife and I were so shocked and saddened to hear of your father's passing.' Mr Hynde, tall and thin, had served Lorrie since she was a girl, and she knew the couple to be honest with their weights and prices.

'Thank you, Mr Hynde.'

'Is there family coming to visit for the funeral?' he asked, as the two women passed him with a nod of goodbye, and his wife came around the counter to join her husband, her kind face full of sympathy.

'No, no family,' Lorrie told him, realising that indeed she was completely on her own now. Tears gathered and, mortified, she blinked them away.

'What about that handsome Italian who was here a few months back?' Mrs Hynde inquired. 'Will he be returning?'

Lorrie's heart somersaulted at the mention of Matteo. 'No.'

If only.

'Well, whatever you wish to order today, it's on the house,' Mr Hynde said. 'I'll get young Eddie to deliver it to you this afternoon.'

'My usual order will be fine, Mr Hynde,' Lorrie told him. 'Oh. No, I don't suppose I will need mushrooms now...' she faltered. 'Father enjoyed mushrooms, but I was never keen.' Emotion clogged her throat, and she took a shuddering breath. 'Forgive me.' From her reticule she pulled out a handkerchief and pressed it to her eyes to stop the tears.

Mrs Hynde patted her hand. 'Nothing to be sorry for, my dear girl. Do you want to come through to the back for a cup of tea?'

'I need to get home.' Lorrie wiped her eyes. 'Thank you for your kindness.'

'We'll make up your order and have it delivered, don't worry about a thing.' Mrs Hynde smiled.

Lorrie made a hasty exit as a woman and her children came in. She hurried back towards the boatyard, not wanting to meet anyone on the way. Another kind word would have her undone.

Head down, she half ran through the yard's gates, having ignored the friendly wave of the baker, who was driving out. The coalman's cart was near the stairs, old Davies, the coalman, was heaving sacks of coal into the coal shed near the office.

Not wishing to chat, she quickened her step to avoid him but ran into Bannerman on the other side of the cart.

'How did it go?' he asked. The gentle look in his grey eyes was enough for the tears to tip over her lashes.

'Fine,' she squeaked.

'Come on upstairs.' He took her arm, and they went up into the flat where he led her to the sofa, before raking the embers in the range and putting the kettle on to boil.

Lorrie cried silently, wishing she could hold herself together, but today it was as though a dam had burst inside her and the tears wouldn't stop. The mention of Matteo, knowing he'd never return, added to the grief of losing her father.

Bannerman let her cry while he made a pot of tea and brought the tray over to her. Silently he poured her a cup and placed it in her hands.

'You are so thoughtful,' she murmured.

His answer was a slow smile. 'Drink. You'll feel better.'

'I doubt it.' But she did as he bid.

'Is the funeral all sorted?'

'Yes. Oswald arranged it all.'

'And you're in agreement?' Bannerman frowned.

'I didn't have the energy to demand he leave it to me, but yes, it is all as I wished it to be.' She drank her tea, aware he had put a good deal of sugar in it.

'While you were out, Abbott and another man came. They were poking about for an hour or so and then left.'

'Did he say anything?'

'Not to me, no. Also a few of the narrowboat men came to the dock, they had boats here for repair. Don Whiteley, Joe Sampson and Les Milton.'

'Oh, yes.' She tried to think how much damage their boats had sustained and how they would be able to repair them and the costs.

'Whiteley's is the least damaged. The fire set in it went out without fully catching anything alight. Paintwork inside is scorched, but it can be fixed. The initial repair was several loose boards below the waterline which Roy had fixed the day before the fire.'

'I see.' Focusing on business dried up her tears. 'So, we need to repaint his boat only?'

'Yes. I told him we'd have it done by tomorrow. I've got Jimmy doing it now. Whiteley said he'll pay his bill in the morning when he collects the boat.'

'That's good of him. He could have rightfully complained about the fire on his boat and not paid.'

'True, but the men of the waterfront are decent, and they respected your father.' Bannerman refilled her cup. 'Joe Sampson, well, his narrowboat has sustained more damage. Jed and Roy are working on it now. It will need one side rebuilt.'

'And we will have to wear that cost.' Her shoulders bowed at the thought of such expenses, not just for Joe Sampson's boat but all the others affected, and it was money she didn't have.

'Joe said he'll find work on his brother's boat until we have his finished. Les Milton, however, isn't happy. He's losing money each day he's not on the water.'

'How badly damaged is his boat?'

'The entire cabin is ruined and one whole side of the hull.'

Lorrie sighed heavily.

'Please don't worry. The pile of timbers, those elm planks, near my hut were left untouched. I can use those to rebuild Milton's boat. It's clinker style. I can do that with my eyes shut and have it done fast.'

'But what with? The tool shed was burnt to the ground with everything in it.'

'I can salvage some of the tools. The iron parts didn't burn. We can clean them up and replace the handles. Jimmy has been to Lowe's Ironmongery this morning and bought a few things we needed.'

She frowned. 'Bought? With what money?'

'Money I gave him.'

'Your money? Oh, Jonas.' His name slipped out easily. 'You can't spend your money.'

'I can and I will.'

'But it's a waste. We can't repair or rebuild all the burnt boats or replace all the tools and sheds. I don't have that kind of money.' She stood, agitated. 'I can't let you spend your money like that. There are enough funds in the bank to pay the wages for two weeks, but the cost of repairing all these boats...' She raised her hands. 'I don't have the money for it.'

'We can work without the sheds. It's summer, the days are bright and long. We can manage outdoors. If it rains, we'll erect tarpaulins. Let me and the lads work on those boats that we can repair easily, and then we can move forward.'

'To do what?' She felt ill. 'No one is going to bring their boats here for repair or commission a new boat to be built now there are no sheds, no tools and my father is dead. We are ruined.' Despair filled her.

'Listen to me, I've thought long and hard about it for the last two days. I thought I'd have to leave and find work elsewhere, but I don't want to do that. I don't want to leave here.' Bannerman took a deep breath, his gaze locked with hers. 'So, I think if I stay, we can slowly rebuild the yard.'

'How and what with? Oswald will want his investment returns each month. I can't afford the wages with no income.'

'We'll think of something. I have money, money I've saved all my life because I had nothing to spend it on, no family and I lived in an attic room in the shipyard. I've earned well for years, and the money has piled up.'

'I can't let you use it for here.'

'Wouldn't that be my decision?' His wry smile softened his words.

'No, it would be Oswald's.' She slumped onto the sofa. 'He has every right to sell up what is left, which is the land, and this building containing the flat and the office. He will want to recoup his losses.'

'You need to speak with your father's solicitor.'

'Yes.' She hadn't thought of that. 'Father might have a will, instructions...'

'And what will you do if Lynch wants to sell his part of the business?'

'I have no idea.' She tried not to cry again. 'Oswald has offered marriage. It might be my only option.'

'*Marriage*? To *him*?' Bannerman blinked in shock. 'Don't be too hasty, please.'

Before she had a chance to answer, a knock preceded Meg and Fliss. Bannerman bowed his head to the ladies and left them.

'How are you feeling?' Meg asked, coming straight to Lorrie and kissing her cheek.

Fliss held back, but Lorrie smiled to her, and she came forward to embrace her.

'We thought you might want some company.' Meg sat on the chair opposite.

'Or we can run errands for you?' Fliss suggested. 'I can do whatever you wish, shopping and such like.'

'I don't need anything, honestly.' Lorrie twisted the handkerchief in her hands. 'I've been to the undertakers this morning. The funeral is on Friday.'

'Do you want to come and stay with us?' Meg asked. 'You can stay for as long as you like.'

'That's so generous of you, but I feel as though I need to stay here. I don't know why.'

'At least you have Mr Bannerman in the yard,' Fliss said.

'Yes, we were just talking about trying to keep the yard open for business, but I don't think it's possible.'

'But if you close, what will you do?' Fliss lowered her voice. 'And what about the child?'

'If I sell the land, and achieve enough profit to pay back Oswald, perhaps I will have enough money left over to start again somewhere.'

'Move away?'

'If I'm to keep the child, I need to go where no one knows me. I can pretend to be a widow.' The idea was beginning to grow on Lorrie. A fresh start. No past memories.

'That does make sense.' Meg's expression turned sad. 'I will miss you terribly, though.'

'Me too,' Fliss added. 'Would you consider going to Italy to Matteo?'

'He was going home to marry. I can't arrive on his doorstep with a baby.'

'Why?' Meg huffed. 'It's his responsibility too.'

'You know it's not as simple as that,' Lorrie stated quietly. 'Or I could stay and marry Oswald.'

'No!' Meg gasped.

'You aren't serious?' Fliss stared at her. 'What would he say about the child?'

'Lynch wouldn't raise a baby that isn't his,' Meg said.

Without knocking, Oswald strode in, and a flame of irritation sparked in Lorrie's chest at his rudeness, but the surprise on his face caused the irritation to wither and be replaced with humiliation. He had heard their conversation.

'A child?' His eyebrows rose nearly to his receding hairline. He glared at Lorrie. 'You are with child, or am I mistaken?'

Lorrie sagged with shame. 'You are not mistaken.'

'Good God!' His ugly face turned puce. 'You slut!'

'Mr Lynch!' Meg snapped. 'How dare you!'

'*How dare I*?' he glowered. 'I thought you to be pure.' His eyes bored into Lorrie's. 'I was willing to offer you marriage, a home, a good life. Were you going to lie to me, hoodwink me into thinking the baby was mine and born early? I know the stories!'

'Oswald, calm down.' Lorrie took a deep breath. 'You're acting as if I purposely lied to you when in truth, I hadn't even accepted your proposal.'

'A proposal I withdraw, madam!' he shouted. 'I'll not be tied to a hussy who is carrying some man's bastard.' He paused, his face twitching. 'It's the Italian's, isn't it?'

Lorrie felt light-headed. Movement at the door made her glance away from Oswald to Bannerman, who stood there looking confused.

'I heard shouting,' he said, his gaze thoughtful, then he turned and looked over his shoulder. 'Abbott has returned.'

Lorrie groaned. It was all unravelling. For Oswald and Bannerman to know her secret was like a kick to the stomach. She wasn't ready for this.

Fliss took Lorrie's hand in support as Senior Constable Abbott came through the doorway, removing his hat.

'Miss Chambers.' Abbott nodded to all three ladies.

'Oswald Lynch.' Oswald stepped forward and shook Abbott's hand. 'What news do you have?'

'Ah, Mr Lynch. I have been wanting to speak to you.'

'I have just this morning returned from London,' Oswald declared, pushing his chest out. 'I am a very busy man.'

'So I have been told.' Abbot consulted his notebook. 'Miss Chambers, I have spoken to Dr Carter. He confirmed your father received a blow to the head from a heavy object, possibly the beam found next to his body, but in his opinion the blow wasn't enough to kill him. He is confident Mr Chambers died of a heart failure.'

Lorrie didn't know what to say. Was any of this meant to give her comfort? What did it matter how Father died? He was gone and she was without him.

'This conclusion means a coroner won't be called to investigate. It is not a murder.'

'Yet the fire was deliberately lit? That must mean something?' Lorrie asked.

'My investigation about the fire continues. I have spoken to neighbouring businesses, but at that time of the morning, there are very few people around and sadly no witnesses so far.'

'But it can't have been an accident for so many fires to be alight at once?' She needed answers. Her father's death wouldn't be swept under the rug. She refused to let the matter rest.

Abbott looked apologetic. 'I don't think so, no. But without witnesses, it will be difficult for me to arrest anyone.'

'So, what happens now?' Meg asked.

'Miss Chambers can bury her father. His will can be read, if he has one, and,' he smiled gently at Lorrie, 'you may begin to rebuild.' Abbott stood and replaced his hat. 'Should I have any more news for you, I will inform you immediately.'

'The culprit must be caught, Senior Constable.' Lorrie jerked to her feet, angry and frustrated. '*Someone* set out to ruin this business and I want to know who and see them locked in a cell!'

'I will do my best, Miss Chambers.' Abbott tipped his hat to her.

Fliss showed him to the door.

'Well, that's that then,' Oswald declared, grabbing his hat. 'My business is nothing but ashes...'

'*Our business!*' Lorrie snapped. Did he think he was the only one affected?

He gave Lorrie a look of contempt. 'We will discuss the business at another time when I feel I can stomach the sight of you.' He stormed out, slamming the door behind him.

'I'll check on the lads,' Bannerman said to no one. Lorrie met Bannerman's gaze, but he turned from her and went out.

Her anger left her as quickly as it came, leaving her deflated and sad. Oswald's opinion of her meant little but Bannerman's disappointment was another thing entirely.

'Will you rebuild?' Fliss asked.

Lorrie rubbed her forehead, a headache simmered behind her eyes. 'I honestly don't think I can. Much will depend on Oswald and his demands.'

Meg tossed her head. 'That man is an oaf.'

'A disgruntled oaf,' Fliss added. 'What if he tells people about your condition? Your reputation will be ruined.'

'He has nothing to gain from telling people.' Lorrie sighed.

'I wish Matteo would dash into the room and sweep you away,' Fliss said.

'It is very doubtful.' For the first time, Lorrie wished she'd never set eyes on the handsome Italian. She was paying heavily for her folly. 'Unfortunately life isn't a romantic poem where lovers are reunited.'

'Do you want to return home with me?' Meg asked. 'Both me and Christian would like you to.'

'Thank you, but no. I will stay here.' In her home, she could hide from the world and grieve in private. She was tired of talking, and if she stayed with Meg, she'd have to talk and be sociable. All she wanted was to curl up in bed and stay there.

15

Jonas buttoned his shirt collar in the small square mirror hanging on a nail in his hut. He'd washed and shaved, combed his hair and dressed in his Sunday best for Ernest's funeral. Outside, the sun shone from an endless blue sky. The birds sang and the river glistened. It was in truth a beautiful day, too beautiful for a funeral.

'Stay,' he commanded Rollo, who lay on the rug by the bed. Collecting his jacket, Jonas left the hut and walked with a heavy heart over to the office, where he paused at the bottom of the staircase before going up.

The news of Lorrie being with child had rocked him to the core. He'd thought of her as virginal, delicate, a true lady. Yet her actions told him otherwise. Despite that, he knew her to be a good and kind person. He'd met the Italian on the day he'd asked for a job, and could easily see why such a tall, strong, good-looking chap could turn a woman's head. Lorrie, an intelligent person, obviously had lost her mind for a short time, and was now paying the consequences.

Could he blame her? If he'd had the chance to be with Jeanie in the only way a man could be with a woman, would he have turned away? No. And for that reason, he wasn't going to be a hypocrite and shun Lorrie for her mistake.

He didn't dwell on any other reason why he would stay friends with her. His budding feelings needed to be squashed. She was a friend only and would need his help in the coming weeks and months. To believe he felt anything more was asking for trouble.

Taking a deep breath, he walked up the stairs and knocked on the door. She opened it quickly, as if expecting him, even though they'd hardly spoken in recent days since he found out about her condition. That was his fault mostly, for he'd stayed away from her door, concentrated on working late into the night on boats that could be repaired, but he also knew she had kept to the flat, hardly leaving it, accepting only Meg and Fliss as visitors. Thankfully, the odious Lynch had stayed away.

However, Lorrie's self-confinement had not done her any favours. The result of days holed up inside was standing before him. Lorrie had lost weight, her face was drawn and her skin pale, shadows bruising beneath her lovely golden-brown eyes. His heart melted, but he instantly rejected the emotion and stood taller. 'Are you ready?' He didn't mean to sound abrupt.

'Yes.' She closed the door behind her. All dressed in black, with a gossamer black veil over half of her face, she looked fragile, and he wanted to hold her and tell her everything would be all right. Of course, it would not be.

They didn't speak as they walked the length of the lane towards the bridge. The church was only a ten-minute walk and Lorrie had refused Meg's offer to travel in the carriage.

'It's a lovely day,' Lorrie murmured.

Jonas only just heard her as a horse and wagon rumbled by. 'We are fortunate the weather has stayed fair. Though Jed tells me a storm is likely this week. We've had too much heat, he says. Funny, isn't it, how some people just know what the weather will do?' He was rambling, he knew, but he needed to get back to the comfortable friendship they used to share.

She stared straight ahead. 'I've been dreading today.'

'I can imagine,' he replied softly, wishing he could hold her arm to give her comfort.

'Funerals make it all real, don't they?' She fiddled with the cuff of her dress. 'The only positive I can take from today is that Father and Mother are together again. That gives me some ease of heart.'

'Yes. It helps us to think of our loved ones being somewhere safe and nice and together. Will you look at that?' He pointed over the side of the bridge.

Lorrie turned to look at the river. Numerous boats had lined up before the weir, the skippers and crews standing on their decks facing her where she stood on the bridge. On both sides of the river, workmen lined the docks and wharves. They all wore black armbands.

Suddenly, a shout rang out and the men raised their hats and three cheers echoed across the water to her.

'They honour your father,' Jonas murmured.

Tears ran down her cheeks. A small sob escaped her at such a meaningful sight. 'My father would have been awed and moved by such respect, as I am.' Lorrie waved to the men, the workers, those who'd known her father for years. 'Thank you!' she shouted back at them. 'I hope they heard me and know how grateful I am.'

'They will do,' he replied.

After a moment, they walked on, Lorrie dabbing at her eyes. 'I've not been a good friend or employer to you, or the others. I have not enquired about the work you've been doing or anything. I've refused to leave the flat and I'm ashamed that I've left the yard to you to deal with. Please forgive me.'

'There is nothing to forgive.' Jonas glanced at her, his voice full of concern. 'You've been grieving.'

'I've been hiding.' She looked away. 'I've been a coward.'

'We all react to painful situations in different ways. Has it helped you to be in the flat?'

'I don't know.' She stared down the road. 'I simply knew I couldn't be with people.'

'And how do you feel now?' He wished he could help her more.

'Numb. Scared.' She continued walking and he fell into step beside her.

'All you need to do is take one day at a time.' He moved aside to allow a woman with two small children to pass by.

'Can I take it hour by hour?' Lorrie gave him a glimmer of a smile.

'That'll do.' He winked.

'I feel better already just being outside and feeling the sun. Wearing black isn't ideal in this heat.'

'No, but the church will be cool.'

They stopped speaking as they neared the church and saw the large gathering outside. Ernest Chambers had been a well-respected man, and many were out to pay their respects. The church was full, spilling out onto the roadside.

Jonas ushered Lorrie into the church as many people wanted to have a quick word with her.

The front pew held Meg, Christian and Fliss, who all embraced Lorrie. Jonas guided Lorrie in beside them and sat on the end. He wasn't a churchgoer but he knelt and stood as the reverend instructed and sang the hymns, but his main concern was being a support for Lorrie. Though, to her credit, she remained dry-eyed throughout and held herself with dignity and composure.

He was grateful when Meg asked him to join them in her carriage to the cemetery. He'd met Christian Henderson only a few times when he came to the yard, but even in that short acquaintance Jonas liked the man.

'Are you sure you don't want to come back with us afterwards?' Meg asked Lorrie as the carriage halted at the cemetery gates. 'You've been in that flat by yourself for far too long.'

'I can't, Meg. Starting tomorrow, I need to get back into the office and sort things out,' Lorrie said as Christian helped her down. 'I've neglected my duties for too long. I've not been in the office for over a week.'

'I'm sure Mr Bannerman can handle things for a few more days?' Meg asked with a glance at Jonas.

'I can, yes, of course,' Jonas added.

'See?' Meg tucked her arm into Lorrie's. 'A change of scenery would do you good.'

Jonas saw the hesitation on Lorrie's face. 'The yard will survive a few days without you.'

'But I've not been in the office to pay the wages.'

'Do you trust me to do it?'

She stared into his eyes and smiled. 'Absolutely.'

'Then that's settled. Spend a few days with Mrs Henderson and I'll deal with the yard.'

Lorrie's look of gratitude did funny things to his stupid heart, and he took a deep breath to calm his racing pulse.

All through the sermon at the graveside, he kept his gaze lowered, but was aware of Lorrie standing in front of him. She needed him, and he'd be there for her, but at what cost to his own sanity?

* * *

Lorrie sat in the parlour at Meadow View House, watching the rain hit the windows and lightning fork the thundery sky. Despite it being the afternoon, the angry clouds had darkened the day and brought her and Meg indoors from the walk around the gardens, which they had done daily for four days straight since the day after the funeral.

'August storms,' Meg said from the other side of the room, where she sat knitting a little white baby's bonnet, not very well. Sitting quietly for any length of time was foreign to Meg and her lack of patience with knitting was demonstrated in a misshapen bonnet.

'August already. This year is going by so quickly.' Lorrie took a date scone from the tea tray and nibbled it. Food didn't always stay down after she'd eaten it and so she was careful in how and when she ate.

'It always does when there's lots happening.' Meg threw the bonnet to one side. 'That's a waste of my time. I'll just buy bonnets. A woman on the market makes beautiful ones.'

'Oh, yes, the stall next to the man who makes leather belts and braces.' She finished the scone as Christian walked in with another man whom Lorrie instantly recognised as Mr Drayton, her father's solicitor.

'I wasn't expecting you this early,' Meg said as Christian bent to kiss her cheek. 'And we have a guest.'

Christian looked at Lorrie. 'Mr Drayton went to the yard and Bannerman sent him to me at the brewery.' Christian made the introductions to Meg before Mr Drayton came over to Lorrie.

'How do you do, Miss Chambers.' He shook her hand. 'Forgive the intrusion.'

'It's no intrusion, Mr Drayton, a surprise, yes. I was going to call on your office next week.' Lorrie was startled to see him.

'Please be seated, Mr Drayton,' Meg said. 'Tea?'

'Not for me, thank you.' He sat on a leather chair near Lorrie. 'My condolences on your father's death, Miss Chambers. A tragic event indeed.'

'Thank you.' Lorrie folded her hands in her lap.

'I have come about your father's will.' Mr Drayton took out a sheaf of papers from his small case. 'Your father's will is simple. Everything he had he bequeaths to you.'

Lorrie's stomach quivered and she hoped the date scone would stay down.

'That includes all his personal belongings at the residence of Chambers Boat Builder and Repairs, Boarman's Lane, Wakefield, and all monies in his two bank accounts at the Yorkshire Bank.'

'Two bank accounts?'

'Yes, a personal one and the business account.'

'Father had a personal account?' Her mouth gaped open in shock.

'Indeed. There is one hundred and seventy-one pounds and nine pence in his personal account.'

Lorrie blinked rapidly, not believing his words. Why would Father have another account with money in it when at times she needed extra money to pay supply bills?

'I shall continue.' Drayton quickly read on. 'Also bequeathed to you is the parcel of land and all buildings within the boundary as listed on the Land Registry Title Deed. I have that deed in my possession.' Mr Drayton glanced at Lorrie. 'Your father had paid off the mortgage, or the remainder of it, at the beginning of this year. I have the paperwork from the bank here.' He tapped the pile of papers on his knee.

Lorrie frowned. 'Father didn't tell me he'd paid the mortgage in full.'

'I believe he used the money that he received from Mr Oswald Lynch when they went into partnership. He preferred to have no mortgage and be a little short of money for a time, than to continue to pay the mortgage for several more years.'

'I see.' Annoyance that her father had not told her surfaced, filling her mind with other questions.

'However, your father also sold a good percentage of the business to Mr Lynch in three separate transactions. Forty-nine per cent of the business in total.'

'Forty-nine? I had no idea it was such a high percentage.' She didn't know what this meant for her and her future.

'The remaining 51 per cent is yours, which you can sell or keep as you wish. Mr Lynch has the right to first refusal should you sell, and he must pay the going price as valued by an independent land valuer, as written here in this agreement which I witnessed and signed.' Drayton lifted up another sheet of paper.

'Was all this agreed before my father had his accident when the wagonload of timber fell on him?'

'Yes.' Drayton scanned another sheet. 'The tenth of January. Both Mr Chambers and Mr Lynch came into my office to request the agreement to be drawn up.'

'And not a word was said to me.' Anger replaced the annoyance.

'I'm sure your father didn't want to trouble you with business matters,' Drayton said with a patronising tone.

Lorrie snorted. 'Yet it was me who worked in the office and kept the business running. It was me who worried about all the bills getting paid, and who ordered all the supplies, who allocated wages, who wrote and sent all the invoices!' She rose and walked to the window, where she watched the rain for a moment, trying to calm herself.

'Miss Chambers, you are in a most admirable position. You own half of the business, which includes the flat, so you have a home of your own, mortgage-free. Many would be envious of such an inheritance.'

'Many would, yes,' she answered dully, fighting the urge to snap at him that she had to deal with Oswald, and that her father had kept things from her. She would have tried to talk him out of

selling 49 per cent of the business. All those little chats he and
Oswald had while she was out of the room, all the times Oswald
called with papers to sign. It made sense now, and at the time she'd
been wary of what went on and it seemed she had good reason
to be.

'Do you have any questions for me, Miss Chambers?'

'I have many questions, Mr Drayton, but none I think you can
answer.'

'Then my business here is concluded.' Drayton packed away
his papers. 'Miss Chambers, if you could find the time to call into
my office, we can finalise your father's wishes and complete the
matter with your signature on the necessary papers.'

While Christian showed Drayton out, Meg came to Lorrie and
wrapped her arm around her waist. 'Be positive. You have a home
and some money to live off until you decide what to do.'

'Yes.' Lorrie sighed. 'But all the secrecy. I'm hurt that Father
would keep it from me.'

'He must have been acting on what he thought were your best
interests. He wasn't an unkind man.'

'No, and I believe he was heavily influenced by Oswald.'

'What will you do about him?'

Christian re-entered the room, his handsome face full of
concern.

Lorrie shook her head. 'I don't know. Oswald and I need to talk
about the business.'

'You know my feelings about Lynch,' Christian said. 'Ask if you
can buy him out. The man should be willing since there is no busi-
ness left to speak of.'

'And use the money Father left me?'

'I predict Lynch will want more than that, and if he does, tell
me, I'll see what I can do to help.'

Lorrie rushed to Christian and took both of his hands. 'You are a true friend. Thank you.'

He smiled and then looked at Meg. 'I'll be in my study if you need me.'

Lorrie sat down by the fire while Meg rang for the butler and ordered fresh tea.

'I need to go home, Meg,' Lorrie said, staring into the glowing embers. Everything Drayton said tumbled about in her mind. Rain still fell outside, and she shivered as if sensing a foreboding. 'I can't hide away here any longer.'

'I understand,' Meg replied, plumping up a cushion behind her back. 'You need to sort things out and make decisions.'

'Yes, so many decisions.'

'Have you any thoughts on the baby?' Meg asked, rubbing her own rounded stomach. 'Will you write to Matteo?'

'And say what?'

'There is a chance he didn't get married, you know.'

'If that's the case then he couldn't have loved me very much because he's not sent for me.' A wave of hurt caught her unawares, she'd been doing so well in burying away any feelings for him. She forced herself to not think of him, to not pine for his touch, his smile, to hear his accent.

'I feel you should write to him and tell him about the baby.'

'And if he's married, what can he do about it?' Writing to him was something she often thought to do, but each time she picked up her pen, she knew she'd never write the words.

Meg's expression became stern. 'If he's a decent man then he'd at least send some money over for the baby's upkeep.'

'Well, I don't have his address in Italy, anyway, so there's no point in writing a letter.' It was a weak excuse because she could simply address it to Falcone Boat Yard, La Spezia.

'Write to your uncles in London. They might know what is happening with him.'

'I'll not write to them, they have not bothered with me all my life, so why should I ask for help from them? Besides, Matteo knows my address. He's not sent a letter to me, that tells me a lot.'

'You don't know what he's feeling. He might be missing you and wishing things were different.'

'Perhaps he is, and if so, he should do something about it, but he left in April and not a word since. I can't spend my life waiting for him to come back.' Abruptly, Lorrie stood, not wanting to discuss Matteo any further. It hurt too much, and she had enough pain to deal with right now. 'I must pack.'

'You're leaving now?' Meg heaved herself up from the chair.

'You've been the very best of friends, both you and Christian.' Lorrie embraced Meg. 'But I need to go home.'

'I'll ring for the carriage to be brought around.' Meg pulled the cord by the fireplace. 'I'll call in and see you tomorrow.'

Lorrie paused by the door. 'Please don't mention Matteo again, Meg. He is my past and it's a past I'm not proud of and one with consequences I've yet to face. I have enough to deal with regarding my future without wasting my time thinking of him.'

'But you love him.'

'Love isn't enough when it's one-sided and can soon wither away.' She thought of Bannerman and all the years he'd spent loving his best friend's wife. No, she'd not do that, not waste her life hoping Matteo would come back to her, living a half-existence and dreaming of someone who'd easily abandoned her. There had to be more to her life than that.

16

Collecting her reticule from the desk, Lorrie left the office after spending the morning working on the accounting ledgers. Outside, hammering and the sound of timber being sawed echoed around the damaged yard.

Bannerman had erected canvas awnings for the men to work under when repairing the tools or when they had their midday break if it rained. In the month since the fire, Bannerman had driven Jed and Jimmy hard to complete the repairs on three narrowboats.

Sadly, Lorrie had to let Roy go for there wasn't enough work for him. However, the boat captains of the waterfront had rallied behind Lorrie, in honour of her father, and continued to send their boats to the yard for repairs or new caulking and paintwork. The jobs were small but constant and kept the flow of income coming in, even if it wasn't the large amounts it used to be. She managed.

Each day she spent long hours in the office. She had placed an advertisement in the *Wakefield Express* to alert people that the yard was open and ready to do business again, even offering Bannerman's expertise of design as he and her father had discussed doing before the fire.

On Sundays, Bannerman, with Jed and Jimmy's help, had begun to rebuild the first open-end shed nearest to the boat ramp and dock. A skeleton of a frame was emerging, thrusting up against the late summer sky. Bannerman wanted it finished before winter set in.

Lorrie's estimation of Bannerman grew more each day. The man worked tirelessly, seven days a week, and late into the night. Lorrie felt guilty at the amount of effort he was putting into the yard, but he refused to slow down. To compensate for all his hard work, she cooked for him, and often they'd share an evening meal, sitting on the dock by lantern light as the sun set a little earlier each day. Eating a meal with him pushed away the emptiness of the quiet flat, of missing her father's presence.

'You off then?' Bannerman said, ducking under the rope that held the awning.

Startled out of her thoughts, Lorrie smiled. 'Yes. I'm meeting Fliss. She's been unwell for over a week, and she sent a note last evening saying she was up and about again and needed to get some fresh air. So, we thought we might walk the towpath along the river.'

'It's a lovely day for it.' Bannerman looked up at the blue sky studded with small white clouds.

'We might not get many more days like today.' Lorrie didn't want the summer to end, to be confined inside in the gloominess of winter. 'I'll be back in a couple of hours.'

'Take care.' Bannerman's gaze flicked to her small bump and back to her face.

Lorrie walked away, her cheeks pink from his glance at her stomach. They never spoke about her condition, but it hung in the air between them, tainting their friendship.

Walking between the mills, their yards busy with workmen, Lorrie headed for Harry's ferry that would take her across the river to Thornes Lane Wharf, where Fliss would be waiting for her in front of the Bay Horse, the public house her uncle owned and where Fliss lived.

On such a warm day, the river was flat, and the boat trade crowded the waterway, eager to make the most of the fine day to move produce and goods. The frenzied activity of the waterfront filled the air with noise. Lorrie watched cranes move cargo from dockside to boats, and men whistled signals or yelled as they worked on the wharves lining the river. She'd lived all her life with the sights and sounds of the riverfront and knew many of the faces working on the boats.

'There you are, lass,' Harry said, helping her from the ferry onto the green slimy stone steps. 'Careful as you go.'

'Thank you, Harry.' Lorrie carefully made her way to the dockside and, shaking out her black skirts, headed for the Bay Horse.

Fliss waved as Lorrie approached. 'I've only just come out. Aunt Joyce wanted me to run errands, but Uncle Terry told me to go out and he'd deal with her.' Fliss looked relieved. 'A week spent inside with my aunt is a week too long.'

'You do look pale,' Lorrie agreed as they fell into step along the lane.

'I'm feeling fine now.' Fliss gazed across the water. 'What a beautiful day. I was determined to be out in it for we'll be into winter before we know it.'

'I said something similar to Bannerman just now.' Lorrie watched a young boy come towards them, leading a shire horse, which pulled a narrowboat along behind it.

'How are you going with everything?' Fliss stepped aside for the boy and horse to pass by.

The horse lifted its tail and deposited manure onto the cobbled lane. Lorrie held her nose, not wanting to retch.

'I'm fine. The business is ticking along steadily, mainly thanks to Jonas.'

'Jonas?' Fliss grinned. 'He's not Bannerman any more?'

Lorrie blushed at the slip of calling Jonas by his first name. 'Well, we spend so much time together, it makes sense to call him by his name.'

At the entrance to a side lane, situated between two malt-houses, a man leaned against the wall smoking a clay pipe. Lorrie recognised him. Saunders.

On seeing her, Saunders grinned, tapped his pipe against the wall and strolled towards them. He motioned to some men standing in the doorway of one of the malthouses. 'Looky here, lads, the high and mighty Miss Chambers,' Saunders mocked.

'Keep walking,' Lorrie whispered to Fliss. She had no desire to talk to him.

Fliss linked her arm with Lorrie and they both averted their gaze from Saunders.

Saunders laughed and stepped in their way to the jeers of the four other men who'd come closer. 'Don't be turning away from me, miss. You're not so grand now, are you? Not with your boatyard in charred ruins.'

'Leave me alone,' Lorrie murmured.

'You see, lads.' Saunders turned to his audience. 'This here *Miss* Chambers was once my boss, or so she thought. She sacked me for no reason, she did.'

The men hissed and heckled.

Lorrie stiffened. 'There was reason enough.'

Bloodshot eyes narrowing, Saunders peered closer to her. 'You didn't like me because Lynch wanted me there.'

Recoiling from the waft of alcohol that emanated from him, Lorrie took a step back. 'Get out of our way!'

'You don't order me around any more. In fact, someone like you shouldn't even have the grace to walk amongst ordinary people.' Saunders glanced back at the men. 'Did you know that this unmarried whore is with child?'

Lorrie gasped.

The men's expressions became similar, all filled with revulsion.

Saunders grinned. 'Your secret isn't so secret any more. The whole town will soon know that a filthy slut runs that boatyard and you'll be ruined.'

The blood drained from Lorrie's face. She swayed.

Fliss gripped her arm tightly, rounding on Saunders. 'How dare you!'

'Oh, I dare. She treated me with contempt and all the while she was lifting her skirts for that dirty Italian!' Saunders sneered. '*An Italian*,' he crowed back to the men. 'Not even an Englishman!'

The men grumbled and spat, growing angry.

'Come on.' Fliss tugged Lorrie about, and they walked away. 'I'll take you home.'

Suddenly, something hard hit Lorrie on the shoulder. She spun to face Saunders as another missile hit her chest. She yelped with pain.

The men, urged on by Saunders, searched along the lane for anything they could throw at Lorrie, stones, sticks, any rubbish. One man even pulled out a weed by its roots and threw that at her. It hit her skirts, showering dirt everywhere. Buoyed on by the sport, the men cheered each other.

Lorrie and Fliss ran, but Saunders and two of the younger men were faster and caught them easily.

Saunders grabbed Lorrie's arm and swung her to him. He

pushed her backwards against a building and started to yank up her skirts. 'I'll have a taste of what the Italian did, shall I?'

Lorrie screamed. She fought him but he easily overpowered her. He kissed and bit her neck. She screamed again at the pain and fought him.

'Saunders, man, you'll draw attention,' one of the others said.

'Let her go,' another said, holding Fliss, who was fighting him like a wildcat.

'Saunders!' the second man beckoned. 'Come on, let her go.'

'She needs teaching a lesson,' Saunders puffed, pulling at Lorrie's bodice.

'I ain't getting in trouble for this!' The younger man thrust Fliss from him and ran back down the lane.

Fliss ran to Lorrie and hit Saunders on the back. 'Get off her!'

'Jesus wept! I'm off!' The third man ran off.

Saunders turned and backhanded Fliss, catching her cheek. She stumbled.

Outraged, Lorrie slapped Saunders's face as hard as she could.

Stunned, Saunders glared at her, hate in his eyes. 'You bitch.'

Fliss scrambled to Lorrie's side and faced him, ready to defend or attack. 'Go on, you bully, try and take both of us on, go on!' she screamed, crying.

A yell came from along the lane. A woman hung out of a window. 'Clear off!'

Saunders lifted his chin tauntingly. He searched in his pockets and found a box of matches. He struck one and watched it burn before smirking at Lorrie. 'Aren't matches so useful? One little box can do so much damage...' He flung the match at Lorrie's feet and strolled away.

Leaning back against the wall, Lorrie sucked in deep breaths. Her whole body shook.

'Let us get back to the pub,' Fliss murmured, wrapping her arm around Lorrie's waist. 'Uncle Terry will get us a brandy.'

'No.' Lorrie held back a sob. 'I need to go to my home.'

'Are you in pain?'

Was she? She couldn't tell. She felt numb. The shock of what just happened gave her wobbly legs. She clung to Fliss as they made their way back up the lane, past the factories and mills, ignoring the sights and sounds that became a blur.

Lorrie couldn't raise her head. She dared not see the faces of other people who might now know her secret. How had Saunders found out? She was shamed, humiliated. Tears fell silently.

Harry said nothing as he ferried them back across the river, waving away Fliss when she offered him money.

Huddled together, they walked through the mill yards, crossed Tootal Street and into the lane leading to the yard.

'What happened?' Bannerman's voice rang out. Dropping his tools, he reached her in seconds. 'Lorrie, what happened?'

'We were attacked,' Fliss told him, crying now herself.

Lorrie fell into Bannerman's arms, and he scooped her up and carried her up the stairs to the flat, shouting orders at the men below to fetch the doctor and the constable.

Placed gently on the sofa, Bannerman laid a blanket over her, his movements gentle, but his body pulsed with tension and anger. Lorrie turned her face away.

'Your neck...' Bannerman peered at her. 'Where else are you hurt?'

'I'm fine,' she whispered. She wanted to close her eyes and shut out the world forever.

'Tell me what happened, Miss Atkins. Are you hurt, too?'

'Only my wrists where they grabbed me. It was Saunders, who used to work here.' Fliss sat beside Lorrie and held her hand.

'Saunders?' Bannerman rubbed his face angrily. 'I'll kill the swine.'

'No!' Lorrie stared at him. 'You'll not be arrested because of that scum. I couldn't bear it. Don't go near him, please. Promise me!'

Bannerman hankered down in front of her. 'Calm down. Think of the child.'

'I don't care about the child.' Lorrie turned away, feeling low and dispirited. 'That's no longer a secret. Saunders knew, and he'll delight in telling all and sundry. I am ruined before I even had a chance to decide what to do.'

'How could he know, though?' Fliss asked. 'Who have you told?'

'Only you and Meg and Christian.' Lorrie stared at Bannerman. 'Jonas and Oswald.' It dawned on her who had told Saunders. Lorrie bowed her head in shame and regret. 'Oswald must have told Saunders. They are as thick as thieves.'

'But why?' Fliss frowned. 'Why would he share that with Saunders, who is nothing to him?'

'I don't know, but it's the only way he'd know.'

'My aunt has a cousin in Leeds,' Fliss said quietly. 'She is kind and works for many charities. I was going to mention her today on our walk. One of the charities she is on the board of governors for is an orphanage on the York Road. I can write to her and see if she will take you in until you've had the baby.'

The idea of living with a stranger filled Lorrie with nausea. 'I can't think of that now,' she murmured.

It was some time before Dr Carter arrived and by the time he did, Lorrie was feeling stronger. After a quick examination, he declared her and the baby to be unharmed apart from the bite mark on her neck. As he packed away his tools into a bag, Dr Carter gave Fliss the once-over.

'I'm perfectly all right,' Fliss said when he asked her questions about the bruising on her wrists. 'Lorrie received more than I did.'

When Senior Constable Abbott entered the flat, he had a quick word with the doctor before Bannerman showed the doctor out.

'Now, Miss Chambers, we meet again,' Senior Constable Abbott said, writing in his notepad. 'An attack, I'm told.' He frowned. 'In broad daylight?'

'Does it matter if it's day or night?' Bannerman snapped.

Abbott raised his hand at Bannerman. 'I need to get all the facts and I'll thank you to be quiet, Mr Bannerman.'

Both Lorrie and Fliss relived the attack while Bannerman made a pot of tea.

'And all this took place on Thornes Lane Wharf?' Abbott wrote as they talked.

'Yes.' Lorrie gave a small nod to Jonas when he handed her the cup and saucer.

'Do you believe Saunders is disgruntled because he lost his position here?' Abbott asked, sipping his tea.

'It's been a while since he worked here, months,' Lorrie said. 'He didn't seem that bothered when I told him to go.' She paused, remembering him lighting the match. 'Saunders said, "Aren't matches so useful? One little box can do so much damage..."'

Abbott frowned. 'What do you think he meant by that?'

Bannerman sprang to his feet. 'That bastard torched the yard!'

'Now, Mr Bannerman, calm down. There is no proof of that. He could have been taunting Miss Chambers because of the recent fire.'

'Or he lit it and was letting her know he lit it,' Bannerman fumed. 'You lot have done nothing about finding the culprit. Have you stopped looking?' He glared at Abbott.

Lorrie went cold. The truth hit her like a bucket of ice water. 'I believe the same as Mr Bannerman. Saunders lit the fire, and he wanted me to know it.'

Abbott screwed up his face in thought. 'Would he allude to arson? Just to prove a point?'

'Have you spoken with him?' Bannerman asked. 'When you spoke to all the workmen here, did you speak to him as well?'

'Yes. Yes, I did.' Abbott went back through his notepad. 'Here, yes, I have it here. Saunders claimed he was playing cards in the Horse and Hounds pub until eight o'clock and then he went home. His younger brother confirmed he was in the house all night as they share a bedroom.'

'His brother could be lying,' Fliss murmured.

'Of course he could!' Bannerman paced the floor.

'We have no proof Saunders started the fires.' Abbot wrote in his notebook.

Lorrie sagged against the sofa. Tiredness and shock made her body heavy.

'You will arrest him for this attack, though,' Bannerman stated.

Abbott tucked the notebook in his inner pocket. 'I will go and question him now.'

'He needs to be arrested.' Bannerman glared at Abbott.

'Allow me to do my job, Mr Bannerman.' Abbott stood. 'I'll call again tomorrow, Miss Chambers. Good afternoon, ladies.'

'Is there anything I can fetch for you?' Bannerman asked Lorrie after the door closed on Abbott.

'No, thank you. I think I might lie down for a little while.' She looked at Fliss. 'Do you mind?'

'Absolutely not. You must rest.' Fliss embraced her. 'I should be getting back anyway. I have a shift tonight.'

'Tell your uncle you're not up to it.'

'I'll be fine.' Fliss shrugged. 'It's best to keep busy.'

'I'm so sorry you got caught up in all that. It's my mess, not yours.'

'I'm your friend. What bothers you, bothers me.'

Lorrie glanced at Bannerman. 'Will you walk Fliss home, please?'

'There's no need,' Fliss said hurriedly.

'There's every need,' Lorrie argued. 'If for nothing else but my peace of mind.' She smiled. 'You were incredible today, thank you.'

Fliss embraced her again and then left the flat with Bannerman.

Alone, Lorrie sighed and closed her eyes, but the scene with Saunders played out behind her lids and so she pushed up from the sofa and walked over to the kitchen table. As tired as she was, she knew she wouldn't sleep. The sun was too bright, the day too warm.

Instead, she rolled up her sleeves and decided to make a cake. Her apron accentuated the small roundness of her stomach and she stared at it for several moments. A baby. Her child. She didn't know how to feel about it. Being unwed and in this condition brought such disgrace. Her reputation would be in ruins once word spread, and Saunders would make sure it did.

Part of her wanted to pack up and move away, far away from the memories, but to do so she'd leave behind the only friends she had. She'd be alone and with a small baby.

Could she travel to La Spezia, to Matteo? Would he help her? Or would he turn her away?

Should she give the baby up for adoption? The woman in Leeds that Fliss mentioned might help her. If her baby went to a good home, some kind family that were desperate for a baby to love. A family with a nice home, or a farm in the country...

Then she thought of all the awful people who could treat her child differently because he or she wasn't their own. What if a farmer and his wife mistreated her child? Or if a wealthy family took the baby and treated it coldly and it was cared for by a cruel nanny like the ones Meg had interviewed?

Half-heartedly, she finished making the cake batter and placed the tin in the range oven. When the knock came at the door, she answered it, expecting it to be Bannerman, but Oswald stood there. 'What do you want?' she asked rudely.

'Charming.' He walked past her. 'We are partners. I am allowed to be on the premises.'

'About that,' she said impulsively. 'Would you be willing to sell your shares to me?'

Oswald grinned slyly. 'Ah, you want me out? After all I've done for this business?'

'It will be years before the business is back to what it once was. Do you want to wait for your returns?'

Rubbing his chin, Oswald strolled to the window and look down at the burnt-out yard below. 'I don't think you could afford to buy me out. No bank will loan you the money.'

'Father left me some money. Depending on what you want for your share of the business, I might be able to afford it.'

'He did, did he?' A devious gleam lit his eyes. 'He never told me that.'

'Why would he tell you something so intimate?' Annoyance sharpened her tone.

'Your father and I were friends as well as business partners. His wish was for you and me to be joined in matrimony. Of course, that is impossible now.' A scathing look was directed at her stomach. 'I am still so surprised you lowered yourself to whore for the Italian, especially when I offered you marriage, respect and decency.'

'I am not a whore,' she murmured. 'I loved Matteo.'

'He obviously didn't want you, though, or he'd have taken you with him as his wife.'

She flinched at the spark of pain that hit her in the chest. 'None of that is any of your business.'

'No, but this yard is.' Oswald shrugged. 'It is worthless.'

'Then you will allow me to buy you out for a fair price?'

'Why would you want to lumber yourself with such a burden? You should be selling too. You'll never making a living from it now. Not enough boats will come in for repairs to pay the men's wages or give you a decent life.'

'That is something I will worry about.' She silently begged him to say yes to the buyout.

'Twelve hundred pounds.' Oswald grinned.

Lorrie's stomach churned. 'That's outrageous. I saw the initial contract when you invested originally last year, and it was only two hundred and fifty pounds.'

Oswald walked closer to her, his smile sly. 'I want my investment back and more.'

'As you say yourself, the yard is a ruin and will take years to rebuild. That offer is ridiculous.'

'Tell me, do the men know of your disgusting condition?' Oswald smirked. 'Do you think they will want to work for such a woman as you when they find out your loose morals?'

Lorrie blanched.

Oswald strolled around the sofa like a tiger on the hunt, his gaze watching her. 'If those men walk out on you, which they will, you'll be left with no business at all.'

'And neither will you,' she snapped, hating him.

'Ah, yes, but I have ways of making money, you do not.' He laughed suddenly. 'Come now, let us part as friends. I will accept three hundred pounds for my half of the business. Deal?'

'I don't have that much money.'

'No?' He smirked. 'How about this then...' He thought for a moment. 'You sign over the land and buildings to me and in return

I will sell you my shares for... two hundred pounds. You can rent the land, the yard, from me as you rebuild.'

'Why would I give away something that I own? I have a home that is mortgage-free, Father made sure of that for my security. You aren't having this land as that would mean I own nothing.'

'But you'll have the business.'

'I will be paying you money for the business and rent.'

'Indeed. However, you will at least have a business completely in your name, which will provide you income, and I will allow you to stay living here so you will have a roof over your head.'

Stunned, Lorrie could only stare at him.

'The alternative is I will sell my shares to whomever I please and you will have to deal with them. They may not be a silent partner as I was and will want to interfere in every aspect of the yard.'

A burning fury boiled in her chest. 'Or *I* sell my shares and the land,' she argued, finding strength from somewhere to fight him. '*You* will then have someone new to deal with, a *controlling* partner being involved in *your* business. That person may not be as accommodating as my father and I have been.' She watched his flabby face twitch.

Oswald collected his hat from the table. 'Don't try to be clever with me. You won't win.'

'I've nothing to lose either.'

'Oh, yes, you have, your home and income. Do you want to be penniless with an illegitimate bastard?' He advanced on her. 'I can make your life hell. One word to Saunders and he'll terrorise you until you beg to die or flee in the night like the filthy slut you are!'

Saunders. Oswald had told Saunders. Did he also tell him to attack her?

Shaking, Lorrie glared at him, not backing down even though

her knees trembled. 'Just let me buy you out for a reasonable price and we never have to see each other again.'

His gaze narrowed. '*Three hundred pounds* by the end of the week and be thankful I'm being generous when you least deserve it.'

When he'd gone, Lorrie lowered herself onto a chair at the table, feeling wrung out and exhausted. Her mind refused to work, leaving her gazing numbly into space. How was she to find such money?

17

Lorrie rose early. As tired as she constantly was, sleep eluded her. In the quiet of the night, her mind wouldn't shut off and allow her the oblivion she desperately wanted. Scenes and conversations replayed in her head. Could she have done anything differently to change the way things had turned out? Giving herself to Matteo would be one, of course, but as her baby kicked gently in her womb, she felt fiercely protective of it. Yes, the baby made her life more difficult, but he or she would be the only family she had, and that gave her some comfort. It also reaffirmed her decision to not give the baby up. No matter what the future held, her baby would stay with her and be loved.

With the fire blazing, she cooked eggs and slices of ham for breakfast, mashed the teapot and tidied the kitchen.

The knock on the door was familiar, Bannerman's short rap.

'Come in, Jonas,' she called, pouring a second cup of tea for him.

'There's a fellow here,' he said. 'He says he's a footman from Meadow View House.'

Lorrie hurried to the door. She knew the footman, Peter, from her visits to Meg. 'Has something happened?'

The footman handed her a folded piece of paper. 'From Mr Henderson, miss.'

Lorrie opened it.

Dear Lorrie,

My darling Meg started her labour last night around midnight and has been in acute suffering since. The doctor and midwife are both in attendance, but I know she'd feel more at ease if you and Fliss were by her side. I beg you to come at your earliest convenience. I've sent the carriage for you both.

Fondest regards,

Christian

'I must go to Meg.' Lorrie dashed into her bedroom and changed her house slippers for boots. 'Jonas, I don't know how long I'll be, maybe overnight.'

'Of course. I'll see to everything here.'

'Eat that breakfast.' She pointed to the food on the range.

'I've just had porridge.'

'Then give it to Jimmy, he eats enough for two people, as thin as he is.' Lorrie pulled on her coat and gloves and pinned on her black felt hat.

Bannerman touched her arm as she passed him. 'I hope everything goes well with Mrs Henderson.'

She smiled. His tenderness was very welcome.

The carriage was at the top of the lane. Fliss waved out of the window. 'The driver came to get me after dropping Peter off to you,' she said as Lorrie climbed into the carriage and the footman went up to sit with the driver.

'Poor Meg.' Lorrie shivered. All that pain Meg was experiencing would be hers soon enough. Would she be strong enough to endure it?

'I've prayed a dozen times since I heard.' Fliss gripped Lorrie's gloved hand. 'Aunt has gone to church even at this early hour to pray for Meg and a safe delivery of a healthy baby.'

'Christian sounds worried.' Lorrie glanced out the window. The driver was pushing the horses to a fast pace.

'He's bound to be. Fathers have no role in this event. He has to sit by and simply wait.'

Houses, mills and factories gave way to orchards and farms as the countryside opened up on both sides of the road. In the distance, the river gleamed in the morning sun. In a short time, they were wheeling through the gates and slowing in front of the house.

Christian burst out of the front doors and rushed down the steps to help them from the carriage, leaving Titmus, the butler, redundant. 'I'm so pleased you came.'

'How is she?' Lorrie asked as they went inside.

'Yelling.' Christian winced. 'It's awful to hear.' He took their coats and gloves, and nearly threw them at Titmus. 'Come up.' He led them upstairs and into the master suite where a doctor and nurse were conversing and Maude, Meg's lady's maid, was standing by the bed holding her mistress's hand.

Lorrie's stomach swooped at the sight of Meg. She lay on the bed, sweating, her face screwed up in pain.

'Mr Henderson, this is no place for you, I've told you before!' the midwife tutted. Her grey-streaked hair was pulled tight into a knot at the back of her head and her starched apron was blindingly white. 'And who are these ladies?'

'My wife's dearest friends. They will help her.'

'The doctor and myself are the only help your wife needs. Now, please, sir, leave the room and allow us to do our work.'

Reluctantly, Christian left the room after an anxious look at Meg.

Fliss and Lorrie went to either side of the bed and, taking over from Maude, held Meg's hands.

Meg peeped at them. 'Where have you two been? It's been hours! If I'd been still at Wellington Street, half the neighbourhood would have been in the room and Mrs Fogarty would have her sleeves rolled up ready to deliver this baby.'

Fliss chuckled at the mention of Meg's old neighbour. 'Mrs Fogarty would be giving out the orders and your Mabel or Susie making cups of tea for everyone. The front room would be full of neighbours sitting around chatting.'

'I miss seeing Mrs Fogarty every day,' Meg murmured tiredly. 'I must visit her soon.' She blinked rapidly. 'I will survive, won't I?'

'Now then, none of that talk,' Lorrie chided gently at Meg. 'Let us have this baby out, shall we? Then you can talk about visiting Mrs Fogarty and showing her the baby.'

Meg squinted up at her. '*I've been trying.*'

'We know, dearest.' Lorrie rinsed a cloth in a bowl of water and wiped Meg's hot forehead. 'Fliss and I will help you.'

'The child is of a good size, Mrs Henderson,' the doctor said, pushing his glasses further up his nose. 'On the next contraction, see if you can push.'

Meg rolled her eyes at him. 'What does he think I've been doing?'

Lorrie and Fliss shared a small grin.

'Do you want to sit up a bit?' Fliss asked. 'Do you need another pillow?'

'Yes...' Meg reared up and groaned deep in her chest as her body worked to rid itself of the baby.

'That's it, Mrs Henderson,' the midwife declared. 'The head is nearly out. Another push, if you please.'

Lorrie watched in utter amazement as Meg strained to push again. Meg squeezed their hands so tight, Lorrie was sure she'd break the bones.

'Steady now,' the doctor, one Lorrie hadn't seen before, told Meg gently. 'Slowly now, Mrs Henderson. That's it. There. The head is out.'

'It burns!' Meg shouted, arching her back. 'I want my mam,' she sobbed.

Feeling so sorry for her darling friend, Lorrie rubbed her arm. 'She's watching over you, Meg. She'd be so proud of you.'

Meg groaned again, her body contracting.

'The shoulders now, Mrs Henderson,' the doctor spoke without looking up from his task. 'That's it.'

Lorrie peeked over Meg's stomach and glanced at the black-haired little baby as it suddenly slipped out onto the bed in a gush of bloody water. 'Oh, my heaven!' She was in awe of it all.

A baby's cry shattered the room. Meg slumped back, exhausted, eyes closed.

'You did it!' Fliss was nearly bouncing in her joy. 'Meg, you did it, you clever thing.'

The door flew open and Christian raced in. 'Is it over?'

'Mr Henderson!' the midwife snapped. 'I will come to you shortly!'

Christian glared at the midwife, and totally ignoring her, came swiftly to Meg's side. 'Darling?'

'I'm alive,' Meg panted, barely heard above the baby's cries.

'My sweetheart, you have done tremendously. I am so proud of you.' Christian kissed her reverently.

'You have a fine healthy son, Mr Henderson,' the doctor declared.

'A boy!' Lorrie cheered. 'How wonderful.'

Christian had tears in his eyes as the midwife stiffly, and somewhat grudgingly, gave the tightly wrapped baby to his father. 'Is he not magnificent?' he whispered to Meg.

'I wouldn't know, since no one has thought to show him to me.' Meg raised her eyebrows at her husband.

'Look, darling.' Christian bent closer so Meg could see the miracle she'd carried for nine months.

'He looks like you,' Meg said happily. 'I'm so pleased. I didn't want him to resemble my father.'

Lorrie glanced at Fliss. They knew Meg had not forgiven her father for his double life, even after death.

'I would ask you all to leave now, please,' the midwife ordered. 'There is more to be done and our task isn't finished.'

'More?' Fliss frowned.

'The afterbirth.' The midwife took the baby from Christian. 'Mrs Henderson may receive visitors again shortly, if she is up to it.'

Like scolded children, Lorrie joined Christian and Fliss on the other side of the bedroom door that the midwife closed firmly behind them.

Christian grinned. 'My, she'd knock any army into shape, wouldn't she?'

'At least it all ended well,' Lorrie said, relieved.

'Thank you both for coming. I know it would have helped Meg.'

Lorrie embraced him. 'Congratulations, Papa.'

Fliss did the same and Christian let out a long, deep breath. 'It is over. Thank God and every saint. I am not a praying man, but I have prayed so much in the last twelve hours I feel I have made up for my past neglect.' He laughed shakily. 'Brandy?'

'It's not even nine o'clock,' Lorrie chuckled, as they made their way downstairs.

'Definitely a cup of tea then.' Christian rubbed his hands

together. 'With a dash of brandy in it, and some breakfast. I am famished.'

Going into the parlour, Lorrie couldn't help but smooth her hand over her own stomach. Her baby was growing under her heart, and she sent up her own small prayer that they would both survive the birth.

'How is it going at the yard?' Christian asked Lorrie as he rejoined them after going to tell the staff the good news.

'Slow.' Lorrie shrugged, not wanting to think of the business after witnessing such a special moment.

'Has Lynch been about?' Christian went to the drinks trolley and poured out three small measures of brandy.

'Yes, yesterday. He offered to sell his shares to me.'

'That is promising news.' Christian gave the glasses out. 'Is he being reasonable about the price?'

'Three hundred pounds.'

Christian frowned. 'That's not a lot. I know the buildings are burnt down, but the reputation of your father's business is worth more than that.'

'Yes, but Father has gone and so have all the buildings.'

'True. I am not surprised Lynch is wanting to leave the business. It was never going to make him rich. I will never understand his reasons for buying into it.'

'Whatever his reasons were, he's changed his mind and I'm glad to see him go. However, I was hoping the amount would be less. I don't have that much money.'

'No, but I do.' Christian grinned. 'I know I said in the past that I needed to invest all my money into the brewery, but in the last few weeks, good fortune has favoured me with a small return on an investment I made many years ago. Now, today, with my son's safe arrival, I feel I should share that good fortune with someone who needs it.'

Tears came to her eyes. 'Are you sure?'

'Very much, and I know it will please Meg. She's been worried you'd sell up and move away because of the child and the past. I want to make my wife happy as much as she has made me and knowing I can help you will be something that pleases her greatly. So, do you wish for me to invest?'

Lorrie rose and embraced him. Her throat caught with emotion, and she struggled to speak. 'In many ways, this is a most wonderful day.'

When the carriage dropped Lorrie off at the end of the lane, she waved goodbye to Fliss and strolled down the cobbles with her mind at rest for the first time in what seemed forever.

Through the gates she heard the banging of industry, the smell of tar and sawdust. She stopped and stared around the yard, black and charred, broken and damaged. Yet, like the frames of the new shed rising into the air, she felt renewed. Christian's investment would see her clear of buying out Oswald and never having to deal with him again. The very thought of that put a spring in her step as she headed for the office.

'You're back,' Jimmy announced, coming around the side of the office carrying timber on his shoulder.

'I am.' Lorrie smiled.

'Thank you for breakfast,' the youth called, continuing on.

'You're welcome.' Lorrie opened the door.

At the back of the office at the draft table stood Bannerman, bent over with a pencil poised above paper. 'Did everything go well?'

'Yes, a little boy. Both Meg and baby are doing fine.' Lorrie joined him at the table which was slightly angled and upon it lay sheets of boat designs.

'I'm pleased.'

'What are you studying?'

'This drawing of the sailboat. I feel there could be alterations, which would improve the keel. Baird was here earlier.'

'Oh? He never sent a note of him coming to visit.' She was sorry to have missed his visit. 'Was he very mad about the fire and sinking of his boat?'

'He is a clever man, Lorrie. He had the sailboat insured for fire.'

'Insured?' Her eyes widened with surprise.

'He's received a sum from the insurance company, and he wants me to design a larger sailboat, one he could take out of the River Humber and into the open sea.'

'Gracious.'

Bannerman raised his eyebrows at her. 'It's a job worth several thousand pounds.'

Lorrie gaped at him. 'And he wants you to do it?'

'Yes, in this yard.'

'Here...' She couldn't believe it. 'Can you do that with the state of the yard?'

'It'll be a struggle and I'll need the shed built to house the shell of it through winter. Baird wants the sailboat ready before March. If we can make it by then, he'll award me, *us*, a bonus payment.'

'That is fabulous news!' She wanted to clap with joy. 'What a day it has been, the baby born safely, and Meg is well, oh, and Christian is going to buy out Oswald and now this.'

'Mr Henderson is buying Lynch's shares?' Jonas couldn't hide his shock.

'Isn't it wonderful news?'

'The best,' Jonas agreed. 'And now the sailboat commission.'

'I'm so surprised, but grateful to Mr Baird for giving us a second chance. I thought he'd stay clear of us after the fire.'

'He was happy with the previous vessel your father built and once he saw my designs and my references from the ship builders in Whitby, we shook hands on it.' His expression changed. 'You don't mind, do you, that I did business without you being here? Baird is returning tomorrow to talk to you, too, about the contract.'

'I trust you completely, Jonas. I know you will only ever do what is best for this yard.'

'And for you,' he added. 'I'm not in this just for myself. My every action is in regard to you, too.' Suddenly, as if he'd said too much, he quickly turned away and shuffled through some drawings.

'I need to make up the wages.' Lorrie went to her desk, feeling conflicted. Jonas was someone she relied on, trusted. After losing her father, and Matteo's abandonment, she'd come to depend on Jonas. Was she relying on him too much, though? Would he soon become tired of working so hard for her? What was his reward, a wage that was lower than he deserved? She owed him so much, his diligence to the boatyard and, more importantly, his friendship.

She glanced over her shoulder to where he worked on the drawings. Her heart twisted slightly, watching him tap the end of the pencil against his chin in that familiar way of his. Did Jonas have affection for her? And if so, how did she feel about that?

Lorrie tipped the coins on the desk to count them out, but her thoughts weren't on making the wages, but on the silent man at the end of the room.

18

Jonas opened the door to the Bay Horse public house and entered the overly warm taproom. The smell of tobacco pipes and stale ale filled his nose. In the golden light from the gas wall lamps, smoke hung above the seated men's heads.

He nodded to those men he knew who worked on the river, or from previous visits, not that he was a regular drinker. A pint or two on a Saturday night was his limit. He'd seen what drink could do to people, including his best friend, Samuel. Too many times he'd witnessed an argument between Jeanie and Samuel after a drinking session where Samuel had drunk too much of his wage and left Jeanie short to buy food. Besides, he couldn't afford to spend time drinking, especially now with all the work he had to do at the yard.

'Evening, Mr Bannerman,' Fliss greeted him from behind the bar where she was serving. 'A pint?'

'Yes, please, and call me Jonas.' He leant on the bar and surveyed the room, looking for one particular man.

'He's not here,' Fliss whispered to him as she took his money and gave him the tankard of beer.

'He's hiding like the rat he is,' he muttered for her ears only.

Since Saunders attacked Lorrie, Jonas had been looking out for the scoundrel with the need to give him a good thrashing. After weeks of subtle searching at different pubs, he'd come to learn that Saunders frequented the Bay Horse more than others, but unusually he'd been keeping a low profile.

'Lorrie wouldn't want you to do this,' Fliss said quietly, wiping down the bar.

'Lorrie won't know.' Jonas sipped his beer, his eyes on the door.

As a youth and young man, he'd been in his share of fights. Samuel had a way of landing them in the shit whenever he'd drunk too much. Jonas could hold his own, but he had to admit it'd been many years since he'd used his fists. He was still as strong as he was but maybe not as fast.

He got talking to an old man, a former narrowboat captain, who'd plied the River Calder for more than half a century. As they were discussing the question of timber over steel boats, Saunders came in, laughing with a mate.

Jonas stiffened, his hand tightening on the tankard he'd nursed for an hour.

Unaware of Jonas, Saunders stopped at the other end of the bar to chat to the two men sitting on stools.

Fliss came to Jonas. 'If you're going to fight, take him out the back, not the front. The odd constable sometimes roams the waterfront. I don't want you getting into trouble.'

Jonas gave one nod, took a sip of beer and straightened. Just hearing Saunders's laughter grated on him. Standing beside Saunders, he waited for the other man to notice him.

Saunders scowled. 'You want something, Bannerman?'

'I do, actually. A word.'

'Sorry, mate, I'm busy.'

Angry at the snub, Jonas grabbed Saunders's upper arm in a

vice-like grip. 'I ain't your mate and I ain't asking. So, unless you want the whole pub to witness our *discussion*, I suggest you follow me.'

He walked down beside the bar, through a door Fliss opened and into a passageway that took him outside.

Saunders followed, grumbling. 'What's all this about?'

'I'm surprised you don't know.' Jonas turned to face him in the middle of the cobbled yard. Light spilled out from the kitchen doorway and window, but the sun had set, and darkness hid the perimeters of the yard.

'What should I know?' Saunders jeered. 'Listen, I don't know what you want—'

Jonas stopped his words with a fist to the mouth.

Surprised, Saunders staggered back, swearing. 'You bastard!' Saunders came rushing back, fists raised.

Jonas ducked the first punch and got another jab to Saunders's cheek before he stepped back out of reach of the returning punch.

Enraged and frustrated, Saunders ran for Jonas, surprising him with his speed, for the younger man was quick. The blow of Saunders crashing into Jonas took the wind from his lungs as they smashed into a pile of empty barrels. They landed hard and Jonas winced at the wood digging into his back.

Pushing Saunders off him, Jonas rolled to one side and scrambled to his feet, fists raised ready.

Swearing, Saunders suddenly bent low and grabbed Jonas's leg, nearly knocking him off balance, but Jonas kicked out at him, connecting his boot to Saunders's shoulder. The other man fell back with a grunt.

'Get up, you dog,' Jonas panted, circling. 'Come on. Fight like a man and not the rat you are.'

Several customers had come outside, Fliss too. Jonas ignored them, but Saunders quickly jumped to his feet, wiping the blood off his lip with the back of his hand.

Seeing the crowd watching, Saunders rushed at him again, but Jonas swivelled sideways and threw his fist into Saunders's jaw. The other man groaned, stumbled then turned for Jonas again. 'I'll kill you!'

'Come on and try,' Jonas taunted, beckoning him with his fingers. 'You're picking on someone your own size now, not a couple of women. It's a bit different, isn't it?'

Realisation widened Saunders's eyes.

'Yes, I know of your attack on Lorrie and Fliss,' Jonas said loudly for the crowd to hear.

Murmurs spread through the group watching, which was growing as more customers came outside.

Jonas circled him, not taking his eyes off the scoundrel. 'Not so cocky now, are you? Man on man. Prefer beating women, don't you?'

'Shut up!' Saunders lunged again, a low punch to Jonas's stomach.

Pain fired through his belly, but Jonas refused to acknowledge it. He jabbed again, hitting Saunders once more in the mouth, splitting his lip wider.

Saunders spat blood. His face screwed up in fury as he stared at Jonas. 'Is she your whore, is she, the Chambers woman? She's had others, hasn't she? The evidence is growing in her gut,' Saunders jeered, glancing at the crowd for their reaction. 'I heard it was that Italian's, but maybe it's yours?'

A red mist filled his brain and Jonas wanted to make Saunders pay for his foul words and what he had done to Lorrie.

'Getting tired, old man?' Saunders mocked.

Infuriated, Jonas advanced in two short steps, punching left and right in quick succession. Saunders blocked and parried. The crowd grew rowdier, urging them on, wanting to see bloodshed and justice done.

They fell to the ground and wrestled. Jonas rolled on top of Saunders and, taking advantage, punched the man's face several times, taking out his frustrations on the pathetic weasel beneath him.

'Enough!' Fliss screamed.

Jonas was hauled off Saunders by two men, one being Terry Atkins, the owner of the pub and Fliss's uncle, and a huge mountain of a man.

'What in God's name is going on here?' Terry yelled.

Panting, Jonas glared down at Saunders, who lay dazed and bleeding. 'A score to settle.'

'Then consider it settled,' Terry snapped.

'You will apologise to Miss Chambers,' Jonas spoke down to Saunders.

'Go to hell and take your whore with you!' Saunders flung back at him.

'You bastard!' Jonas sprang and pulled Saunders up, ready to fight again, but Terry yanked Jonas away.

'You'll pay for this. I know people.' Saunders scrambled backwards along the cobbles, blood dripping from his busted lip. 'I have protection.'

'Protection?' Jonas sneered. 'You're going to need it. I ain't finished with you and I'll make sure you'll always be looking over your shoulder.'

'And I'll tell Lynch about you, and he'll have you in prison before sunrise.'

'Oh, aye?' Jonas stilled. 'Why would Lynch do that? I've no problem with Lynch.'

'He owns half that boatyard. I'll have you sacked.'

Jonas advanced on him, fists poised. 'You *dare* to threaten me, you filthy swine!'

'Wait!' Saunders held his hands up, cowering on the cobbles. '*Wait.*'

Jonas, his rage barely contained, dragged Saunders closer by his shirt, his voice low so no one else could hear. 'How about I have *you* lying at the bottom of the river by sunrise, hey?'

'No, no!' Saunders's eyes were wide in his bloody face.

'I think I'd be clearing the town of a filthy piece of rubbish if I did, don't you? No one would miss you, Saunders, no one.'

'I didn't mean it. I'll not tell Lynch anything.'

'Don't believe you,' Jonas said, his nose only inches from Saunders. 'You're pond-dwelling scum. I wouldn't believe a word you said.'

'I mean it,' Saunders pleaded.

'You're going to leave town, understand? Either that or end up in a cell or worse, the bottom of the river.'

'Leave town?'

'Exactly. You've caused enough strife to Lorrie, and you'll not be a thorn in her side any more.'

Saunders panicked. 'I've nowhere to go, and me mam's sick.'

'Not my problem.'

'I have to stay for me mam.'

'You should have thought of that before terrorising Miss Chambers,' Jonas snarled. Thinking of Lorrie hurting made him tighten his grip on Saunders's shirt. He'd never forget that bite mark on her neck.

'I didn't want to do it. Lynch told me to, gave me money to do it.'

'You took *money* to accost a woman with child?'

'No! The money was for the fire!' Saunders blurted out.

Shock froze Jonas. He blinked. His heart somersaulted in a

chest suddenly tight. 'The fire.' He could hardly say the words. Jonas lifted his fist to punch him again. 'What kind of animal are you? You don't deserve to breathe the same air as everyone else. Maybe the stink of a prison cell will suit you better?'

Terry came closer. 'Now then, men, let's be finishing this.'

Jonas kept his grip on Saunders, his mind whirling. 'Tell him. Tell Mr Atkins what you just told me.'

'No, I can't. I'll go to prison.' Saunders was crying now.

'What's going on?' Terry murmured, then seeing the seriousness in Jonas's face, he turned and clapped his hands. 'Come on, you lot, back inside. Get some drink down you. The show is over.' Terry glanced back at Jonas. 'Go into the snug.'

'Bring the constable.' Jonas marched Saunders to the back door.

'No!' Saunders skidded his feet, refusing to go inside. 'No, not the constable. I'll tell you everything but not the police.'

Jonas banged him up against the wall. 'You've just admitted to starting a fire that killed a man and ruined a business. You'll be telling the constable everything, or I'll kill you myself.' He'd never done such a thing in his life, but his anger burned so brightly, not only for Lorrie but for Ernest, who hadn't deserved to die.

Lorrie was blackleading the range early the next morning, determined to get as many chores done as she could before going to visit Meg and the baby later in the afternoon.

A knock preceded Jimmy sticking his head around the door. 'Miss Chambers?'

'Yes, Jimmy?' Lorrie knelt in front of the range.

'Er... Is Mr Bannerman here?'

'No.' Lorrie got up and wiped her hands. 'Is something wrong?'

'Rollo is barking like mad in the hut. I can't find Mr Bannerman anywhere in the yard.'

Frowning, Lorrie took off her apron. 'Perhaps he's gone into town.'

'Without Rollo?' Jimmy looked sceptical.

'True. I'll come down.'

At the bottom of the stairs, Lorrie sent Jimmy to look around the yard again, while she went to the hut. After knocking and receiving no answer, she opened the unlocked door and Rollo came running out, jumping up at her skirts.

'Calm down, boy.' She patted his head and then he raced off to pee against the washing line pole. 'Where's your master then?' she asked the little dog as he came trotting back to her.

Inside the hut, the stove was cold, the ashes dead. Bannerman's bed was made, his coat gone.

Jimmy met her outside. 'He's not here.'

'Then he must have gone into town,' Lorrie replied, and with Rollo at her heels headed back across the yard.

'Here he is now.' Jimmy pointed at the gates, where Bannerman came walking through.

'What happened to you?' Lorrie hurried to him, frightened to see Jonas sporting a black eye and a ripped shirt under his coat.

Rollo made a fuss, running about in circles barking. Jonas bent down to him to give him a belly rub. 'Sorry, old fellow. I didn't mean to leave you all night.'

'All night?' Lorrie stared at him. Something bad had happened and she didn't know if she wanted him to tell her. How much more could she take?

'Sorry, I don't wish to worry you.' Jonas ran a hand over his sore face and winced. His tired features and the state of him spoke more than any words.

'Were you in a fight?' Jimmy asked, surprised. 'Did they keep you in a cell all night?'

'Yes, I was.'

Lorrie blanched. 'You were in jail?'

'No, no, not that bit.' Jonas held up his hands in apology. 'A fight, yes, and at the police station, but not in a cell.'

'You'd better come up and tell me about it,' Lorrie demanded, not pleased. She thought Jonas would be the one person she could depend on to not get into trouble. 'Jimmy, go to Jed and he'll give you work to do until Mr Bannerman joins you.'

Upstairs, Lorrie packed away the blackleading and tidied the kitchen while Jonas sat at the table, Rollo at his feet.

'I'm sorry if I've upset you,' Jonas said. 'It's the last thing I wanted to do.'

'Fighting?' She shook her head in despair. 'Why?'

'Saunders.'

'Saunders.' She lit the range fire with jerky movements. That man's name sent shivers down her back. Why was he always the cause of trouble?

'I wanted to teach him a lesson for harassing you.'

She struck a match and set it to the twists of paper. 'Did you think that I'd want you in danger? Fighting with Saunders could have seriously harmed you. He could have had a knife and killed you. Do you think I want that to happen to you?' Her heart pumped wildly at the notion of Jonas being in danger, or hurt.

'Lorrie, he needed to know he couldn't attack you and get away with it.'

'But instead, you got into trouble with the police.' She didn't know whether to be angry with him or pleased he'd stood up for her.

'No, I didn't get into trouble.'

Lorrie added kindling, watching the fire take hold. 'Then why were you gone all night?'

'I was helping Senior Constable Abbott.'

She glanced at him, the story was becoming crazier by the minute. 'Are you going to explain, or do I have to drag out every word from you?' she snapped.

'Forgive me. It's been a long night. Come and sit down, please.' He waved to a chair, his tone gentle.

She did as he asked. The grave expression on his face worried her. 'Jonas, please, you're scaring me.'

He took her hand, and she jumped a little in surprise, for they never touched. However, she liked the feel of her hand in his callused one.

She noticed his bruised knuckles. 'Thank you for defending me, my honour, but I would never want you in harm's way.'

'I can look after myself,' he said wryly. 'I might be heading for my forty-sixth birthday soon but I'm not a decrepit old man just yet.' He grinned, then quickly turned serious. 'I have something to tell you.'

'You're not leaving me, are you?' she blurted out.

Jonas scowled. 'Leaving you? No, never.'

She sagged. 'Oh, thank heavens.'

'Lorrie, Saunders admitted to Abbott that he assaulted you.'

'Good.' She was pleased about that.

'He also admitted to... to torching this place.'

She gasped, her hand flying to her mouth in shock. 'The fire? Saunders did it?' She couldn't believe it. 'Why? Because he lost his position? He did it to get back at me for sacking him?'

Jonas let out a long breath. 'He confessed to Abbott that he was paid to do it by Oswald Lynch.'

Stunned, Lorrie stared at him. Those words refused to sink into her brain. 'No...'

'Abbott told me that Saunders confessed to taking money from Lynch to burn this place down.'

'But why?' Lorrie couldn't comprehend it. 'Oswald wouldn't benefit from the business being ruined.'

'He would if it was a fire. Abbott will investigate it today and speak with Lynch, likely arrest him, too. Abbott believes Lynch must have taken out fire insurance. He'd receive a large payout.'

'But he couldn't have done that. I would know. It would be in Father's papers. Such a certificate would be in the safe in the office...' Even as she spoke, she knew she was being foolish. Oswald didn't tell her anything. He might not have even told her father.

'If Lynch didn't tell your father and did it solely in his name, how would you know? With your father no longer here, Lynch could make the claim and take the money, and no one would be any the wiser.'

Nausea rose and Lorrie dashed to the sink to throw up all her breakfast.

Jonas came beside her and rubbed her back. 'I'll get you some water,' he said as she retched.

Minutes later, Lorrie allowed him to lead her back to the table. She sipped the water, eyes stinging with unshed tears.

'Abbott will come and speak with you later, after he's seen Lynch. He'll want to discuss all this with you and make sure you weren't involved.'

'Involved?' Lorrie spluttered. 'My father died because of that fire! He should have been safe in his bed, not running about on damaged legs trying to save boats from burning!'

'I know, but Abbott will have to be thorough and question you. You need to tell Abbott everything you know.'

'Oswald asked me for three hundred pounds to buy his shares.' An anger was building. 'Three hundred pounds... Yet he was also going to claim insurance. Insurance I knew nothing about.' She rocked back against the chair. Her thoughts were ragged, splintered with rage and hate and the savage grief that Father had died because of Lynch, a man he had trusted.

'Lynch will go down for this, and so will Saunders.' Jonas rose and attended to the range fire. Once it was going sufficiently, he set the kettle on to boil.

'I need to buy his shares,' she murmured, feeling light-headed. 'I cannot be tied any longer to that horrid beast.'

'We'll speak to Abbott and see it gets done before Lynch is sent down. If I have anything to do with it, you won't be buying them at all. Instead, Lynch should just sign them over to you and beg for forgiveness at the same time.'

'Oswald may not admit to it. He will say Saunders is lying.'

'Saunders swore under oath, and he has information he'd only know from Lynch telling him.'

'All this time, Oswald was here, knowing the truth. He paid Saunders to ruin us. How could anyone do that?' Lorrie shivered, her mind racing with unanswered questions and wild thoughts. 'Oswald paid for Father's funeral.'

'Guilt money.'

Her chin trembled as she tried not to cry. 'I felt so *grateful* to him for being supportive during the funeral. I truly believed he liked Father.'

'I think Lynch did respect Ernest.'

'Did he? No, he played Father for a fool. Oswald planned to burn all this down and destroy the one thing that Father loved and had worked years to achieve.'

'Men behave strangely when money is involved. Lynch was desperate.' Jonas made two cups of tea and brought them over to the table. 'Abbott knew Lynch had creditors to pay. He'd gambled heavily in the past year.'

'Yes, I heard that from Christian.'

'The fire insurance money would save his neck from some nasty people he owed money to or would have done. Nothing will save him now from a prison cell.'

'I still can't believe it. Father died at the hands of Oswald Lynch and Saunders.' Sadness grew heavy in her chest. 'Two people who we knew. You don't expect that, do you? You think of death being done by the hand of an accident or illness, never by someone you know.'

'It's a shock. Even Abbott was surprised.'

'What happens now?'

'I believe Abbott will arrest Lynch and interview him over Saunders's allegations. It will go to trial. You'll need to be prepared for that.'

Lorrie flinched. 'It'll be reported in all the newspapers. It'll be common gossip. Father's good name dragged through the mud...' Her shoulders slumped. 'People will talk about me, too. I'll have to go to court, won't I?' She bit her lip in despair. 'They will see me, my stomach... Lord above, I'll be vilified.'

'You'll get through it.' Jonas took her hand and this time she didn't jump at his touch. 'When all this is over, you can start again, Lorrie. I will help you.'

She took a long moment to reply. 'I'm not sure I want to. I'm with child and unmarried. What future do I have?' For the first time, she said it out loud to him.

'Maybe so, but you're still a good person, Lorrie. One I am honoured to call a friend.'

'I do not deserve your friendship.'

'You do in my eyes.'

'People will be gossiping about me, about this child.'

'And I'll continue to defend you. I won't let anyone hurt you.'

'That's something you can't control,' she whispered. She

slipped her hand from his and stood. 'You should go and get cleaned up. I've work to do in the office.'

'Very well.' He rose from his chair, his gaze lingering on her.

'And thank you, Jonas, for confronting Saunders. It couldn't have been easy.'

He shrugged. 'I simply wanted to teach him a lesson for hurting you, but we got so much more. I never expected a confession about the fire.'

'I still can't accept it. What Oswald has done. I begged Father not to become his partner.'

'We all make mistakes, Lorrie,' Jonas said quietly. 'Don't be too hard on your father or yourself over something you had no control over.'

Once Jonas had left, Lorrie rinsed out the teacups, her mind spinning. Oswald had betrayed them. His actions, his instructions to Saunders had concluded in her father's death. She would never forgive either of them, and she would face them in court and watch them learn their fates and do it with her head held high.

19

Head down, concentrating on tallying up the ledger, Lorrie tried to ignore the wind banging against the office window. She should have gone upstairs hours ago, but with the small fire burning brightly, and with the gas lamps flooding the office with light, she was disinclined to go up to the silent flat and to bed. Although she had been reading several books lately, she was beginning to dread the nights being on her own.

The wind slapped the front window and something in the yard rattled along the cobbles, likely a bucket. All day the gales had caused havoc with the construction of the large shed Jonas and the men were building. The roof slates were on now, but the walls had yet to be boarded. Jonas worked long hours to get as much done as he could while the weather held but the strong winds today had held them up.

She rose and added more coal to the fire. The day had been overcast and a little cool. She hoped the summer hadn't disappeared entirely. She wasn't ready for the coldness of winter yet. But it would be September in a few days, and the trees were changing colour, and the days were growing shorter.

Another bang sounded outside and, sighing, Lorrie closed the ledger. She really should go upstairs and call it a night. The baby moved as she stood, and she rubbed her stomach. Its little kicks and flutters gave her much joy.

Opening the safe, Lorrie placed the bags of coins she'd counted for wages inside just as another bang sounded. She swung around as the office door was flung open and Oswald stood there, wild-eyed and desperate. Her ordered pile of papers flew off her desk and swirled in the air.

'Oswald?' Shocked, she stared at him. It'd been two weeks since Jonas had fought with Saunders, and he'd confessed. Two weeks since Senior Constable Abbott and his men had been searching for Oswald and unable to find him. Rumours circulated he'd gone to London, others said he'd gone to France or America. No one thought him to be in Wakefield still.

'I need your help,' Oswald panted as though he'd run miles.

'My help?' She nearly laughed at him.

'I have to get away. The net is closing in around me, thanks to Saunders squealing like a stuck pig.' Oswald inched his way in, closing the door. He'd lost weight, looked haggard.

The papers landed either back on her desk or on the floor, but she gave them no heed as Oswald took a step towards her.

'Stay away from me!' She held her hands up to ward him off. 'How dare you come here after all that you've done!'

'I never meant for Ernest to die.'

'But he did. You burnt down our business! Why? For the fire insurance money?'

His eyes nearly popped from his head. 'You know about that?'

'I know.' She folded her arms, not frightened of the pathetic creature before her. Anger gave her strength.

'I need to flee, Lorrie.' The frantic expression appeared once more. 'I need money.'

'More money?'

'The insurance company hasn't paid out,' he whined. 'Abbott has spoken to the insurance company and put a stop to it. He told them I'm under investigation for committing arson. It was *Saunders.*'

She could have laughed at his pathetic tone. 'At *your* behest.'

'I need the money for my shares. We made a deal. Give it to me.'

'You want me to give you three hundred pounds now?' She did laugh this time. 'Are you utterly mad?'

'Listen to me!' He advanced on her, no longer pathetic and scared, but determined and menacing. 'I want my money.'

She gripped the side of the drawing desk, wishing Jonas was here to help her. 'I haven't got that kind of money.'

'Look!' He drew out of his coat pocket a folded sheet of paper. 'A contract, selling my shares to you. It's all here in writing.'

Lorrie took a step back on seeing the glint of silver metal of a pistol in Oswald's pocket. *He had a pistol.* She went cold.

'I've signed it and it's witnessed by my solicitor.' He waved the document at her. 'All you need to do is give me the money and this business is wholly yours.'

As tempting as it was, she didn't trust him. 'I don't have the money here. How could I have?'

'You knew I was coming back for it,' he snarled and then swore violently.

'No, I didn't. The police are looking for you. No one has seen you for two weeks. Everyone thought you had gone. Senior Constable Abbott has been here to see me nearly every day asking me if I'd received any correspondence from you.'

The wind howled down the chimney, sending smoke into the room.

Oswald glanced at the safe. 'How much do you have in there?'

'The wages for three men. Hardly a fortune.' She didn't tell him that, upstairs, she had twenty-five pounds from a finished repair job which she was taking to the bank in the morning. Father never liked all their money being in the safe in case it was taken in a robbery. He told her many times to spread the money about, so if someone came to steal, they'd believe all the money would be in the office safe.

'Give it to me. I need to get away.'

'Before you're caught and must pay for what you did?' she scoffed. 'And you think I'll help you?'

'If you want the business in your name then yes, you will.'

'Let me read the document. Is it legally witnessed?'

'Yes, by my solicitor, I told you.'

'Forgive me for not trusting a word you say,' she snapped.

He flung the paper at her feet and pushed her aside to reach the safe.

Lorrie slipped the paper under the desk with her foot and faced him. 'Take the men's wages, but that's all you'll get.'

'I don't think so,' he mocked, stuffing the small bags of coins into his coat pocket. 'I know there will be some money upstairs. Your father told me he liked to spread it around the place.'

The blood drained from her face. Oh, Father! Why?

Oswald laughed. 'Exactly as I thought.'

He raced outside into the darkness and the wind. Lorrie followed him, the wind battering her, taking the breath from her lungs and flattening her skirts against her legs.

Upstairs, Oswald crashed open the door and like a madman began searching the flat. He wrenched open the dresser drawers, flinging them and their contents over the floor. He swiped everything from the kitchen cupboards, before upturning the sofa and ripping the material from underneath.

'Where is it?' Oswald yelled. 'Tell me, by God!'

Frightened, Lorrie backed towards the door. 'I don't have any money!'

Demented, Oswald ransacked the living area and then dashed into her father's bedroom.

'No!' she screamed. 'Leave my father's things alone.' At the door, she watched him haul the drawers out and empty her father's clothes over the bed. Clothes she'd not been able to face giving away. Next, Oswald tipped up the mattress, searching for the treasure he thought he'd find there.

'Where is it?' In one swift move, Oswald took Lorrie by the throat. 'Give it to me. It's only fair. You have the shares!'

'Fair!' she gulped, terrified. 'Fair? You killed my father!'

'And I'll kill you tonight, too!' His fat fingers closed tighter around her throat.

Lorrie struggled to breathe. She sucked in air, wheezing. Dizziness came in waves. She closed her eyes as her lungs fought to work. The room was growing dark...

Suddenly, there was a huge commotion, shouting and yelling. The hand around her throat released her and she slumped down against the wall, gasping, her throat burning.

The room was abruptly empty.

She struggled to stand, but pulled herself up and, holding on to the wall, carefully made her way out of the bedroom. The door to the staircase was open, banging in the wind.

On the landing, she searched into the dark night. A lantern bobbed down by the dock. On the wind she heard shouts.

Cautiously, one step at a time, she went down the staircase. The gale whipped her hair into her eyes. From a lifetime of knowledge of the yard, she felt her way between the old destroyed sheds and the new constructions towards the dock. More yelling reached her. Who was with Oswald?

Her eyes strained in the darkness. The lantern stopped moving.

Inching closer, hidden in the shadows, Lorrie kept her gaze on the men on the dock. One of them was Jonas.

Heart skipping several beats, Lorrie wanted to call out to him, but then she saw Senior Constable Abbott. In the dim light of the lantern, Oswald raised his pistol and waved it wildly about, first at Abbott, then at Jonas. Her throat clenched in fear. No! *Not Jonas.* She couldn't lose him as well.

Abruptly a growl and a flash of cream shot past her and sailed through the air at Oswald. Rollo sank his teeth into Oswald's leg. The pistol went off. Ducks on the river edge quacked and flew up into the blackness in alarm. Jonas rushed for Rollo as Oswald kicked at the little dog. Abbott tackled Oswald to the ground, shouting for Jonas to help him.

Dashing forward, Lorrie scooped up Rollo, for the little dog was being kicked and squashed under the weight of three men. 'Shush now,' she soothed him, but he wiggled and yapped, determined to get back into the fight and save his master.

'You're under arrest, Oswald Lynch.' Sitting on top of Lynch, Abbott panted. 'Bannerman, go to the station, I need more help and the cart.'

'I'll go.' Lorrie put Rollo down. 'You stay, Jonas, and help the constable.' She hurried along the dock and up through the yard. She walked and half ran as fast as she could, but once over the bridge, a stitch gripped her side. The pain bent her double and she huffed.

'Nay, lass, are you hurt?' A couple came out of the darkness on the street corner.

'I need the police. Senior Constable Abbott needs more help. Chambers Boatyard,' she told them, breathing deeply.

The woman came forward. 'Let me help you, lass. George, get off to the station. Chambers Boatyard you said, lass?' The woman's kind face was shadowed in the street light, but instinctively Lorrie trusted her.

'Yes, hurry, please.' Lorrie leant on the woman's arm.

'Come on, love. Let's get you home. Are you in labour?'

'What? Oh, no, no, I can't be, I'm only five months. It's just a stitch in my side.'

'Right then, we'll take it nice and slowly. Gently does it.'

It seemed to take forever for Lorrie and the woman to reach the flat's staircase and forever again until more constables came rumbling into the yard on the caged cart.

'Shall I make us some tea?' the woman said, straightening an up-sided chair and lowering Lorrie onto it.

Seeing the smashed teacups and the destroyed furniture, Lorrie hung her head and let the tears flow.

'Now, everything will be just dandy soon enough, lass,' the woman crooned, holding Lorrie's hand. 'We'll stay quiet up here out of the way and let the men do what needs to be done.'

Eventually, Jonas came upstairs. His face registered the state of the flat but then his focus was on Lorrie. He knelt beside her. 'They've taken Lynch to the station. Abbott will come and see you tomorrow.'

Lorrie sighed. 'I'm so tired of dealing with Senior Constable Abbott, good man that he is.'

Jonas gently lifted her chin to inspect the bruising on her neck. He swore under his breath.

The woman and her husband stood by the range. 'We'll be off now, lass,' the woman said. 'If you're feeling better?'

'Much better.' Lorrie gave her a small smile. 'Forgive me, I don't know your name. I'm Lorrie Chambers.'

'We're George and Flo Ingram. We live on Doncaster Road. We'd been to the theatre tonight and had to walk home as we couldn't find a hansom for love nor money, could we, George? But it's just as well we didn't, or we wouldn't have been able to help you now, would we?'

'Thank you both.'

'Think nothing of it, nothing at all.' Flo came and patted Lorrie's hand. 'Can I call in tomorrow and see how you're faring?'

'I would like that, Mrs Ingram.' Lorrie smiled again.

'Right, I will then.' Flo nodded vigorously. 'Come along, George,' she said as though her husband had been holding her up. 'See you tomorrow, lass, ta-ra.'

When the door shut on the Ingrams, Jonas began to straighten chairs and pick up broken items off the floor.

'Leave it.' Lorrie waved him away. 'I'll see to it in the morning.'

'You will not. You need rest and lots of it.' Jonas placed the sofa upright and gathered the fallen cushions. 'I could throttle Lynch for scaring you, for hurting you. Coward that he is.'

'Jonas.' Tears filled Lorrie's eyes. She held out her hand to him and he hurried over to take it. 'Oswald shot at you.'

'I think he was aiming for Abbott.' He grinned with a shrug. 'Rollo put him off his aim.'

'You could have died tonight.' The very idea of that frightened her senseless. She couldn't lose him. He meant too much to her. Impulsively she threw her arms around him and held him tightly.

'I'm fine, darling girl,' he whispered into her hair, holding her just as tightly.

'I can't not have you in my life,' she murmured.

He pulled back to smile softly. 'I'm not going anywhere.'

'But you might, one day.'

'Only if you tell me to go.' He delicately brushed a strand of hair back from her face.

She leaned her face into his hand, enjoying the comfort, the touch of another. It had been so long since she'd been touched so tenderly. She sighed deeply and closed her eyes.

'You're tired,' Jonas whispered.

She was, desperately so.

'Did Oswald damage your bedroom, too?'

'No.' She gazed into his grey eyes. 'But I don't want to be alone.' She glanced around the ruined flat. 'I don't want to be here alone.'

Jonas stood and held out his hands. 'Let's go to the hut. You can sleep in my bed, and I'll take the floor with Rollo. He'll be beside himself with happiness.'

'He was such a good boy tonight, so brave.' Lorrie took her coat from the door and went out onto the landing with him.

'Rollo is named after a Viking warrior, of course he's brave.' With his arm around her waist, Jonas led her down the steps into the cold, windy night and towards the hut where for one night she could sleep close to another person.

A part of her wanted Jonas to be in the bed with her, just to hold her, but she knew she could never voice such a thing. She carried another man's baby. Jonas deserved more than that.

20

On a rainy day in late October, Lorrie exited the courthouse on Wood Street and stood under the portico to regain her composure. Her legs were a little wobbly, but she kept upright. People hurried by, horses and carriages splashed through puddles as the rain fell from a grey sky.

She had given her evidence to the judge in a packed courtroom. The trial of Oswald Lynch had proved a crowd-pleaser. The upstart getting his just punishment. Though to Lorrie it had brought her attention she never craved.

Under the questioning she had wilted a little, but a quick glance at her support in the stalls, Meg, Fliss, Christian and Jonas, even Jed and Jimmy, plus others from the waterfront, gave her courage. However, she got through it all by keeping her focus on Oswald. Her attention hardly wavered from him as she told them all her side of the story.

She'd attended the trial of Saunders the week before. He'd been convicted for arson and bodily harm on her. Fliss had been a called witness and the pair of them had relived the assault. Saunders was sent down for five years.

Today Oswald had been given the prison sentence of three years for fraud and assault.

Was it enough? Lorrie couldn't answer. Somewhere deep in her chest, a rage simmered at the injustice that Oswald's underhand dealings had led to her father's death.

'There you are.' Meg came out of the black doors with Fliss.

'How are you feeling?' Fliss asked.

'Numb.' Lorrie shivered as the rain fell harder.

'It's over now,' Meg said, glancing up the street. 'Lynch and Saunders are in prison where they belong.'

'It doesn't bring my father back, though,' Lorrie murmured sadly. Today she had thought about him constantly, hoping he'd be proud of her for standing up and saying her piece.

'No, it won't.' Fliss gave her a small smile. 'Thankfully, you won't have to see or hear from them for years.'

Meg held on to her hat as rain gusted under the portico. 'We'll be out of this weather shortly. Christian has sent for the carriage.'

'And Jonas?' Lorrie wondered where he'd got to. 'Has he not come out yet?'

'He went through a side door. Jonas is walking back to the yard with Jed and Jimmy.'

'Walking back in this weather?' Lorrie frowned. 'I could have caught a hansom with him.' She didn't like being away from him.

'We offered for him to join us in the carriage, but he said no.' Meg shrugged. 'He seemed very quiet today, not that he's a big talker anyway.'

'I might walk, too,' Lorrie said, wanting to go home and be where Jonas was. Being near him she felt safe, but more than that, she simply enjoyed being in his company.

For weeks now she had come to realise that Jonas meant so much to her. Every day she would stand for an hour or two and watch him work, and she always cooked them a meal to share in the flat before he went to his hut for the night. Her fondness for him was turning into something more, and she didn't know what to do about it.

'You're not walking in this weather in your condition,' Meg scoffed.

'Shall we go somewhere for a cup of tea?' Fliss suggested.

'We can go back to Meadow View,' Meg offered.

'I would prefer to just go home.' Lorrie smoothed down her black skirts. The black cape she wore only emphasised her bump. She felt enormous, though everyone disagreed. She calculated she only had about twelve weeks to go before the baby arrived. The thought terrified and pleased her at the same time.

'Here's the carriage now.' Meg linked her arm through Lorrie's and as she did so, she slipped an envelope under Lorrie's cape. 'Read it at home,' she whispered.

Startled, Lorrie gripped the envelope with her arm and pulled her cape closer around her. She didn't speak in the short carriage ride home, letting Meg and Fliss plan a small dinner party for next week.

It was a relief to escape the carriage and hurry down the lane to the yard's gates. Work on the new structures was coming along well despite the shorter days. The large shed was now a working space undercover, and the smaller tool shed was completely rebuilt as well. Another shed was rising from the ashes and the yard was filling up with boats to be repaired. Jonas worked hard and long into the night. Sometimes, she would come out and sit with him as he sawed, planed or sanded wood by lantern light.

Although they didn't always talk much, the company was soothing, a comfort for them both, Lorrie liked to think.

Inside the flat, she tore open the envelope. A folded piece of paper slipped out along with another smaller envelope.

The note was from Meg.

Dearest Lorrie,

Firstly, I beg for your forgiveness if I have done the wrong thing.

Many months ago, I wrote to Matteo and explained to him your predicament. I didn't know his address and hoped for the best.

Yesterday, his reply came. I haven't read it. I left it sealed. You can either read it or throw it in the fire.

Never would I want to hurt you, but I felt something needed to be done, once and for all, so you can move forward in your life without wondering about the past and what might have been. You needed answers. I hope you find them.

Your loving friend always,

Meg

Lorrie sat on the sofa, her stomach a quivering knot of apprehension. She stared at the envelope, at Matteo's handwriting, writing she'd seen before when he was here. How she used to watch the flow of his hand as he wrote or drew a change on a design. Those same hands had held and touched her so deftly, eagerly, with desire and longing.

Her pulse racing, she carefully opened the envelope and pulled out the note within.

Dear Mrs Henderson,

Thank you for your letter. It came as a surprise when it eventually reached me some weeks ago. It had been delivered to many members of my family before I found it waiting for me at home when I returned from my honeymoon in Florence.

I am shocked and saddened that Lorrie is with child. I would never wish to put her in that situation. My actions were not of a gentleman, and I pray she forgives me and still looks upon me with kindness for she will always be a fond memory.

I will endeavour to establish a bank account through my uncle and place money at her disposal to use to educate the child, should she keep it. My uncle's address is on the back of this letter.

Please give Lorrie my sincerest regards. I wish her and the child nothing but happiness and good fortune for their future.

Your humble servant,

Matteo Falcone

La Spezia

Lorrie read the letter three more times before tears blurred her vision. He'd been on his honeymoon. He was married after all. Her heart thumped with a mixture of sorrow and rage. Matteo had dismissed her and their child to his past. A mistake. A mistake he could fix with a bank account.

She jerked to her feet as the door opened and Meg and Fliss stood there, their expressions similar, of worried expectation.

'I'm sorry.' Meg rushed to her and embraced her, but Lorrie couldn't return the embrace.

'Why, Meg? Why did you write to him?'

'I thought I was doing the right thing,' Meg cried. 'I wanted you to be happy.'

Lorrie thrust the letter at them. 'Read it.'

'We couldn't.' Fliss's eyes widened in alarm. 'It's private.'

Lorrie snorted angrily. 'It's not even to *me*, it's to *Meg*!'

Scowling, Meg took the letter and both she and Fliss read it.

Upset, Lorrie paced the room, not knowing what to think or feel, only knowing she felt cheap and ugly. The baby kicked and for an instant she hated it.

'He is not worthy of you,' Meg declared, full of anger.

Fliss nodded. 'How dare he write such an insipid letter?'

Lorrie smirked. 'He can because I mean nothing to him. I never did. I was just too stupid to see it. I wanted him to love me as much as I thought I loved him, but now I can tell what I felt for him was nothing solid, nothing real. It was desire, a passion that turned my head for a moment. None of it was real.'

'You did love him, don't tarnish your feelings,' Fliss said. 'Matteo might be a cad, but that doesn't mean you were acting on anything but love for him.'

She didn't have an answer to that, but there was a spark of something dying inside, hope perhaps. 'How foolish it was of me to still believe, to still imagine that Matteo might come back and declare his love for me and marry me.'

'That's not foolish,' Meg whispered.

'He's married!' Lorrie yelled. '*He married another.*' Her chin trembled as emotion coursed through her.

'He didn't deserve you,' Meg whispered, her pretty face sad and upset. 'I'm so sorry. My thoughts were that he'd come back to you.'

Lorrie sucked in a gulp of air. 'He was never coming back. Deep down I knew it.'

'I can stay the night if you wish?' Fliss offered. 'It's been a long, arduous day for you, and I can keep you company.'

Taking a deep, steadying breath, Lorrie reached out and took their hands. 'Thank you for being such dear friends.'

'Even me?' Meg said shyly.

'Your heart and intentions were in the right place, I understand that.' Lorrie kissed Meg's cheek. 'In some ways I'm glad the letter came. You're correct in that I need to move forward. I've been waiting, wasting my days, wondering if Matteo would ever come back. Now I know for sure. For that I thank you because tomorrow I can put it all behind me.'

'And what will you do with the child?' Fliss murmured.

'I shall raise it.' The decision became final in her head. 'This baby didn't ask to be created. It is not at fault.' Lorrie rubbed her belly, the love returning. 'I shall love it.'

Meg relaxed slightly. 'We all shall love it.'

'Both of you go home.' Lorrie kissed their cheeks. 'I'm completely fine. I'll have something to eat and go to bed early.'

'Are you absolutely certain?' Fliss asked at the door.

'Yes. I'll see you both at church on Sunday.'

When they had gone, Lorrie went to the range and stirred the embers. A cup of tea and some toast was exactly what she needed. She built up the fire in front of the sofa as the rain lashed down outside.

The warmth inside the flat and the light from the gas lamps created a cosy atmosphere as she sat down to eat her toast, but the letter placed at the end of the table repeatedly drew her gaze.

Reluctantly, she read Matteo's words once more. He sounded cold, uncaring. Did he really feel that way? Tears shimmered in her eyes as she recalled their night together. How could such tender feelings mean nothing to him now?

'A honeymoon in Florence,' she whispered. He was married, starting a new life with a new woman. He'd eventually have more children...

She wrapped her arms around her stomach and spoke down to her baby. 'Don't worry, little one, my love will make up for his lack.'

A knock on the door brought her head up. She knew it would be Jonas.

'Come in.'

With a gentle smile, he came towards her, Rollo prancing at his feet. 'I just wanted to make sure you were all right?' He frowned, staring at her face. 'You've been crying.'

She quickly wiped her eyes. 'It's been a horrid time.'

'It has.' He sat down beside her at the table.

'Do you want some tea?'

'Not really.' His wry smile held a hidden meaning. 'To have tea would dilute the whisky I've had for courage.'

'Courage?' She didn't understand.

'Lorrie, today saw the end to a difficult chapter for you, at least I hope it has.' Jonas ran an unsteady hand through his grey hair. 'I want you to know that I'm here for you, no matter what, in any capacity you need.'

'I know that.' She sat straighter, knowing this conversation was important. Abruptly, she had a sudden fear. 'Has something happened? Are you going away?'

'What?' He grimaced. 'No. No.'

'You're being so serious. You're worrying me.'

Jonas jerked to his feet, tapping his fingers on his thigh as if in torment.

'What is it?' Lorrie dared to whisper.

Swiftly he was beside her again. 'I love you,' he blurted out.

She stared at him.

'I fully understand you don't love me, but,' he held his hand up as she went to speak, 'but if you listen to my proposal and think about it for a little while, you might see some benefits.' He rubbed his face with one hand, gathering his thoughts. 'I love you, and I want to take care of you, to cherish you as you deserve. Now I know your feelings are still involved with the Italian, and that is understandable, for you're carrying his child. However, I'm willing, very willing to marry you and give the child my name, should you want that, and should you believe there is no chance of you marrying the Italian.'

'Jonas—'

'Let me finish.' He looked pained. 'I will honour you all of my days. I'll work hard to show you how much I love and respect you. I will love the child as my own and treat him or her with the same regard as I would my own flesh and blood. I've wasted my life loving a woman I couldn't have, and I've gone and done it again with you, but maybe, just maybe, this time it might be different. If you can bear to be with me, as husband and wife, I will do my utmost to make you happy until I die. Of course, you couldn't be expected to feel the same and I understand that and accept it and—'

She cut his words off with a kiss.

He broke away and stared at her, his pewter-grey eyes confused.

Her heart melted. Before her was a man who adored her. A man who had fought for her, worked hard for her, and treated her with such devotion. He made her feel safe, appreciated, treasured. How could she not love him?

Lorrie smiled. 'I once said I never wanted to be without you. I meant every word.'

'But the Italian?'

'My feelings have changed for Matteo, are still changing, and will continue to do so.' She gave Jonas the letter to read.

After he read it, he frowned. 'What a fool he is to give you up.'

'I was never his to give up, that is clear to me now. We were passing fancies with no real connection, no deep love to hold us together. I think I was in love with the idea of love, of romance. I was so lonely. He was the first man to make me feel like a woman and not a girl. That is intoxicating. Yet Matteo couldn't commit to me. He didn't want to, which tells me we were never meant to be.'

'And does that make you sad?' Jonas asked quietly.

'It did, it still does a little, but not so much now. Like a seedling, love needs to be nurtured, tenderly cared for; without care, it dies.'

'Then maybe we have a chance of true happiness?' Jonas's vulnerability touched her heart.

She wrapped her arms around him. 'I believe we have a very

good chance of happiness.'

'And lots of children,' he grinned.

'More children? I need to have this one first!' She grinned and then gazed seriously into his eyes. 'You will not treat this child differently because they are not yours?'

Jonas placed his hand on her stomach. 'This baby is yours. She could be a little girl with your sparkling golden-brown eyes or a quiet little boy with your father's talents or could have your mother's dark hair. This child will be a little bit of many people, not just Falcone's. More importantly, it's your baby that I will see from the very first moment it takes its first breath and for that reason I will love it.'

She hadn't thought of it like that.

'But,' Jonas rubbed her stomach again, 'the one thing this child will definitely have is me as its father and I will do everything I can to love and raise him or her alongside you.'

Lorrie raised her hands to cup his face, enjoying the freedom of being able to touch him. 'I don't know when I started to love you, but I do, most sincerely.'

'Good. I'd hate to be second best to the Italian.'

Her heart swelled with love. 'You aren't second best, I promise you that. You've shown me so much care, so much affection and tenderness, thoughtfulness... I will never compare you with another, and if I do, it will be to praise you and not them.'

He kissed her for a long time before raising his head and whispering, 'You are the love I've been waiting for.'

'And you are the one to heal my heart and give me the family I've always wanted. Thank you for loving me.' She kissed him deeply, holding on to him tightly.

Jonas whispered against her lips. 'We'd better hurry up and get married.' He kissed her again as Rollo barked and jumped up at their legs.

ACKNOWLEDGEMENTS

Dear Readers,

Thank you for delving into *The Dock Girl's Shame*. I hope your enjoyment matches the pleasure I had in crafting it. As I mentioned in Book 1, *The Waterfront Lass*, I chose to set this series in Wakefield's waterfront area due to its fascinating history. Although my parents hailed from Wakefield, they never spoke of the riverside, likely because our ancestors were coal miners on the opposite side of Wakefield, disconnected from the boats and waterfront.

In my genealogical quest, I discovered ancestors living in the impoverished Kirkgate areas, north of River Calder and the train station. Surprisingly, one forebear was a mariner in the early 1800s, with his son recorded as working on a Wakefield boat. While details remain elusive, I envision it might have involved the River Calder or perhaps a narrowboat.

Watching a recent video showcasing the revitalisation of the waterfront stirred my imagination about the bygone industries and the inhabitants who once thrived there, particularly those from vanished streets. Thornes Lane Wharf persists but in an altered state. The once-prolific malthouses and mills along the waterfront have vanished, save for a fortunate few repurposed into retail or office spaces. The Hepworth, a modern gallery, now stands on the site where I imagined the brewery and Chambers's boatyard, overseeing the weir. Victorian maps depict the waterfront teeming with industries, while slums housed the multitude employed in these endeavours.

While I've meticulously researched historical records, I've also exercised creative freedom, like fabricating scenes such as Harry's ferry, to serve the narrative. This tale is fiction, yet I've utilised maps and historical data to root my characters in a factual context as much as possible.

Thank you once more for exploring Lorrie's story. Fliss will soon have her own tale, where Meg and Lorrie will reappear, allowing you to catch up on their lives.

I'd like to take this opportunity to thank the whole team at Boldwood Books, especially my editor Emily Ruston, for all their efforts to help me bring this book to publication.

I'd like to thank my family for all their support and love.

Best wishes,

AnneMarie Brear

2024

ABOUT THE AUTHOR

AnneMarie Brear is the bestselling historical fiction writer of over twenty novels. She lives in the Southern Highlands in NSW, and has spent many years visiting and working in the UK.

Sign up to AnnieMarie Brear's mailing list here for news, competitions and updates on future books.

Visit AnneMarie's website: http://www.annemariebrear.com/

Follow AnneMarie on social media:

𝕏 x.com/annemariebrear

f facebook.com/annemariebrear

BB bookbub.com/authors/annemarie-brear

⊙ instagram.com/annemariebrear

ALSO BY ANNEMARIE BREAR

The Orphan in the Peacock Shawl

The Soldier's Daughter

The Waterfront Women Series

The Waterfront Lass

The Waterfront Women

The Dock Girl's Shame

Sixpence Stories

Introducing Sixpence Stories!

Discover page-turning historical novels from your favourite authors, meet new friends and be transported back in time.

Join our book club Facebook group

https://bit.ly/SixpenceGroup

Sign up to our newsletter

https://bit.ly/SixpenceNews

Boldwood

Boldwood Books is an award-winning fiction publishing company seeking out the best stories from around the world.

Find out more at www.boldwoodbooks.com

Join our reader community for brilliant books, competitions and offers!

Follow us

@BoldwoodBooks

@TheBoldBookClub

Sign up to our weekly deals newsletter

https://bit.ly/BoldwoodBNewsletter

Printed in Great Britain
by Amazon

43824828R10155